# THE DRIFT

ALSO BY JOHN RIDLEY

*Stray Dogs*

*Love Is a Racket*

*Everybody Smokes in Hell*

*A Conversation with the Mann*

# THE DRIFT

John Ridley

# THE DRIFT

ONE WORLD
BALLANTINE BOOKS • NEW YORK

*The Drift* is a work of fiction. Names, places, and incidents either are a product of the author's imagination or are used fictitiously.

A One World Book
Published by The Random House Publishing Group


Published in the United States by The Random House Publishing Group, a division of Random House, Inc., New York, and simultaneously in Canada by Random House of Canada Limited, Toronto.



www.ballantinebooks.com/one/

Library of Congress Catalog Card Number: 2003093362

ISBN 0-345-44348-9

This edition published by arrangement with Alfred A. Knopf, a division of Random House, Inc.

Manufactured in the United States of America

First Ballantine Books Edition: November 2003

10 9 8 7 6 5 4 3 2 1

George Plimpton was up, angry. Doing work. George was a badass. George was a head smasher. And though some tried, George Plimpton was not to be trifled with.

George's belligerence was necessitated, this time, by a weepy-bitchy scream in the night, shrill enough to be heard above the steel wheels rolling across the joins of the rails and the diesel-electric GE Unit some fifteen cars up hauling us eastward across the American Middle West. The scream was weepy-bitchy shrill enough you'd almost think it was a woman doing the "please, oh God"-ing. Almost. Not quite. Not quite weepy-bitchy shrill enough for that. It carried just enough bass to be the cries of what passed for a man; the cries of Yuppie Scum. Some day-trading, dot-com-ing bastard who was bored with his Benz and instant millions and figured—for whatever reason logical only to Young, Upwardly Mobile Scurf—that hopping Old Dirty Face, riding the rails, would be a romantic, nostalgic way to see America: swapping harmonica songs and open fire–cooked canned beans with some white bearded hobo who regaled with recountings of endless travel over wide-open spaces.

Yeah.

The screams were most likely courtesy of a romantic dick to his ass. Maybe the product of an old-fashioned shank to his ribs.

Fine.

Not my problem.

Yuppie Scum's in the wrong place, Yuppie Scum gets what it deserves. I was just trying to make Iowa.

Except

All that weepy-bitchy screaming . . . it's just got a way of edging you up.

Others, the other tramps and 'boes in the car—catch-outs to Iowa were always heavy the second weekend in August—kept to themselves. Others were smarter than me. I made for the commotion.

A full moon cutting through slits in the metal of the boxcar helped me read the situation. Fetaled up in a corner of the car was a floppy blond-haired white guy still "oh, Jesus. Oh God, please, God don't"-ing. He was sporting Dockers—actual honest-to-Christ Dockers—and a shirt that had previously been another color but was now blood-reddish from the red blood that flowed from cuts and slashes, defensive wounds, decorating his arms and upper body. Standing over him were a couple of 'boes. Black bandannas on their necks. Could still smell the piss.

Fuck.

Not 'boes. Freight Train Riders of America. FTRA. Meth-snorting peckerwood gangers. One was demonstrating a blade, the other the smile of a patron enjoying a show.

To the both of them: "Knock that shit off."

Real-life violence is not like movie violence. Movie violence is most times preceded by lots of snappy dialogue from $20 million action star #14 concerning how he's going to do some nasty things to the stuntman who's paid union wages to go down on cue. Real-life violence is mostly unescorted by tough guy remarks about driving somebody's nose bone up into their brain. In real life, violence is just very suddenly with you.

Suddenly the FTRA with the blade was slashing for me.

And it was then that George Plimpton got up, angry. Did work. George greeted the FTRA where his arm and hand joined. The wrist, technically speaking. George greeted the FTRA at the wrist, and the FTRA's wrist replied with a squeal and a deafening snap and a fountain of blood from where flesh got torn open by breaking bone. George swung around, catching FTRA in the face, across his cheek. What teeth weren't smashed from his mouth were driven through the skin of his jaw.

FTRA One was done for the day.

FTRA Two, who'd come to the party without shank or sharp

object or goonie stick, gave me and George some fearful looking-over.

I said to him: "Got money?"

The FTRA's head—poked like he'd tried to block buckshot with it. Brittle skin peppered with a beard that wouldn't grow right—shook his head no.

"Got food stamps?"

The head with its shitty excuse for a face gave me "no" again.

My eyes shifted away from the FTRA. In a flinchy style he looked to where I was looking: the open door of the boxcar. Not a word spoken, but my meaning was clear.

FTRA number two started in with some begging. "Please. . ."

One pitiful word, but at least he didn't sound the bitch Dockers Boy did.

Didn't matter. "Get out."

"Plea—"

George raised up.

That was it for FTRA Two. He'd seen George Plimpton doing work.

George Plimpton was not to be trifled with.

Using what was left of his free will, FTRA Two sailed himself into the dark that waited just beyond the door.

The boxcar now de-FTRA'd, my attention was pulled by the sick whimpers of the yuppie scum.

"Th—thank you."

Those goddamn Dockers. And I'm pretty sure his shirt was Banana Republic.

"Got money?" I wanted to know.

On the floor of the boxcar, Yuppie Scum was just a little ball of confusion. ". . . Wha . . . ?"

"Got money?"

". . . No . . ."

"Got food stamps?"

"No, I don't."

He was lying. Not about the food stamps. Yuppie Scum didn't

know a WIC coupon from a welfare check. But money . . . Those FTRA fuckers hadn't had time to roll him properly. They hadn't had time to get to his wallet; his cash or his traveler's checks. Yeah. Believe it. Goddamn Yuppie Scum caught out with traveler's checks. And this one had to go and pretend like . . . I save his less-than-useless pink hide, and he doesn't have the decency to compensate me?

I grabbed at Yuppie Scum, grabbed his wallet, pulled it free, taking a swath of Dockers with it. Gripping his bloody-moist BR shirt, I hauled him for the boxcar door. Knowing what was coming, he went spastic—flailing, clawing at me. All that gift-wrapped in more of his girlie yells. He'd made his choice. He'd picked lying over truth-telling. Couldn't he just take what was coming?

George helped him with that. George knocked him limp.

Out the door with Yuppie Scum. Into the night, into the howling air that swept past the rushing train. If not for the noise of the Unit, the constant chatter of the couplings, it would have been quiet enough in the city-free nothingland west of Iowa to hear the coo of tall weeds petted by the night breeze, the hum of crickets and power lines as they sang at each other. It would have been quiet enough to hear if Yuppie Scum bitch-screamed as he flew groundward, if his neck cracked when he hit terra firma from a train doing sixty-plus, or if he just smacked earth, picked himself up, and hollered "To hell with you, you nigger tramp!" as he dusted his Dockers off. Not knowing which was true, I imagined my reality of favor. I imagined Yuppie Scum's neck to be shattered beyond repair. Not killing him. Leaving him a quad for life. And I was happy for it. Yuppie Scum reproduced at a rate just slightly below fungus in a dark cellar. He would be replaced. He would not be missed.

I know.

I had been Yuppie Scum. I had been replaced in the world. No one missed me.

With George I returned to my corner of the boxcar, the other tramps and 'boes not even daring to look our way. I went through Yuppie Scum's wallet.

Shit.

No money. He wasn't lying.

Anyway.

I was jangled and I needed some of Lady K to set me straight. Needed her, just wanted her. Didn't matter. I had some of her. Calmed down, George and I curled up together. I did not sleep. As always, I was scared to death of what waited for me just the other side of being awake.

Charles stood, stared. He stepped back. Stared. Stared. Stepped forward. Stared. Squatted. Turned a little. Stared some more. No doubt. It was there. No doubt about it. When he squatted, turned a little, he could see the dent just above the rear wheel well on the passenger side of his car. No paint gone. Just a dent. You did have to pretty much stare to see it. And squat down. You had to be really looking for it. Most people would never even know it was there. Know, care. But Charles knew. The knowing was an irritant, dull but constant.

Prickly heat on flesh.

So that meant getting the dent fixed. That meant driving crosstown to the dealership in Santa Monica, but they weren't open weekends, so that meant taking the car in Monday to Friday from ten to four. I worked . . . Charles. Charles worked nine to five. That meant driving all the way from his office downtown during his lunch hour. Downtown to Santa Monica. And back. In an hour.

Impossible.

A breath from Charles: "Shit."

And it was new, that was the thing. A new BMW. A month old. Not even. How long had he wanted one, never felt like he was driving what his colleagues expected him to without one, didn't even have the thing a month, and then someone—some asshole in the Ralphs parking lot—had to go and back into it. Or maybe it was some asshole at SavOn. Or that asshole valet at that play at the Pantages he didn't want to go to, but Beverly did so they went. A dent on his Beamer is what he had to show for it.

Charles let down the garage door. It squealed. He'd fix it this weekend, he told himself. He'd been telling himself that nine weeks running.

Charles walked through the laundry room into the kitchen. No dinner cooking. Of course. Chinese tonight, or Mexican? He had a taste for neither. He couldn't remember which he had more of last week. Picking, he settled on Mexican. Couldn't find the takeout menu. Ordered fried rice instead. House special. No shrimp in Beverly's.

From the kitchen into the living room. Bad scrape on the wall that needed filling, repainting. The guy Charles'd hired to do it kept not showing up when he was supposed to. He did once, but had the wrong color paint. Outside, the front yard: there was that brown patch in the middle of the lawn. Neighbors were over last week, made a comment about it. Slight, but rude as if they expected Charles to get that taken care of ASAP. He tried to get the gardener to do something, but the gardener only spoke Spanish, or at least pretended to only speak Spanish, so the patch stayed brown. Charles'd go to OSH and get some lawn feed, see if that helped. Next weekend. Right after he fixed the garage door.

The house was quiet. Beverly was home. Somewhere. Later he'd look for her. After the food arrived. Had he ordered Chinese or Mexican? And after that Beverly would expect them to watch *Ally McBeal* so they could pretend they'd spent some quality time together.

Pretend.

Not like

Remember that vacation, the first one you took together? Cayman Islands. And all you did was lie around together. Couldn't lie around together enough. Took all the time in the world doing it. Time was cheap. Jesus was it ever.

Should've felt happy remembering that vacation. He should have.

Charles went upstairs, went into the bedroom, sat on the edge of the bed. Okay, so food was coming. Ally was waiting for him. He had work to do on the Whitaker estate plan. A lot of work. The Whitakers had a lot of estate.

God, people like that . . . Charles knew what kind of dough they had, how they lived. They lived good. They lived easy. Sure they did. People like that didn't lift a finger for anything. They had other people to run their cars to body shops across town when they got whacked.

Other people to make sure other other people did reconstructive surgery on marred walls. They had other people to plan their estates, no matter how much time that chopped out of that other person's night. It would chop time out of Charles's night for the next three nights running. He was expected to have the plan done by the end of the week.

Anyway

Charles figured if he managed things right, didn't let too much of his night get hacked away, once he finished all the things he was expected to do, he'd make it to bed near midnight and maybe get something in the neighborhood of five hours' sleep. A truer approximation calculated his getting to bed well after one and less than four hours' sleep. So to do all he needed to do and hit the sack at a decent hour Charles figured right then he had about . . . half an hour to call his own.

One-half of one hour.

How to spend it?

Watch TV? Waste of time. And Ally would waste his time later.

Watch the news so tomorrow at the office he could fake like he knew what was going on in the rest of the world? But the news wasn't relaxing.

Read? A book? Charles could barely remember where he left off in whatever he was reading last.

Magazine? *Vanity Fair*? *Esquire*? Ads for stuff he couldn't afford. Interest pieces on people he had no interest in. *Time*? *Newsweek*? Wasn't it easier to just watch the news?

Maybe he should just go ahead and work on the garage door. OSH was still open.

What did he want to do?

The clock: all his thinking had shaved two minutes from his thirty.

"Christ."

How had he

Charles wondered how he had

The line from the Talking Heads song. How'd it go?

And Charles thought: What I want, all I truly want

And the line from the song went

And there she was, just outside the bedroom door. Beverly didn't enter. Charles had told her—and told her and told her in an effort to buy himself just a sliver of personal space—when he's sitting alone in a room, even if it looks like he's doing nothing, he might be giving a deep consideration to something, so don't, please don't, just wander in and bust his train of thought. She didn't. Instead she'd taken to skulking around outside of a room as if that were somehow less annoying.

Prickly heat on flesh.

And all Charles truly wanted

And Charles looked up, acknowledged Beverly. She came into the bedroom, little smile on her face, hands behind her back. Hiding something. Something gift-wrapped.

And Beverly said: "I have a surprise for you."

I am Brain Nigger Charlie.

In this incarnation.

In this incarnation I am.

In my previous incarnation—my previous incarnation before my most recent incarnation—I was Charles Harmon. That was a few years ago. A few years, another life. Miles and miles of rail.

Who

No

What

What I used to be, at the age of thirty-three, was an ACC-bred tax lawyer for a Big Eight accounting firm in Los Angeles, California. Charles Harmon, despite his—in spite of his—light-skinned blackness, led a very nice upper-middle-class life along with his wife, the equally light-skinned, surpassingly upper-upper-middle-class Beverly. They had a three-bedroom, one-full / two-half-bath home in the Los Angeles suburb of Woodland Hills—if that doesn't stink of upper-middle-classdom, then I'm unfamiliar with what does reek of it—with a pool and a small greenhouse and a big, freshly remodeled kitchen that sat unused except for the microwave. Neither of them cooked. Takeout was more convenient, and left them with just that much more time to self-obsess.

Charles met his wife at some mixer for black profess . . . excuse me, African-American professionals. She was—is—an attractive woman. Just under five feet six inches in height, slender, a very pretty face with dark eyes. He was attractive, too. It might have been nice if he was a little taller than six feet. It might have been better if he weighed more than one hundred seventy-five pounds. But he was all right, and she was all right, and the two liked each other enough; their relative attractiveness, each other's corporate positions, the fact that they both spoke the white dialect of assimilation and shared the touchstones of their indoctrination: Salinger over Morrison. Kiss not Parliament. They got *Police Woman* over *Christy Love.* So they married after spending just enough time together to be fairly sure there was nobody else they wanted to be with more—her whining him all the way to a preacher for a nice-sized church wedding no matter neither of them particularly believed in God—and together they, Charles Harmon and Beverly Baker hyphen Harmon, lived the great American delusion: that toiling at their easily downsizable jobs for the money they earned was the greatest good achievable. That the smiling faces in the Prada and Pottery Barn ads sold them exactly what they needed. That the somebody-elses of the world would do the volunteer work and community service and on the first Tuesday in November turn out to vote for the guy who would have his finger on the nuclear button. The Harmon/Baker-Harmons were too busy building up their myth of being to care about such things.

Their myth was good.

Their myth was nearly perfect.

Then Charles went and got Beverly knocked up. He did it because Beverly wanted a baby and because it's what he was supposed to do; having a baby, having a family is what was expected of him. You mate, you procreate. You share boring tidbits of your day at the dinner table and wake up ungodly early to go to church Sunday mornings 'cause eons ago that's what someone said you were supposed to do, civilization functioned pretty good that way and who was Charles to argue otherwise? Anyway, Charles would have time to enjoy life the way it was. He figured it would take months of trying to get Beverly pregnant. At their fancy restaurant dinner parties that they filled their weekends with, all their couple/friends ever talked about was how hard they had to try to get pregnant.

Try.

When you're young, when you're in high school, your biggest fear is accidentally getting a chick in trouble. When you're old, when you're married, you have to *try* and have a baby.

Charles got Beverly pregnant on the first official baby-trying fuck.

The very first.

The first.

Charles nearly fell back when he heard that. Actually, he did fall back onto the bed where he sat after Beverly presented him with a cute, gift-wrapped little bib that read I ♥ DADDY as way of telling him a cocktail of sperm and egg was fermenting inside her and he might as well forget every other plan, every other idea, every dream he'd ever dreamed in life. His essence, his existence, was about to nexus around some suckling, crying, diaper-filling humanoid. Charles had never given much thought to a kid, the totality of parenthood, until he was on the eve of having one. A kid is with you, it is always with you—if not physically, then emotionally—until the end of your life, unless it dies before you do and then the guilt of raising a kid just to have it kick off is shackled to you in the kid's place. And the weight of that reality hung on poor Charles like a lead designer Kipling backpack stuffed full of shitty thoughts.

Things were suddenly bad.

And then they went

from

bad

to

worse.

The very night Charles was told of his wife's pregnancy he had a dream of the unborn child. He dreamed it was a happy, healthy caramel-colored kid. With a third eye in its cheek. Other than that it was in the baby's cheek, it wasn't really a mutant eye. It was fully functioning. Didn't roll around uncontrollably. Wasn't deformed. It was a nice, normal third eye. But it was blue. Crystal blue, like one of the eyes of that baby at the incomprehensible end of *2001: A Space Odyssey*.

A baby with a cheek-eye.

A black baby with a blue cheek-eye.

No matter the image had probably been conjured by the lake of booze Charles'd drained into his stomach to ease the anguish of being told that he'd fucked his way to the end of his life, that blue-cheek-eyed baby was the most disgusting thing he had ever conceived. It was so vivid, so real, it cut into his mind and remained like a scar. It was tattooed on the back of his eyelids so that every time they closed the cheek-eye was there waiting for him. Sleep at night grew to be an impossible chore. Who wants to sleep when a cheek-eyed baby waits in your dreams? Lack of sleep made concentration on the highly difficult task of tax lawyering during the day impossible at best. But the baby, his unborn baby, remained an image uncleansable.

Uncleansable by any means yet known to him.

So Charles went to work. Like an AIDS doc doing overtime looking for the cure, Charles went to work looking for the thing that would sandblast his brain to a sparkling, mutant-baby-free shine. Booze helped. The same thing that gave birth to the monster helped bury it. Soft liquor dulled the image and hard liquor made it damn near fuzzy. But booze also made Charles pass out, and in the gutter of every bender that blue cheek-eye was there giving Charles a cold stare. There would be no escaping his dreams. The only thing for Charles to escape was sleep. And that's when he met the two most fantabulous women he would ever know: Lady E and Lady K. Ecstasy and ketamine. Drugs. Designer drugs, of course, for his designer lifestyle. No meth for Charles. Meth was white trash shit. No coke, with its weak high and hard crash. No heroin. No needles. Just the E and the K. The E fuel-injected serotonin into his brain. It kept him awake so he couldn't see the baby, made him too happy to care on the occasions that he did catch z's. The K mellowed him out, anesthetized him to the harshness of life. Yeah, the cheek-eyed kid was still growing in his wife's stomach, but his designer mix helped him to not mind and the non-minding made his middle-classdom perfect again.

Except

The requisite number of hours Charles needed to be high during the day to keep himself steady added up to all twenty-four of them. When you're high all the time or crashing from a high or working your way back to being high from a crash it tends to affect the other aspects of your life: the job that's no longer important to you. The wife you're too fucked up to get a hard-on for. The child you'd be just as happy were it stillborn as born at all. You can fake like you care about those things, for a while, but whatever else drugs do for you they are like honesty drops. Sooner or later the truth comes out of you. You puke out the truth because you just don't give a shit anymore. Not about reality. Reality is a poor substitute for the surreality of a fucked-up brain.

But large, stodgy accounting firms don't like it when their employees are tweaked and functionless, so Big Eight gave Charles the boot. And wives don't like it when their husbands won't slip it to them anymore and say nasty things about the child they're carrying, so Beverly gave Charles the boot. And after a few months of staying juiced and jagged day/night/day—in addition to being jobless and basically homeless—Charles was, in an incredibly short amount of time relative to the years of building himself up, penniless. Literally without a cent and living on the streets. So, he gave Los Angeles the boot.

Tried to.

But same as a species getting left behind in a tar pit, Charles could not extricate himself from the city. When you have no money at all, getting from point A to point A-and-a-half is nothing short of a Sisyphean chore. Charles tried panhandling, begging—oh, is it such fun when you accidentally try to cop a dollar off a guy who used to be subordinate to you at the office. Desperate, or close enough to it, Charles gave stealing a thought. Was too scared to really try. Visions of prison gang rapes danced in his head. He was optionless. Years of living white had not prepped him for the rudeness of real life. He learned something then: for those without money, money is nearly impossible to come by.

LA, once his home, was now his prison.

Then

Then, on one of the city's trademarked hot and smoggy summer days, in the rail yards downtown, while scrounging for empties to be rusty-shopping-carted over to the nearest recycle center for their IA, ME, VT, NY, OR, MA, DE, CT 5¢, MI 10¢ CA cash refund, Charles saw a couple of Julios catching out; hopping a freight.

Hopping a freight.

Why not? It cost nothing. And no matter where the train was headed it was somewhere besides Los Angeles. And the way those Julios just eased alongside the train as it slow-rolled from the yard, then swung up onto a flatcar . . . If they could do it, couldn't Charles?

Sure he could.

And once on the train he could finally have what he truly wanted: that extra minute added to the one half hour a day he called his own. A minute. Ten minutes. Ten thousand. Just time enough to take a deep breath.

And once on the train he could finally get rid of what he truly hated: being a collection of other people's expectations.

Freedom. Freedom is what the rails are for.

The first time Charles tried to catch out he got bagged by the slack of the line and nearly had his arm torn off. But he made the train. The train made its way from LA. Charles decided he wanted to go to New Mexico. He'd never been to New Mexico before—there were a lot of places he'd never been—but New Mexico was the first one that popped into his head; so very much land, so very few people, so greatly different from LA.

He got as far as Barstow.

Barstow, California, was a step down, not up, from Los Angeles.

From there Charles would only slide lower.

The rails were a whole new thing for him. A society that coexisted with, but not among, the rest of the world. Bugs under a rock. Rodents in a dark closet. A collection of the undereducated, or uneducated, or psycho vet. Or pure white trash. And into that, into all that, stumbles Charles Harmon, brain-fried but still functioning on a higher plane than the average tramp. He could read at a college level, and speak like Peter Jennings delivering the evening news. He could remember train schedules and was too stupid to keep to his own and *not* tell every tramp and 'bo when they were wrong about which train was going where when. And when the other tramps and 'boes didn't care, would tell Charlie to shut his yap, he would insist he was right anyway. And for that, for all that, Charles became

I became

Uppity Nigger Charlie. That was my most pervious incarnation. Everyone on the rails gets tagged. You get a new name because you are a new person. The life you lived before is left behind. You get tagged, but you do not tag yourself. Yuppie Scum do. When Yuppie Scum Eddie-Bauer-does-the-rails thrill-ride, they tag themselves; Train King,

Unit Master. Shit no 'bo would ever call another 'bo under any circumstances unless to piss him off and possibly get killed in the doing. But since no one is interested in tagging Yuppie Scum and since they're only on the rails because they're living out some masturbatory head trip anyway, they tag themselves. It is arrogant and it is false. How can you give yourself a new name when you don't know who you are? And you don't. If you did, you wouldn't be on the rails living like a vagrant in the first place. You wait. You wait for someone to read you and assess you and in an offhanded moment break you down to what you really are from the obvious to the sublime: One-Legged Joe. San Francisco Mad Boy. Cow Fucker Ralph.

Charles Harmon? Uppity Nigger Charlie.

Thing is, uppity niggers get beaten down.

Charles got beat down. He got beat down for talking wise to the wrong people. He got robbed for not being smart about hiding what little money he was able to beg and keep. He got brutalized on a near regular basis because he was weak and easy, and because he jungled up or caught out with the wrong sort of people. Wrong being the crazed, the vicious, the easily incited. The black haters.

There was a good number of those; black haters.

The rails belonged to disenfranchised whites. Poor ones. Stupid ones. Redneck ones. Whites so far down the food chain, so excuseless for their failures, they looked to put anyone beneath them for any reason to be used as a rung for pulling themselves one slight step up from the bog of their own valuelessness. The FTRA was the first of the wayward to band together in a train gang and give fierce voice to the polloi of the rails. They dealt drugs for money, killed tramps for fun. Other gangs would follow, new and improved only in the depth of their racism, level of violence. Charlie learned that niggers were seldom welcomed in the yards and jungles, and uppity niggers were like a piñata with a bull's-eye painted on its stomach.

Or its ass.

Uppity Nigger Charlie got raped. Quite often he did. On the rails, same as in prisons, forced sex was the chief tool of degradation. You cannot imagine the sick feeling accompanying objects being inserted into you, be it flesh or glass or wood. You cannot comprehend the humiliation that comes with having your manhood . . . No. To hell with that. Manhood is just an icon of pride. It is your humanity that is torn painfully, bloodily from your anus with each debasing, demeaning stroke. Filthy hands clawing you, the stink of cheap liquor choking you. And all that soundtracked with hoots and hollers thrown out rodeo-style, and backed with crazed unending laughter. That was the worst of it; the mocking cackles from mouths that owned more gum than teeth. Laughter sharp as razors, razors that tore through the flesh and sank to the bone. Laughter, as if such an act so vile and violent was the most humorous thing this side of a tea party between Stooges One, Two, Three and the Brothers Marx.

And when they were done with you, when they tossed you aside like you were nothing more than a cum rag, when you lay, alone, in the corner of a boxcar, you felt . . . you felt . . . I felt . . . poor Uppity Nigger Charlie felt like crawling onto a track, stretching his neck across the rails, and waiting for a hotshot running full on to free him of all the pain and suffering of his nonexistence. He felt like doing it.

He did it.

Freedom. Freedom is what the rails are for.

Freedom came rolling at Charlie on a Conrail line at seventy-plus miles an hour.

Freedom

Two times Chocolate Walt saved Charlie from dying. At least two times he did. The first time was simple. Walt just reached down and snatched Charlie up out of the way of that oncoming Conrail and the eternal liberty it was going to deliver him to. The second time took some doing. It took some learning on Charlie's part. Chocolate Walt taught Charlie about who you did and did not jungle with, how you did and did not catch out. He taught Charlie how to hide whatever money he came across and what worked better than money on the rails; food stamps, booze to barter with. He taught Charlie how to use his smarts instead of just flaunting them.

And then Chocolate Walt introduced Charlie to George Plimpton. Having George around changed everything. George was tough and undeniable. In a fair fight George was nearly unbeatable. In an unfair one, George had his trick which was nearly unstoppable. And quite suddenly, with George by his side, when situations grew troublesome, it was Charlie who was beating instead of getting beat. It was Charlie who was kicking ass instead of getting fucked in his. Quite suddenly he was, I was, reborn again and for the last time.

He was
I am
Brain Nigger Charlie.

Not a lot of places on Mother Earth willingly throw open their arms to transient, near-destitute tramps, hoboes. Britt, Iowa, couldn't throw its arms wide enough. It'd been trying for more than one hundred years. For more than one hundred years it'd been home to the annual Tourist Union No. 63. Commonly: the National Hobo Convention.

Yes. Really.

Britt, Iowa. Founded by rail, the city slogan went, sustained by the plow. Sustained, but not much. Not well. The city—a couple dozen square miles of low-rise brick buildings, grain silos, small ranch houses, and a Casey's gas station that also called itself a general store—was like a just opened time capsule buried in the Ike era. Signs posted at the city entrance: Kiwanis Club. Rotary Club. Lions Club. Future Farmers of America. Ladies' Auxiliary Bingo Committee. The Britt Industrial Development Corp. boasted the city had a pool at the elementary school, two—count 'em *two*—dentists, a municipal building *and* library.

Though, compelled to be honest, I do like libraries.

Other than that, the city had all the comforts of home. If you lived in a home built in the eighteenth century. Perfect place for a gathering of fringe dwellers who traveled using yesterday's technology. Perfect, provided the convention itself conformed to certain conventions. The gathering was as much for tourists as for hoboes. Maybe tourists more. Tourists brought money to the city. Hoboes just brought their stink. So, it was no good for the Britt hobo to be a scary hobo. The Britt hobo was not the drifter with drugged-out brains, or the vet that was convinced Charlie was hiding out in the Junior Miss section of Wal★Mart waiting to finish what he started at Khesanh. He was most definitely not the nigger-hating FTRA ganger who would goonie-stick any black face he saw into a puree of skull and brains, then piss on it for good measure. Or fun. The Britt hobo had his belongings tied up in a bindle that was slung over his shoulder, whistled a public-domain song from a mouth ringed by a precision-groomed three-day growth of beard, had a comical patch on one knee, a humorously ill-fitting jacket, and a lovable dog with a spot over one eye that was always faithful and wasn't so stupid it ran in front of a westbound UP and ended up a blend of fur and flesh and internal matter spread like a coat of paint over fifteen feet of rail. The Britt hobo was the Disneyland version of hobo. And just like the Hall of Presidents at "the Happiest Place on Earth," you didn't see Jefferson fucking his black slaves, and in Britt you didn't see hoboes getting lifted on MD 2020, meth, or—hell—glue in a bag and sticking their dicks in any hole of any thing that happened across their paths. The National Hobo Convention in Britt, Iowa, was a once-a-year-every-year whitewashed tourist-attracting good-time lie dragged out over three days to maximize the town's bilking potential. The final and climactic day of the convention got going with a Hobo Parade that pulled in dignitaries from far and wide. Mrs. Iowa International made an appearance. Same with the Hancock County Pork Queen. The Britt High Class of 1950 had a reunion float. Mar's Taxidermy had a float. The American Legion had a float; five old guys who'd survived one of the wars. For my money, which I didn't have any of, the highlight of the parade was the massive John Deere 9400 series tractors that lumbered down Main Street like Soviet tanks in May Day parades from Cold War days gone by. Overgrown Tonka toys man-sized enough to make the most die-hard of money-grubbers shit on their stock options and get into the ag business.

Parade done. Lunchtime. Everybody, hoboes and tourists the same, walked the couple of blocks to Municipal Park—the park was named Municipal Park—and stood in long, long lines for some piping hot mulligan stew. Tourists ate it because it was fun eating an authentic phony hobo meal. Hoboes ate it because it didn't come out of the garbage. To help choke down the food some local kids put on a talent show—were compelled to put one on by parents whose failed dreams of something better were now being forcibly recombinated into their offspring. One kid did a tap routine to "Zoot Suit Riot." Another didn't completely ruin "You Light Up My Life."

Off to the side: a couple of vets starting talking about their time in Korea and how people didn't appreciate them risking their lives for the American way. They ended up talking about how the Jews were behind and had profited from every war in the history of man.

The mayor took up a microphone under the gazebo that shaded him and several other local officials from the blazing August sun. He kicked the afternoon's festivities off by asking for a moment of silence for Alabama Hobo, who had just got himself killed somehow.

Didn't know Alabama Hobo.

Stayed quiet for a minute anyway.

That done, it was time to get down to business: the picking of this year's royalty: The King of the Hoboes. All other touristy bullshit aside, this *was* business. The King of the Hoboes was an honorary thing, yeah, but most times it went to a 'bo who'd spent a lot of hard days out on the rails. Spent them, and survived them. For that reason alone they deserved something. All they got was a cheap cape made out of red felt with white trim, a straw hat with a crown cut out of a Folgers can. They got a little respect, too. Probably for the first time in life. Probably for the only time.

Electing the king is straightforward, brainless: each guy who wants to wear the crown is allowed to speechify on why he should ascend to the throne for a scant two minutes. The winner's chosen by applause from the gathered audience. The race for His Highness was a six-way affair among Hobo Joe, Texas Madman, Captain Dingo, Luther the Jet, Dante—who'd obviously prepped for the election with a few extra slams from a bottle of muscatel—and Chocolate Walt. Walt was easy to spot. He was the only guy running I knew. He was the only black man in the bunch. The orations mostly centered around undeliverable promises of getting more appreciation for hoboes, getting the Bulls to quit beating our heads every time they found us wandering their yards, getting the rail companies to hand out free food and drink. Dante just stood and laughed for his two minutes. Walt went the humble route, talked about how honored he was to be in Britt and how honored he was to be among the nominees for King of the Hoboes, and what an ould be to be elected King of the Hoboes, but if he wasn't it real honor anyhow. In his two minutes, Captain Dingo y courted the vet vote, made solemn references to Alabama Hobo as well as his own deceased grandparents in nearby Mason City, Iowa, and still had time left over to play a little guitar ditty about Dumpster divin'. It was a piece of political showmanship so slick it could've had Nixon jumping up from six feet under and doing a jig. The clapping poll resulted in no clear winner. It would come down to a speech-off between Dingo and Chocolate Walt. Showing a bit more beltway savvy, the Captain co-opted Walt's previous speech, spun it just enough to make his words seem fresh and new and his own: he was humbled, he was honored by the great people of Britt, who were part of the great populace of America; the greatest nation on the face of the planet, or any other known planet for that matter. If there'd been a baby nearby to kiss, or a Commie's neck to twist, he would have. Didn't need to. The salt-of-the-earth midwesterners loved him just the same.

Chocolate Walt stepped to the mike.

Quietly, he said that the Captain had given a fine speech, a real fine one, and that he didn't think he could compete with the Captain's words, but that he would try to find the right phraseology with—he took off his tattered cap—the help of his Lord and Savior Jesus Christ. Because if Jesus gave him the words, then he knew that Jesus truly wanted him to be king. If not, that was fine too, because all things were part of the Good Lord's plan and he was happy just to serve the one true King, Jesus, and as King of the Hoboes his first and only obligation would be to travel the rails and spread the Good News about Christ to all those who didn't know Jesus, because only by bowing down and supplicating to the Almighty can any of us achieve true salvation through His gift of everlasting grace and forgiveness and God and Jesus and Jesus and God and on and on and whoops and hollers went up, wild shrieks and drunken whistles and near-endless applause. Captain Dingo swore visibly. A couple of 'boes did a previously never-before-seen jig. A couple more got into a fistfight whose origin may or may not have had anything to do with what was happening around them at that moment. Other than that, generally there was a Thunderbird-fueled good time to be had by all.

. . .

When those who wanted to wish well to the newly elected king had scattered off to jungle up, or eat and drink, or just drink, I approached Walt. He was a book of years, his body the pages, the text written in harsh verbiage. Walt's hide, though deep black from birth, was tanned from long days spent in unshaded sun and dried from the constant massage of unblocked air driven over him by rolling trains in the dead of winter. The skin that was exposed was almost uniformly scarred. Every scar told a story. Some mundane; flesh ripped trying to open canned food without benefit of a can opener. Other stories were horrific: tales of surviving the assault of goonie sticks in the middle of the night or at high noon or at any other time of day as violence did not respect the clock. His gravest wounds were his eyes. They carried no life or light. In their time they had seen many things, few that held any wonder. They saw now, at all, because they had no other purpose. Nothing else to do with themselves. But each blink of their lids was slow and long as if they hoped, mercifully, Walt would one day allow them to close and remain so forever.

Those dead eyes looked at me.

From the expression Walt gave, you would not have known he was about the only person riding the lines I would call friend; the only person I would consider turning my back on in a rolling freight car long after dark. His look was dry and disassociated. He once-overed me up and down in the manner of a horse trader gone to market. Finally, satisfied with his inspection, he gave me a smile that was two-to-one gum to teeth.

"Brain Nigger." Diesel locomotives didn't rumble as low.

Walt had deteriorated since I had last seen him. It happens like that. On the rails there was no gradual decay. You were vital, then you were old. One, then the other, without passing through the transition land of middle age. Vital, then old. Walt was old. He still had size, but his muscle had sagged toward fat. What was left of his hair—or, now, the better way of saying: what parts of his bald head where hair still grew—was a deep gray; a Brillo pad dragged through soot. The rest of him was ashy where it wasn't just plain dirty, hunched where he didn't simply stoop. "Brain Nigger Charlie," Walt said again. He liked using my tag. He was the one who'd modified my previous name, gave me my new one. Saying it made him proud, as if recalling an appointment he'd once generously given me to a high station; lord mayor. His Holiness. Brain Nigger. To hear him say my name was a reminder that I was in Walt's debt. I owed him. I owed him several. Made me uneasy. When you owe someone, sooner or later they hand you the bill. I had more than a feeling payment due was the reason Chocolate Walt had called me to Britt.

Walt asked: "How's George treatin' ya?"

I hefted up George Plimpton. "George is treating me well."

George Plimpton was my friend and partner. My traveling companion. There was no place I would think of going without George. He had saved my life more times than Chocolate Walt. He had saved my life more times than I could recall.

George Plimpton is not a person.

George Plimpton is a person.

My George Plimpton is not.

George Plimpton is that writer guy who's always doing different things and trying different things and writing about them. My George Plimpton is a narrow piece of wood. Four feet long. Maybe that. Maybe an inch in diameter. But like the living breathing George Plimpton, my George is many things. My George is a walking stick and he is a poking-around stick and he is, most importantly, a goonie stick. On the rails a goonie stick is about the only protection a tramp or 'bo has—good for beating people and bashing people and making people take a step back when they're thinking no-good thoughts. An innocuous-looking shaft of wood, drilled, lined with metal, George had made many men step back. George has protected me well. And when all else failed, George did his little trick and with great rapidity all ill-advised conversations were ended.

"You, Brain Nigger; how you been?"

"I'm alive."

Walt nodded to my comment, added with weight, giving false profoundness to: "And sometimes that's the best you can say."

Chocolate Walt sat. Just below the chatter around me, the swapping back and forth between 'boes of rail stories concerning this adventure or that which, if not embellished, wholly untrue, I could hear the cracking of Walt's rusted knees. I remained standing. Didn't know royal etiquette, but could guess you didn't just park your ass with a king because your feet hurt.

I offered Chocolate Walt congratulations on his democratic coronation, complimented his winning speech.

He shrugged. "Shit, Charlie. Go on and on about God, and there ain't nothin' in this country you can't get. Long as it's the Jesus god, and not the Jew god or the Muslim god or that cow god they got over where you can't kill cows."

Yeah. True. Anyway: "King of the Hoboes. That's something."

"King of the Hoboes," Walt said. "King of the Hoboes," he mused. "I ain't no hobo, Brain Nigger. Not no more I ain't. A hobo travels somewhere. Travels to work; travels to contribute somethin'. He don't just take, he contributes. A hobo's got reason to go where he's goin'. That ain't me no more. I'm old, Brain Nigger. Look at me an' you can see that." Slowing, giving measure to his words: "The rails is for young men."

That was not true. Not necessarily. Most men on the rails tended to be older. But I understood what Chocolate Walt was getting at. He wasn't strictly talking about the years of a man, but rather of the Wick of Life inside him. His had burned nearly to the end.

"Still got a lot of miles left in you," I offered.

To that Walt shook his head, raised his left hand. There were four fingers and what remained of a thumb. Just above the second knuckle it was gnarled, and not in any pleasant manner. If there was a pleasant manner for the gnarling of a digit. It looked like the majority of the meat and bone had been amputated with a sudden violence that was not content, merely, with the taking, but also gained satisfaction from leaving an ugly, shredded, mangled reminder that marked its territory.

Walt, by way of explanation: "Catchin' out in St. Lou. Train wasn't rollin' any more than ten miles an hour, an' still I took it wrong."

"Happens." I patted my left leg. Walt knew the scar that ran the length of my flesh under the fabric of the pant.

"Yeah it do, but you either lie on the ground or you get up. You got up, Charlie. When this happen," waving his thumb-stump at me, "I lay where I was, hand all done in. I just lay in the gravel by the rail bleedin' an' bitch-cryin'. Musta laid there near on forty minutes. Four-an'-oh minutes."

My feet hurt. Royalty or not, I sat with Walt. "You had your thumb mangled."

Chocolate Walt threw a gurgled "Aaaaah" at me and swatted in the air at my talk that, for him, amounted to nonsense. "When was the last time you wasted forty minutes of livin' on cryin'?"

Didn't recall.

"Can't remember, can you?"

I told Walt what I'd already been thinking: "Don't recall."

"Babies an' old men cry." Walt gave a longing stare at the space the majority of his thumb no longer occupied. Gone, ripped away with his prime. "An' neither ride the rails. I can barely ride. Shit, after this," indicating to his thumb, "I just pretty much stayed in St. Lou. Even if I could ride I run outta places to go an' things to do when I get there. Don't go nowhere, got no reason to be anywhere. Know what that make me?"

The question wasn't meant to be answered. Not by me. I left it for Walt.

"A hobo rides the rails to work, a tramp just rides the rails, an' a bum don't do nothin' but set on his ass. I don't do nothin' but set on my ass in a trailer park in East St. Louie. That make me a bum. King of the Bums. Of all the people who got nothin' in this world, I'm king of 'em. Got nothin' . . . but family. Family, they always part of you, always inside. Shit, you can't get rid of family if you tried. Blood flows, Brain Nigger. Blood flows."

Blood flows. Sounded good, but the sense of it was lost in Walt's effort to be profound. I noticed that Walt was making an effort at adding profoundness to a lot of things he was saying. Not having been around him for well more than a year, I didn't know if it was a by-product of acquired age, or if royalty just naturally went out of their way to make everything they said ring important.

No matter. He was king. Let him proclamate.

"Got no control over family, Brain Nigger. Get what God gives.

The ones that talk too much, the ones that want too much, the ones that leech to ya. Cling, Brain Nigger. They cling an' they need. But no matter that bullshit I was spoutin' that got me made king, I do believe God give you family for a reason. Love 'em, hate 'em; it don't matter. You gotta be there for 'em. Got to, Charlie."

Walt looked to me for affirmation.

"Got to," I agreed.

"Got to," Walt rejoined. "Blood flows. They inside you, an' you inside them. When you got nothin', you got family. When they got nothin', they got you."

For a sec, part of me hurt.

Walt hesitated.

An obligation was about to be laid upon me.

"I got a niece. Brother's daughter. Brother ain't much." Walt stopped, bit at his lip. A little boy caught in a lie. "Shit, Brain Nigger, he is much. More 'n I am. Works in the post office. He don't haul mail around. Hell if he do that. Supervisor or somethin'. You know they got some thing where they can't much fire you once you in the post office. He makes somethin' near sixteen dollars for an hour, he could fuck the president's lady an' they can't fire him. Yeah. Next to me, he's a whole hell of a lot."

Walt paused. Maybe he paused. Maybe he was milking the moment.

Whichever, I helped him on with: "He's got a daughter."

"He's got a daughter. My niece. Sweet girl. Young. Seventeen. About. Jesus, Brain Nigger. A girl at seventeen . . . she's a whole other kind of animal. Maybe this girl is a little wild, but only some. An' like I say, she sweet. She the only one, in the whole of my family, she the only one that ever give a damn about me. Christmastime every year she get me a card. A card at Christmas. You know how good that feels?"

For me, for five years now, Christmas had been just another cold day.

"See how sweet she is?"

I saw.

"She in my manner more than my brother. Little wild, like I say. Just some. An' got the rails in her blood."

More blood talk. I noticed that Walt was referring to blood in a lot of things he was saying. Not having been around him for well more than a year, I didn't know if it was a coincidence, or if royalty just naturally equated everything to bloodlines.

No matter. He was king. Let him equate.

"Maybe I fed her some stories, told her about ridin' to here or there. Yeah, I made it sound good. It can be good; ridin' the rails. Sometimes it can. Told her all about ridin' around with you, ridin' with Brain Nigger. Those was good times. But I told her the rough bits, too. Didn't matter. Couple of months back she started ridin'." Walt stopped, then added the kicker: "Went ridin' on the High Line."

My unease had been creeping upward and talk of the High Line pushed it to critical mass.

"You know your body loses, like, two, three billion little parts of your skin every day?"

Walt did that sometimes, made a left turn without signaling.

I said: "No. Didn't know that."

"Them little parts of the body, what them called?"

"Cells."

"Two, three billion of 'em every day. Every damn day your whole body's fallin' off, an' gettin' made up new at the same time. Don't even know that shit's happenin'. It's goin' on, an' you don't even know it."

"Skin is the body's largest organ. It's nearly twenty percent of your total body weight."

"Talkin' about my niece, Brain Nigger." Walt had swerved back into the lane of relevance. "Not tryin' to talk about how much skin weighs. I don't give a good goddamn about that."

Walt was my friend. In a corrupt world, he was the least amoral person I knew. Though there was no one as familiar with rails as him, though he was now King of the Hoboes, as I had not seen him in a long while, I had to remind myself that he was crazy.

I wondered if, right then, he was reminding himself the same thing about me.

"She'd been sendin' me letters, postcards. Got three a week first off, then a couple. Haven't had nothin' in more than a month."

"Got tired of writing," I said. I said: "Stamps aren't cheap when you're Tap City."

Walt shook his head to my notions. "We're too close. She wouldn't just stop for nothin'. She find a way to pay for the mailin'. Even if she only wrote once a week, she find a way. She was excited about bein' on the rails, those first batch of letters she sent . . . But then . . ." Walt looked hard for a way to explain himself. The best he could do was: "She changed. You could hear it in the words she wrote. Two months, an' she changed."

"So she changed. She changed into the kind of girl who doesn't want to write her uncle. She still loves you, Walt," I smoke-screened. "Be happy with that."

And then Walt gave me his imperative: "Find her. Find my niece."

My response was a cold statement of fact, known and obvious, previously left unsaid, now in need of voicing. "She's dead. A little black girl riding the High Line? She doesn't have one chance in a thousand."

Me giving credence to Walt's fears only served to add to the sag age and life had already saddled on him.

Heavy is the head, baby.

Never minding the reality of things: "But if there is a chance . . . She like my own little girl. She needs me. You don't abandon your child."

Jesus. Just take some rusted metal and shank me.

I said: "I don't know the High Line. Not like you do. Why don't you—"

"Goddamn it!" He put that up in front of me like a brick wall. "Don't you think I would? I'm wore out. I'm fallin' apart. Can't hardly even catch out no more without tearin' myself up. No way I can ride the High Line. Not ride it and live."

"So I should ride it and get myself killed?"

"You Brain Nigger Charlie. You got more smarts than all other tramps an' 'boes out there. Ain't nothin' the Brain Nigger can't do."

"All the brains in the world aren't any good against a blade or goonie stick."

"A brain'll keep you from facin' one first off."

Walt did a hand-to-pocket, came up with a photo. Old. Sort of. Only by a couple of years. Edges were taped. Not to repair a tear, but to keep it from tearing. The picture: a high school photo, it looked like. Yearbook picture; kids marched into the gymnasium, handed a plastic comb, and told to primp. Stood in front of a blandish backdrop firing-squad-style and snapped. It was of a girl. She did not look like Walt. Not just in features. She did not look like Walt in tone; her skin was light as his was dark. High, high yellow. She was plump if not fat. Her hair was sandy brown, wavy no matter it was pulled back. She smiled. Some. She wasn't ugly. By no means was she, oh, say, Elle Macpherson. All in all she was passably pretty.

And she was a child.

Walt said: "Corina. Corina Leslie. Didn't tell you that before. Corina's her name."

From the corner of my eye: again Walt's hand went to his pocket.

I looked.

He held food stamps. The currency of the rail. They could be bartered or traded, easily hidden, and were mostly unwanted by common thieves. Or, if nothing else, they could be used as God and Uncle Sam intended: for food.

Walt told me: "Sixty-seven dollars' worth for your trouble. For . . . I don't know, whatever."

Sixty-seven dollars in food stamps. Who wants to be a millionaire indeed.

Lifting the coupons to my eye level as if they were a shiny distraction: "Find her for me, Brain Nigger."

The coupons were icing, but unnecessary. Not that I wouldn't take them—even at my lowest, I could calculate my worth to be at least sixty-seven dollars in government aid—but I'd already made up my mind. Or, my mind had decided things for me.

To Walt, like a vow: "I'll find her. Find her, or find what's left of her."

*Dear Uncle Walter,*

*Well, Uncle, I'm sending you this coresponding to let you know that I'm doing it. I'm finally doing it! After all the stories you've distributed to me over the years, after reading so many picture books of so many beautiful destinations, I'm finally catching out and riding the rails. I can guess that your response is predictable. "Don't be riding the rails, Corina. The rails is no place for a girl. You're likely to get cut up and raped."*

*Well, with no doubt, a certain decree of truth is in that, but bad things could happen to me crossing the street. And Milwaukee is no place for a woman with ambition, and I have a head full of those.*

*Don't worry, Uncle Walter. I'll be well and safe, and I promise to catch out carefully and mind who I jungle up with (See? I even know how to talk just like a real tramp). And I promise to write to you every chance that I get. I'm hoping to have some exciting stories for you, just as you had for me.*

*Safe rails,*

*Corina*

*PS—I am neglecting to tell Mom and Dad I'm going off riding. I will leave them a note, and no doubt they will blame you for my transactions, so excpet an angry letter from them in the near future.*

*Corina*

The measure of my life: 4 feet 8.5 inches. It was determined centuries ago by people dead so many times over it's pointless to even try to calculate the exact amount. Imperial Rome set the standard for Roman war chariots. The gauge of the wheels: 4 feet 8.5 inches. When the dagos were in their heyday taking over Europe, they built the roads to fit their chariots to allow for more convenient travel and slaughter. All the wheel ruts in the empire got gauged at 4 feet 8.5 inches. Then England got brassbound. Pretty soon they were the new superpower. No matter. They kept on building wheel ruts gauged at 4 feet 8.5 inches. And when they started building tramways they gauged them at 4 feet 8.5 inches because, apparently, fresh ideas are hard to come by. And the guys in England who built the tramways built them so well that when the colonies—which were no longer colonies, but the United States of America—wanted to get into the railroad game they hired limeys to come over and do the job. The Brits gauged the rails at 4 feet blah blah inches. And they kept gauging rail at 4 feet and some inches right up to the time Charles Harmon lost his marbles and started hopping trains.

Read all that in a book I found in a library.

I like libraries. Like to read. Reading works out the mind, keeps the brain in Brain Nigger. It is the intelligent way to kill time. Factor in the hours I can't sleep, I have much time to kill.

I like to read about trains. After I stopped getting beat up, as it was my mode of transportation, as it was my new way of life, I wanted to know about them. Time was traveling by rail was good and decent. After the early, early days of train travel, when passenger cars got loaded with amenities like springs on their wheels, cushions on their seats, it was the classy way to go. The cars were handcrafted works of art. At times, as many as six men could spend as much as sixty hours carving and polishing the rosewood or ebony or mahogany. Gold leaf was the standard inlay. There was marquetry and satin spilling out of the coach cars, parlor cars, Pullman and dining cars.

Dining cars.

Restaurants at most whistle-stops were not as fine as a dining car on the Baltimore & Ohio, the Denver & Rio Grande Western. Meals cooked fresh, made to order. Crab Imperial. Rocky Mountain Trout. Steak Diane Flambé. Get that at a drive-thru on I-15. Get that in cattle class on Southwest Airlines. That was in rail's golden age, right after the Civil War when HOe BOys—disenfranchised Yanks and rebs—would catch out and ride the rails looking for work. Looking for opportunity.

Looking for something.

The morning after the day Chocolate Walt was elected King of the Hoboes I caught out from Britt. Before going, I found a wall, tramp-tagged, and added my mark with the edge of a rock: YOU CAN'T OUT-THINK BRAIN NIGGER.

The rail yard in Britt was friendly. Tramps and 'boes could light onto a train before it started rolling, not even worry about Bulls scratching for you. I checked my rail book; a collection of trains I'd clocked over the years. A local would take me east to a BNSF union where I could catch out north to the High Line. I found an open and empty boxcar to call my own for me, George, and my pack. I carried a JanSport. Found it by the side of a road. Some road. Somewhere. When I was in grade school JanSports were what all the rich and cool kids had. I did not. I was made fun of for the off-brand I carried. It made me hate rich and cool kids, made me want a JanSport more than anything in the world. Mine, now, held my world. Cardboard; light, easy to carry, good for bedding. Few bottles of clean water. My radio. Ladies E and K. Stolen toilet paper. Whatever food I had. Maybe a couple of other things. A couple. Maybe. Mostly, that was my estate.

Rolling, I took the picture of Corina from the breast pocket of my shirt where I had determined it was least likely to get crushed in my travels. I took it out and stared at her, Corina giving her best Mona Lisa: am I smiling, or am I not? Walt had told me what little there was to know of her. There was very little to know. Seventeen, and would have been starting her senior year of high school. Beyond that, Walt had said, as close as he was to the girl, on the occasions they spoke, their conversations were built on fanciful musings of possibilities and places yet traveled. Corina was incessant in her debriefing of Walt and where he'd been and what he'd seen. His adventures on the rails, if you call digging rotted food from Dumpsters and using last week's *Time* magazine to wipe your ass an adventure. Be that as it may, Corina would listen in rapt attention to each detail, her breaths on the other end of the collect call coming as raspy as a perv's. She would listen, she would share dreams of the future, but what Corina did not do was reveal herself. She spoke very little of her present reality, or her childhood. That, especially, seemed to be lost to her. "Forget her past," Walt told me. She had, and that should tell me all I needed to know about it. Seventeen and desperate to bury what little youth she owned. Sad.

Blessing:

That I was looking for a girl was the good news. Women were rare on the rails. Even with the volume of her looks dialed to "just okay," Corina's womanhood would get her noticed; get her talked about. It shouldn't take much question-asking in the jungles, Sallys, and Goodys to get some kind of line on her—find out if she'd been tagged, who she'd been rolling with and where to.

Problem:

That I was looking for a girl was the bad news. Corina's womanhood would get her noticed; probably get her raped.

Probably?

Definitely.

What was done to men on the rails was sickening. I knew. I had front-row seats for those parties. Sometimes been the specially invited guest. What was done to women, a person who owned any humanity did not care to think about. What would be done to . . . what might already have been done to Corina made me unable to look at her little face in that little picture, knowing the eyes that stared at me might, now, be locked in an infinite gaze if not just rolled back into her head, filling the sockets with cold white.

I took out Corina's letters and postcards she'd sent to Walt, Walt had given to me. Read them. Married the words with her picture. The spelling was poor. The syntax and grammar shit. I wondered if Corina was stupid or just lacked education. Either/or, didn't matter. I didn't judge her on it. Where once a command of English seemed so important—a tool for scaling the corporate structure—in my present universe it was vestigial and even laughed at. In my years of travel, away from my cloister of people-like-me, I had come to believe that language is music: there are ten thousand different songs in existence that range in sound from interesting to ignorant, but all are equally genuine. It's only the simple-minded, indoctrinated by hand-me-downs from the King's English with no recourse but to think as told, who cannot sing for themselves. Corina's voice, though it stumbled, was beautiful in its virgin enthusiasm for all the world had to offer. Her first letter was dated April and postmarked from Milwaukee, WI. The last was stale by almost four weeks, postmarked in Williston, ND. Four weeks. A month since Walt had heard from the girl.

The High Line. What in the holy hell had she been thinking?

I looked at the picture in my hand, wondered what it was that would drive a girl from her home out onto the rails. Could her life have been that bad? Did it matter? I thought of Charles Harmon. His life had been . . . his life had been good. Comfortable. Soft. Lived in a certain blissful myopia until psychosis gave him a mugging and left him rolling on the pavement. I looked at the picture in my hand and wondered if I would ever know the true story of Corina Leslie.

The light faded from the sky and shadow hid the features of Corina's picture. I repocketed the photo, lay back on the floor of the boxcar, tired from conjecture over dark possibilities. For a time I listened to my Silvertone radio; an offering from a tramp who once had a big mouth, but learned better than to sass George Plimpton. It was AM. I was fine with that. Frequency modulation held no fascination for me. I was not particularly interested in the reigning teen pop queen's take on love, life, and the world. I did not care to listen to yet another wigger rage against the oppressive powers that held all young white men down. I listened instead to the AM talk that flowed through Middle America into my radio along the white cord to my monaural earpiece until my Silvertone lost signal altogether. Then I listened to the static. In short order, as I rode, as the car found a rhythm on which to sail a sea of steel, The Drift arrived silent as Death. As my eyes closed I found myself looking into the crystal blue cheek-eye of my unborn child. I tried to fight the vision, but its stare was hard and sure and I could only put it down with a couple of kisses from Lady K.

I lay awake through the night as the train rode west.

*Uncle Walt,*

*No matter that so many times I had seen and read about so many wonderistic places in books and on TV programs, I never new that the world was, for real, so beautiful. I rolled thorugh Nebraska today which was mostly flatish and fairly brown at that, but it was not Milwaukee and was therefore the most beautiful place I had seen. The land is very lonely. I mean by that there are so few people around. Just the plains and trees and stuff. There are some animals—I think I saw a wolf! But it might have just been a dog. Some cars pass the roads just beyond the rails, but if you squint your eyes you can harldy see them as cars, more like bright colored animals traveling there blacktop trails. Other than that this is lonely country. I don't mean that in a bad way. It's lonely so I can hear myself think. It's lonely so I can listen to the things I tell myself. It's lonely, but lonely in a beautiful way. I don't have to tell you how I mean, not all the years you've been riding. I don't have to explain how amazing things are. Funny to me, now that I'm out here—people are so afraid of being alone, but when you diverse the word, alone is really just being all one. The ironisissm of that is very deep. I feel that, out here. I'm all one with me, Uncle. I feel real good.*

*Well, I'm losing light, so I'll end this letter for now, but I promise to write again real soon.*

*Safe rails,*
*Corina*

The train began to slow-roll for Williston, and I let down inside the BNSF yard. It was an easy yard, light with Bulls. Rail police. Private cops employed by the transport companies to patrol their property. They were the guys too old, too fat, too mentally unstable . . . too something to get themselves hired by an actual municipality to do actual law enforcement. Instead they drove around in their modified Ford Tauruses enforcing their fake laws on—and only on—company-owned land; their little Barney Fifedoms.

The time of my detraining was more or less early afternoon, 1:40 according to the Lady Armitron day/date watch with the expansion bracelet I'd rescued from the bottom of a garbage can in Reno. The watch was, when found, in perfect condition except for a crack in the crystal, which was not crystal but cheap plastic. Still, that was apparently defect enough for someone to no longer want it. But wound once a day the watch had never let me down in a year and a half of wearing. If my Lady Armitron said it was more or less 1:40, then I took it to heart.

About a quarter mile from the edge of the BNSF property was the Williston jungle. Not nearly as large as the jungles in Harve or outside Spokane, it'd still managed to spread itself like a human swamp. It was a haphazard shantytown. A camp for societal refugees. The primary material of construction: plywood and sheet plastic welded with duct tape. Those who could not scrounge plywood made do with just the plastic. Those too lazy to build even remedial housing got by with cardboard boxes or settled for the sky overhead as shelter enough. Within the jungle, from pipes and sticks pressed into service as standards, territories were marked with flags that raised slightly in the light wind, flapped halfheartedly, then lay again, having made themselves barely noticed. Anarchist flags. MIA flags. A Confederate flag. Flags with swastikas and lightning bolts and an NVA flag. Almost as an afterthought someone flew an American flag. Mixed with the others, it hardly added up to a patriotic gesture. Just more pretty colors that rose on occasion, then lay back down. Campfires dotted the jungle. From most came the smell of things cooking. Literally, *things* cooking. Particular smells nearly indistinguishable beyond that, familiar only to those who've roamed jungles with regularity. Even then barely. This guy's sizzling up sausage. That guy's BBQing a hen. A meat, but none that could be readily named. A stew with vegetables rotten to the point of being just edible. And if I had a slight bit more hunger to me and had been of the mood to mingle with others there isn't one of those fires I wouldn't stop at to try and barter a plate of whatever was being roasted. But I was good for the minute, having made a meal on the journey of picked apples, a Snickers, and a couple of Little Debbie snack cakes whose shelf life of infinity made them the perfect traveling ration.

Stomach full, I avoided the jungle. I circumvented its shacks and goonie-sticked tribes and primal law: survival of the fittest or craftiest or nastiest motherfucker who refused to die no matter how many times you beat or bludgeoned or stabbed him. Moving away from all that, I headed for town.

The walk into Williston proper was not particularly long. With George Plimpton aiding me, my Armitron clocked the hike at twenty minutes. It had been nearly a year since I had last been to Socket Mama's. Five more months since the time before that. Memory was a competent guide. Only a couple of wrong turns on the way to my destination.

Any other neighborhood, Socket Mama's house would have been a well-built toilet. Any other. But on a block of run-down duplexes next to crack houses butting up against condemned houses, it was the Taj Mahal. No rusting junk in the front yard. No dead cats out back. You could sit inside her place nearly three minutes without spotting a rat, roach, or something that crawled. Socket Mama lived good. She could afford to live good. She was a whore of the uniquest variety. Her foremost quality was her ability to suck, fuck, or ball-lick any man, without regard to his look or stink, who had five dollars to offer up. Shitty as her house was, at five a trick it boggled the mind how many organs had to pass her lips just for the down payment. Mama's other uniqueness was that she was missing an eye. Her left eye. She wore a glass one, but for a mere four dollars above the price of a BJ she would pop out the prosthetic and give a customer a rim job with her socket.

Her tag didn't come from nowhere.

Arriving, from a distance I saw Socket Mama's house was sporting some new fixtures: bars on the windows. A big metal door.

The house next door—a jumble of wood, brick, and mortar: someone sat on the porch. A little boy. Or a midget. I yelled: "Socket Mama around?"

I got nothing from him.

Again: "Hey, is Socket Ma—"

Ignoring me, the little thing got up, waddled away.

Midget.

I finished the walk to the metal door, knocked. Waited. Knocked again, harder. Waited.

A peephole opened. Mama's good eye looked me over. Her glass one stared at something past my shoulder.

She asked: "Who it?"

"Brain Nigger Charlie."

"Nigger!" Mama's voice smiled. Her good eye lit up. Her glass one stared at something past my shoulder. "Didn't recognize you."

"Get that many blacks around here?"

With pride: "Oh shit, Nigger. I bring 'em in from all over. All over." Real quick the light and smile went away from her. "You alone?"

"Yes."

Real quick the light and smile came back to her. "Well, shit, Nigger, c'mon in."

On Mama's side of the door a bolt got slid back. Three or four locks got thrown. The door opened enough, just enough, for me to slip through.

I said: "Banks should be this secure."

Mama said: "I'm good as a bank, Nigger. Bank of Sweet Fuckin'. I earn my way and I live nice. You see anybody else on the street that got shit worth stealin'?"

"No."

"No. Goddamn right, no. Fuckers come in here and steal my shit awhile ago. Invaded my house." Mama swung an arm like a game show prize girl indicating her abode.

My eyes trailed Mama's arm. I saw no television, no nice furniture, art, or decent knickknacks. I thought back, couldn't remember Mama ever having anything of value. If they didn't get cash, the guys that hit Mama's put up a lot of effort for a bunch of nothing. Cash I knew she had. Yes, Mama did good business despite her rough looks. She was certainly no, oh, say, Elle Macpherson. A tiny woman. A fat woman. Her makeup looked as if she had operated by guesstimation concerning how much to put on and where to apply it: rouge closer to her jaw than cheek, lipstick that skirted her nose. Her eyebrows, shaved, were drawn in in a nonuniform fashion—one was raised in question, the other furrowed in denouncement.

And none of that mattered.

The men Mama serviced weren't looking for a pretty face. Not necessarily. Not particularly. Just a rentable hole that was ready and eager to take what they had to offer. And that Mama wa—

From a blind spot to my backside came the sound of a shell being chambered in a shotgun. The sound of such a weapon being readied for work is hideous. It is like the sound, magnified ten times ten thousand times, of dried leaves being crunched as someone walks on your grave. On the rails, Death tends to come at you from out of the sun; from where you can't see it and cannot fight it. For a second I thought Death was coming for me in the house of a one-eyed whore.

Mama read the fear on my face, yelled: "Lester, what the fuck you doin'? You see you scarin' Nigger." To me: "That's Lester. My sister's boy. Dumb as a box of hair. Ain't good for nuthin' but movin' furniture and killin' people, and one he does only a little better than the other." Yelling again: "Lester, git your ass out here and say sumthin' to Nigger!"

I turned slightly, slowly.

Behind me a closet door opened. Lester shuffled out. He was big by all applicable standards of height, weight, and girth. He was all that and stupid-looking, and those were the only polite things I could think to say about him. He also held a sawed-off shotgun. I didn't bother saying anything at all.

"Say sumthin' to Nigger," Mama prompted.

Lester let out kind of a grunt.

Staying cool despite my sweat: "Getting paranoid, Mama?"

"Told you, Nigger. They come right up in my house. Invaded my house. One of them house invasion robberies. Like 'em to try that shit again."

We all stood for a moment.

Mama: "Well, go on, Lester. Git on back to work."

Lester shuffled back into the closet. Closed the door.

Mama got right down to things: "What you want, Nigger? You want five's worth," she reached fingers for her fake eye, "or you want the full nine?"

"Don't want any of that, Mama. Something else. I'm looking for a girl."

"Well shit, Nigger, I'm all the woman you need."

"I'm out here about a girl in particular."

"Seem like every 'bo on the rails is out here 'cause of some woman in particular."

I took out the picture of Corina, held it up for Mama. "Started riding the rails a few months back. If she's got a tag, I don't know. Otherwise she goes by Corina."

Mama took the picture, not at all careful about holding it by the edges. That bristled me some.

Mama said: "Pretty girl."

"Yeah," I said.

"Got all her teeth?" Mama asked.

I answered: "Far as I know."

A beat.

"Bitch."

"You seen anything of her? She come through here, or the jungle?"

"Ain't seen her. I'd know if I had. Ain't too many women on the rails."

"That's why I'm coming to you. Lot of men pass your way. Any of them talking about some new flesh?"

Mama, shaking her head: "Nobody said nuthin'. An' any tramp that even come close to baggin' this woulda had stories to tell. I ain't heard none." Mama gave the picture of Corina a good looking-over, her stenciled eyebrows expressing jealousy, most likely over Corina's dentition. "She special to you?"

"Not particularly."

"Then why you lookin' for her? Didn't know Brain Nigger to ever stick his neck out for nobody."

"She's Chocolate Walt's niece."

"And you gonna go get yourself kilt 'cause he did you solid one time?" Mama laughed. At me. Had herself a good laugh, shook her head "poor pitiful you"-style. "Shit, Nigger. I got too many men I gotta cuddle after they cum, and they cryin' and carryin' on and confessin' shit. Men always wanna confess shit after they fuck. And I gotta lay there and lissen like I care. I lissen to you confess shit plenty."

I shifted, one foot to the other. Tried to find comfort.

"Next time you go confessing shit, oughta give yourself a lissenin' to."

"Next time we fuck, remind me to keep my mouth shut."

"God, would that be some pleasure. How long she been gone missin'?"

"Nearly four weeks."

Matter-of-fact: "She's dead," no pause, "You see any trolls outside?"

"A midget."

"I know what a goddamn midget is, Nigger. That thing ain't no midget. It's a troll." Mama moved from where she was to a front-facing window. Inching back the curtain, she spied outside, her head bobbing around as if her functioning eye was too self-important to do the job of looking all by itself. "Fuckin' troll. Always watchin' me. Gonna jack me if I give him half a chance. Let 'em. Let 'em try 'n jack me up. I'll take another three inches off of him." Yelling: "Ain't that right, Lester?"

Something got mumbled on the other side of the closet door.

Mama kept bobbing at the window, but said to me: "Anyway she's dead. There's some Death on the rails."

"Always is."

Mama turned from the window, gave me all her attention. She had a look, emotions so deep even her fake eye conveyed it. "Not like this, Nigger. Not like this." A little softer: "Know the CCR?"

"Know of them."

"They got some girl riders. Maybe they seen this bitch you lookin' for. Got a commune over on Lancaster. Fuckin' sickos."

"Compared to what else is on the rails they're harmless."

"Harmless? Livin' in those sex communes, fuckin' all the time . . . Nuthin' but drugs and fuckin'."

I didn't quite see the ground Mama was standing on. I said: "How's that different from the way you live?"

"Oh shit, I fuck for money, Nigger. That's capitalism. Them CCR kids just fuck to fuck. Fuck for free. Fuck whoever. That ain't right."

I offered Mama ten dollars in food stamps for her help. Not wanting to go through a stamp dance, she asked for ten in cash and said she'd throw in a socket job. We settled on five in stamps and five in cash. No sex. I left. Lester still in the closet, Mama still on the lookout for trolls.

*Well, Uncle,*

*What can I say? I did not know it was possible too be so hungry. Until this point I have tried to avoid writing to you about my present plight. I didn't not want to come across as just another pretender out riding the rails—some conolation of Yuppie Scum. But I have not had a decent meal in days. Decent, I don't mean a sit down at the IHOP. I mean something not cold and days old dug out of the garbage at the back of a craphole diner. Diving has been hard at any rate. The rain has been falling steady and to go diving is to get wet with no good way to get dry. I'm trying to be chalant about the situation, and I tell myself that its going to get better. I tell myself that everyday, but it every time I say it, it just makes me realize how long I've been hungry and wet. Oh, well. Don't disparage. I know, I hope, that things will get better soon.*

*Safe rails,*

*Corina*

Along the road George Plimpton and I walked, off to one side, standing in deep weeds, was a guy. White guy. But he wore a shroud of dirt that tinted him brown and rotted his flesh with patches of fungus. The wind carried his stink. I could smell him from a distance. Gripping a long thin branch, the guy swatted at the weeds. Continually. Over and over again.

"Hey," I called to the guy.

No reply.

I moved closer thinking I was too far for him to hear me. Then I saw: wasn't weeds he was swatting. It was a dog. The dog, on its side, legs extended, jerked after catching each blow. Couldn't tell if it was jerking in pain or jerking 'cause that's what carcasses do when you hit them with a stick.

I called again: "Hey!"

Ignoring me, the dirty white guy kept up with the dog-whacking. No anger. No rage. He just hit the dog to hit it. Emotionless. Dispassionate. He smacked the animal like it was nothing more than his minimum-wage gig.

One more time: "Hey!"

The guy took a break, turned to me.

"CCR; you know 'em?"

He nodded.

"They got a place around here. Know it?"

Pointing a dirty, fungused finger: "Another mile up the road. Maybe less. See a horse farm you gone too far. There's a split off toward a house. You'll know it. You can smell the pussy." He turned back for the dog, stopped, turned again to me. "Ever start doing something and you just can't stop?"

I went on up the road.

Less than a mile, like the dog beater said, a split off; a trail into a thicket of trees. I could catch whiffs of pine and evergreen. No pussy.

A hundred yards from the house—an old, run-down Victorian thing—I could see kids lying around on the porch: young pale lawn jockeys proclaiming the house CCR territory.

Different from the FTRA, NLR, STP, the CCR were three letters that abbreviated nothing. Or at least, if they did, no one knew what. Should be that way. CCR—the name—didn't mean anything. CCR—the group—didn't stand for anything. Slackers they were. Tattooed grunge punks and their pierced girlfriends who were too lazy even for sitting around drinking mochaccinos at Starbucks bitching about how the world had handed them less of something for nothing than they deserved for all they'd never done in their too few years of living. So they took to catching trains, spreading their slackerness along the rails like a lazy virus slow-crawling through veins and co-opting flophouses where the woefully disenfranchised white youth of America could go and do not a single thing. But also different from most train gangs, they counted women among their numbers. Birds of a feather flock together. Chicks in trouble look for other chicks in trouble.

No matter that they didn't know me, no matter I was a black drifter approaching, the kids outside the house—six of them. Five guys and a girl—did not move. They just slothed where they lay, looking bored. It was their version of cool: when you've got all your shit together, the world fatigues you.

"Could use a little help," I announced. If that got their attention they didn't show it. "Looking for somebody."

"We ain't seen him."

That came from one of the boys. One of the kids I thought was a boy—big, beefy, hair shaved in a bowl. But at close range he . . . she had small tits and no visible Adam's apple. That confused my speculating on its sex. Sitting in a chair, feet propped up on the porch railing, he . . . she leaned back and looked through me same as if I were a puff of smoke.

Me: "How about I finish asking the questions before you get wise?"

"How about: you're finished now. So bounce your ass on out of here."

The Shemale laughed. The other boys laughed. The other girl kinda laughed, but was timid about it.

The thing about CCR kids: they might talk big, they might act tough, but that's all it was; an act. Measured against everything else on the rails, they were only kids, nothing more. Sometimes they just had to be reminded of that.

George Plimpton got up, angry. Did work.

Guided by my hand, George whipped out, grabbed a leg of the chair the Shemale was sitting in, pulled it out from underneath it. The beast smacked the porch, smacked it hard. Its head bounced up from the wood and was met by my swinging foot. That sent the Shemale's head back down simultaneous with the opening of a bloody crevice across its lip.

The others, the boys, got some movement to them, but it was up and away from me. Four of them. They could've jumped me. Even with George on my side, they probably could have done me some damage. They were too scared to even consider the possibility. All children ever think of is how to avoid getting spanked.

I did some eye-fucking with the blob of unisex flesh below me: "You got something wise to say, or you just going to lay there and bleed?"

The Shemale's act of bold defiance was to stay where it was and do nothing more than try to look angry. Try, but not make it beyond looking beat-up and scared.

I said to them all, but kept up my stare at the Shemale: "I'm looking for a girl." Corina's picture came out of my pocket. I fanned it in a slow arch before me for all the kids to see. "Her name's Corina. She would've passed through these parts six or eight weeks ago. Any of you seen her?"

Nothing. Not a word from a one of them.

"She's gone missing. She's probably in trouble and I'm trying to help her."

More nothing. Maybe they'd seen her. Maybe they hadn't. Most likely they were too anxious to say one way or the other. They kept up nervous stares at George, afraid of what he might do next. For a second I gave thought to handing one of the kids a beating to see what kind of information would come spilling out.

Thought about it.

Instead I opted for: "Her uncle sent me out here. Her uncle is worried about her. I know that doesn't mean much to most of you. Most of you don't give a fuck about your families, or," looking square down at the Shemale, "they don't hardly give a fuck about you. But maybe one of you's got a family that was decent. One of you's got a mother or father who misses you. Maybe you miss them."

One of the kids, the one that was a girl, definitely a girl—not just, different from the Shemale, because she had sizable tits, a plump ass—she was a girl because she couldn't have been much beyond fifteen years old. Along with some body piercing and a good collection of bad tattoos—the conformist accessories of individuality—the girl sported a purple-black fist-shaped bruise on her shoulder. She had a matching one near her left eye.

The girl saw me sizing her up. She looked down, shuffled her feet. Bit at her lip. Looked back at me.

Forgetting the others, I started talking to her. "You know what it's like to be in trouble? I don't just mean a couple of bucks are the only thing standing between you and some food. I mean the kind of trouble that'll get you smacked or fucked if you're not careful, and if you're really unlucky it'll get you killed. That's the kind of helping out this girl needs. She needs it badly."

The girl looked down, shuffled her feet. Bit at her lip . . . she looked away from me. Maybe she knew things. Maybe she would talk. Maybe. But no use trying to force it, trying to get tough with her. It was obvious toughness was all she ever got. So how much was me being the thousandth person to get rough with her going to buy?

Nothing.

But there were other ways to work her.

I said to the girl, regarding Corina: "Just trying to help her, that's all." Going soft: "I'm just trying to get her back to people who give a fuck about her."

A little more feet-shuffling from the girl, then: "I seen her."

From down below me, from the Shemale: "Shut up!"

"When did you see her?"

The girl started to answer. The Shemale cut her off.

"Fuck him! You don't tell him shit!"

I looked the thing straight in the eye, spoke to it in a way that was more growl than dialogue, like I was talking to a dog that didn't know my language and could only get my tone. "Keep your mouth shut, things'll go easy. But if I have to hit you once, I'll beat you near to death. There's no middle ground."

Yeah, it got my tone.

The others, the boys, they hadn't said word one since I'd dumped the she/he on its ass and kissed its lips with my boot. They kept their mouths closed and their eyes locked on George, praying he didn't get salty and come after them.

To the girl: "What's your name?"

She looked around to the other kids.

"Forget them. Your name?"

"Dumb 'Ho."

"I didn't ask your tag. Your name?"

"Margaret."

"You're a stupid slut, and you're gonna be a sorry little bitch if you dongrahhh . . ."

My foot came down hard on the Shemale's throat, choking off whatever it had to say.

"She give you that tag?"

The girl's eyes followed my leg down to the she / he, gave a little nod.

"So is that what you are then? 'Cause she says so, you gotta be a dumb whore?"

Still looking down, the girl asked me, real quiet, real careful: ". . . What's your tag?"

"Brain Nigger."

"And that ain't wrong?"

"Nothing wrong with the brain part. I'm smart, and I claim it. Same with nigger. I call myself that; call myself a nigger. Any redneck, any WT, some racist piece of shit wants to call me a nigger . . . you see how it doesn't mean much? I own my name, I own myself. What about you? You just a dumb 'ho, or are you something better?" I gave her a beat to think on that. Again: "When did you see the girl?"

"Four weeks ago. About. Think it was her. She was thinner than in that picture."

Thinner. Thinner from not having the money to buy food or the means to get it.

"It was over in Shelby. We were catching out. I talked to her some. She wasn't doing too good, you know? Wanted to invite her back with us, but she," looking to the thing under my boot, "said no. Said she wasn't CCR, so she couldn't ride with us."

"That the way it was?" I asked the Shemale. "You wouldn't help her because she wasn't CCR? Or did you cut her off because it was a piece of her pussy she was holding back?" I ground my foot into the Shemale's throat.

The Shemale spat blood back up at me.

The girl said: "I gave her the address here, told her to come if she got real desperate. She wrote once. Said she met a guy on the rails who was giving her work."

"She give a name?"

"Keller . . . Kelner, maybe. It was something kinda Jew-sounding. I don't know what she was doing for him, but she came off happy just to be making money. She had a tag, too. I think he gave it to her." The girl made a grand show of hard thought. All she could come up with was: "Ocean Girl . . . or something. Maybe."

That was it; all there was to be had from Margaret, and all there was to be had from Margaret was only slightly more helpful than useless. I reached down and gave a quick frisk to the Shemale—a pocket held a plastic baggie with six or eight blue tabs. Lady E. Papa Smurfs. Don't mind if I do—before lifting my foot off its throat. It gasped and gurgled, rolled on the wood of the porch fish-on-dock-style.

I went to the girl, "Thanks," put a hand to her back, slipping a couple food stamps along the curve of her ass into her pocket. I hoped the other kids didn't see that. Once I was gone they'd snatch them from her with no more thought than a bullet gives to snatching a life.

I was done. I started off the porch. Not two steps from it I heard the Shemale lumbering to its feet, moving. Not for me. Wasn't even worried about that. It was moving for Margaret. Moving and screaming at her every variation of "fuck" it could think to yell—the word distorted by a fat lip, spat with fresh-flowing blood and half buried under the sound of flesh smacking flesh; a fist smacking Margaret's face.

Could've gone back. Could've broken it up. Could've, but it was pointless. The Shemale would only finish the job later, and whatever more I gave it, it would just give to the girl times six. I felt kind of bad, the girl taking a beat-down for helping me. For a minute I felt that way. Thing was, nobody told her to open her yap. And if the girl wasn't smart enough to shut up when she was told to shut up . . . She wasn't Dumb 'Ho for no good reason.

I walked my way back for the Williston rail yard.

*Uncle—*

*I don't know what to say, except that I'm at a crossroads and don't know what to do. I got choices to make, and they are not good and they are not easy. I can't believe so short ago all this was like living the dreamlife I always wanted and now it nothing like a dream. Its all so disorientating. I'm doing things I know I shouldn't, Unc, but I got to do to live. I know you wouldn't want me to, but I just got to do to live. Sorry for that, but you been out here so you know what it's like, and I know in my heart you wouldn't blame me for anything I did. I'm hungry and I'm cold and all that is just extending the situation. What I'm doing, it's work and it's pay, and later on I can worry about the right and wrongness of things. I've got to, well, like I said. I've got to do to live.*

*I'll talk to you later.*

*Safe rails,*

*Corina*

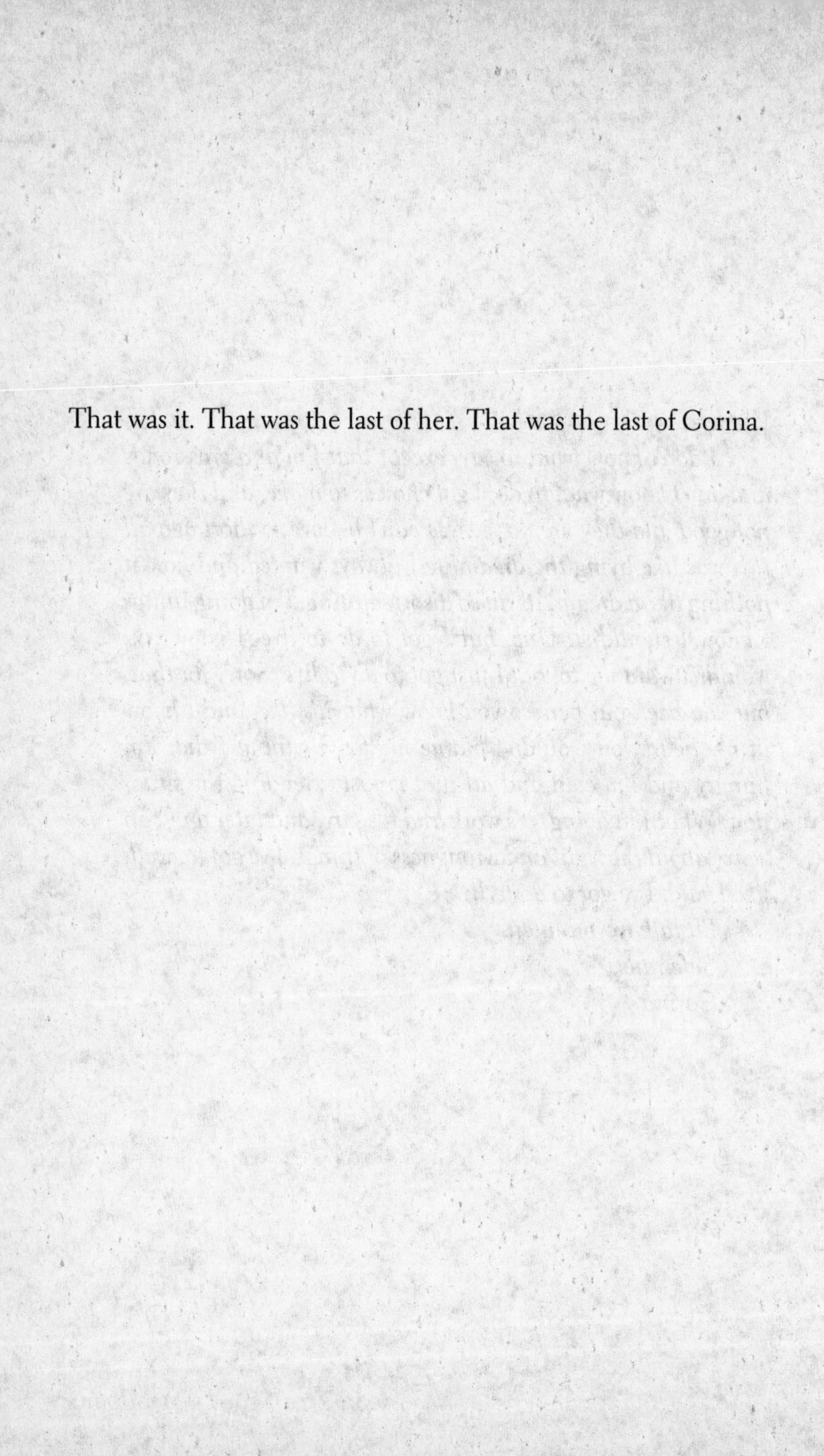

That was it. That was the last of her. That was the last of Corina.

I had a name.

Kind of.

A destination.

Sort of.

It had cost me ten dollars in food stamps, five in cash to get that little bit of noninformation. I wondered a second what the bill for finding out things that were actually useful was going to run.

Catching out of Williston: I hoped my rail book had not gone stale; there was still a train rolling about the time I had last clocked a year ago. My book would be no good from here on. Williston was as far along on the High Line as I'd ever been. As far as I felt safe traveling. Where I'd be heading was new territory. Darkest America. The yard was heavier with Bulls than when I'd rode in. They were scratching around something fierce. No way I'd hop a sitting car. I'd have to catch out on a train that was rolling. Didn't care for that. Didn't have a choice.

Beyond the property, crouched, a good grip on my pack and on George, I was ready to bolt. Once a train left a yard it would get speed. When it was rolling more than twenty-five miles an hour, if not impossible to board, it was attempted only as an act of pure idiocy. That was a fact of physics generally held by 'boes, but that I also had learned on my own. It was forever scrawled up and down my left leg.

I waited.

It would be nice to catch a boxcar. It was cool for an August night. A gondola, a flatcar, or even a piggyback wouldn't be bad. But inside is always better. Except in the heat of July, high noon. Heat of July, high noon, an oven at Bergen-Belsen would be better. But it was an August night. It was cool. It would be nice to get a boxcar. An empty. Something near the head end, or rear so the tensioned springs didn't read the tracks too well; the ride wasn't too rough. Yes, that would be nice. It would also be nice to have, oh, say, Elle Macpherson pick me up in her Ferrari and drive me to Shelby as I rested. I would ride in whatever part of the train I could catch.

I waited.

In the yard I could hear a switcher humping—picking up speed, pushing cars, the sound of them banging and banging and banging. Echoing off invisibly as if they existed on a whole other plane than myself.

I waited.

Above me, darkness pinholed a billion times over. Around me, near quiet broken only by nature: owls and critters and the solo of a wild dog. Stillness. With so much unseen and unheard there was a vacuum of substance that seemed to invite and accept only more emptiness. It was like being on the event horizon of a black hole that inspired, never expired. That was, all of that, ingredients for The Drift. And it was out there. It sat in patience where the rails ran together, their point of convergence, far off in the night. It was where I was headed. I looked toward it disquietly.

From the yard: the sound of a locomotive. The low rumble of a train. Thoughts of The Drift let me get caught off guard. Quick, I was up and moving for a cyclops light that macheted a path for the train to pass through. Running, running for it. Crossing track. My foot caught rail. I went down. My chest smacked ground, punched the air from me. I lay where I fell, sucked hard two, three times before I could catch breath. I struggled up to hands and knees, I oriented for the train. It was picking up speed. If it wasn't moving twenty, it was close.

I could skip the train, let it roll on. I could stay where I was. Stay down. Catch out on another train. Tomorrow. Sometime.

Except

Corina.

If she was already dead, tomorrow she wouldn't be any less so.

But

If she was still alive, a day, a few hours, might keep her that way.

I looked down the train: a boxcar rolling my way fast. Door open.

A gaping mouth screaming at me: "C'mon, Brain Nigger! Let's go, Brain Nigger! Show me something, nigger."

I did not care to be mocked, especially by inanimate objects.

I got up. I ran. Breath still short, I tried to match speed and trajectory. I stumbled some in the soft gravel. Didn't go down. Couldn't. Couldn't let myself go down. Making the door, I tossed in my pack, George. For a few yards I ran with the train, reached up locked on one hand, the other, got purchase with my foot. Three points. Felt safe. An illusion. Wasn't safe. Wouldn't be safe until I was in. I pulled up, keeping my limbs close—so they wouldn't get smacked off by a passing track sign—but not too close—so they wouldn't get tangled in brake cable. I hauled, hauled myself into the car: a sack of flesh being self-loaded as freight.

And I lay. And I breathed. And I rested.

Catching out on the run was not something you got better at, just something you survived.

And I lay. And I breathed. And I rested.

I rolled. I looked up. I saw him. A bum. He was about my age, which meant he was generally too young to be riding the rails. Clean-cut for a bum, too; hair shaved tight. Not skinhead tight. He wasn't Yuppie Scum, either. His clothes were filthy, worn, and from him I caught an unmistakable days-without-a-bath reek. And different from Yuppie Scum, he had enough rail wits to hop a train, no matter the scratching Bulls, in the yard. He had that over me.

Pieces of moonlight kicked off the wet of his eyes. They were open and ogling me. But all the bum did was look. He said nothing. I was fine with that. It was always better to ride alone. Generally you didn't slit your own throat and rob yourself blind in the middle of the night. But single-occupancy accommodations were never guaranteed even in boxcars pulling out for all points in the dead of night. Sleep, avoided by me anyway, was no longer a consideration. I wasn't going to shut myself down around an unknown quantity. But as long as he kept to himself and didn't try to come near me so that I would be forced to beat him just about dead with George Plimpton, we would do real well together.

I longed for drugs.

I fingered the freshly acquired Smurfs in my pocket. On autopilot, my senses fantasized about bumping one: so fucking bitter to the taste, held under the tongue as hot spit broke it down and passed it into the circulatory system. In time, in a short amount of time, would come the flush skin and full-body tingle and the philosophical conviction that no matter you were gamy and hungry and riding in a rickety, squalid boxcar, life was beautiful, man. Life was soooo beautiful.

"Smoke?"

I looked up, looked over. It was the bum ruining our perfect relationship by talking to me, offering me a cig.

"Smoke?"

"No," I said. That's all I said. Curt. Short. Hoping he would get I wasn't looking for conversation.

He didn't. "Mind?" He lifted the cigarette, asking if it was okay to light up.

I didn't answer.

He lit up.

Train rolling near fifty miles an hour, air hacking through the car, I could still smell the bum's smoke. Dirty as I was, as many odors as I carried, as many smells as I'd encountered digging for edibles among putrid garbage in back-alley Dumpsters in the hot days of summer, the stench of cigarettes was something that I still managed to hate.

Of course, the bum had to say: "Love a good smoke." He took the cig from his mouth, gave it the same longing look a NAMBLA freak would give a prepube dick. "All anybody ever talks about on TV is how this shit's bad for you. Don't even got that Jim Camel anymore, or whatever. Fuck 'em; telling me what to do. I won't even watch TV anymore."

I was sure the entertainment industry suffered the loss.

The train slowed. We were siding. Fabulous. That's all I needed. A little more quality time with my new bud.

"Shit kills me, so what? Something's gonna get you sooner or later. Every day you live, you're just one day closer to dying."

Every day you live, you're just one day . . . The notions of a railroad philosopher never ceased to underwhelm me. They were so loony or so high they figured there was something in traveling place to place on an outmoded form of transportation on the fringe of society that gave them a particularly significant insight into the human condition. The only revelation I'd had in my five years was that as shitty as life was there was always room for it to become just a little bit more so.

"You military?" he asked.

Again I didn't answer, and again it had no effect on the conversation.

"I'm military. Don't serve. Not now. But I say I'm military. It never leaves you. A part of it never does."

On a parallel track a train rushed by in the opposite direction. Amtrak. The Empire Builder. Flashes of light through the windows of the passenger cars. Glimpses of people moving too fast to be distinguished, then gone.

As the Amtrak dopplered off: "Part of it never leaves you." The bum picked up where he'd left off almost to the syllable. "I quit it, though. Had to. Didn't hate it. Makes a man of you, that's for goddamn sure. Made a man of me. What I couldn't take was the regimen. Always someone busting your ass; telling you what to do. What to do," he repeated. "Couldn't take that shit. Don't got that shit on the rails, know what I'm saying?" he asked. "You know what I'm saying," he insisted.

Our train started rolling again.

"Out here you got no regimental organizational shit. Out here you don't have to . . . you just, what you got is—"

"Freedom."

"Freedom. Yeah." He marveled at my ability to sum up a collection of ideas into a single word as if it was a strange science that bordered on magic. "Freedom. Shit. Freedom's a hell of a thing. Still, even at that, the military never quits you all the way. Some of the shit I seen . . ."

The bum killed his smoke, flicked the butt for the open door. Air grabbed it, swatted it right back into the car.

The bum: "I was in the Gulf. I was right in the heart of that shit."

I got myself ready for an "oh, how war fucked me up" story that I'd heard from the occasional Korean War vet still riding the rails, and the too-goddamn-many Vietnam War vets, and from one vet who claimed the invasion of Grenada forever changed him. How you go mental spending half an hour wiping out farmers I don't get.

But I was wrong. This bum didn't have any of that for me.

"Tell you this: I ain't saying war is any good. It's not. Not one good thing about it. But as a person, as an American . . . that shit was the most proud moment of my life. Maybe, you know, it wasn't like World War Two; wasn't like we were going after Nazis and shit. The Gulf was just about freeing up oil so Yuppie Scum could gas up their little German cars. But I was . . . we were—and that's what it's about, you know. We. Us. All of us over there; we were fighting together for something. We were standing up for some shit.

"Do you know, serious, do you know how good it feels to stand up for some shit?"

Stand up for something. Be honorable and fight for something, instead of just tossing it aside as a matter of convenience.

"No." Forgetting my burning desire not to say word one to the bum, I said to the bum: "Tell me about it."

"I get asked about it; people find out I fought, they want to know. I try to explain things, but unless you were really there . . ."

"Try." I was suddenly desperate to know. "Were you scared?"

The near dark was lit by the "you dumb fuck" look the bum flashed. He said, harsh: "You dumb fuck. Them motherfuckers had nerve gas and a bigass cannon gun and those fucking Scuds *with* that fucking nerve gas on 'em . . . was I scared?"

"Sorry," I was compelled to say to the tramp. In my mind I had upgraded him from bum to tramp.

Still harsh: "Was I—"

"Sorry."

Still harsh: "You bet your ass I was fucking—"

"Sorry."

He went quiet. For nearly a minute there was the roll of the trucks over the rails, the groan of metal and the creak of wood as the train was dragged westward. But there was nothing from the tramp.

He was so quiet for so long that I finally almost said, again, "sorry," and prepared to go from that right into begging to be told what war was like for him when, finally, he said: "But that's the point; to be scared and not fucking run like a girl. Shit, if the whole dealy didn't scare the shit out of you, then what the hell's the point? If it was like opening a gift on Christmas morning . . . every motherfucker can do that. That don't make you feel good about you. Doing what shit everybody else can't, that's what makes you feel good about you."

I started to ask something.

He stopped me with: "Thing of it is, when the whole dealy was over I did kinda feel like a girl anyhow 'cause you're scared and it turns out just about nobody got killed anyway. Hardly none of us got killed, and they were like surrendering to CNN. Got all worried for nothing."

"Fighting man?" I asked.

"We were all fightin' men," he said. He said it in his "you dumb fuck" manner.

"Were you, I mean, infantry?"

"Nah." In the dark his head nodded to the negative. "Air Force. Was with the Fourth Wing at Al Kharj."

"Did you kill anyone?"

The tramp went quiet for another full minute. Nearly. I wasn't sure if he was thinking on my question, ignoring me because my question had been one more in a string that were obvious and annoying, and, thereby, offending.

Eventually: "I killed people. Don't know for a fact, but I'm pretty sure I did. It's not like I was looking anybody in the eye when I offed 'em. Days of looking the other guy in the eye when you take 'em out are just about done anyhow. But I flew a strike over the highway at Al Jahra."

He paused, waiting for a response from me. I gave none. He took that, correctly, to mean I had not one idea in hell what he was talking about.

"Last day of the war. I mean, like, last day, last hour just about. Had the Iraqis on the run. Iraqis, you see how I said that? Not sand niggers or desert monkeys. They were the enemy, but that don't mean I go for all that mind-hate bullshit the military tries to feed you. Anyhow, last day and all, and we had them fuckers running. We were flying over Al Jahra. There was, easy, an unbroken couple of miles of people streaming out of Kuwait on this one highway. Like a . . . like a line of ants. Ever see that?"

"I've seen it."

"Know how ants move in a line?"

"I know."

"That's what it looked like swooping down in our F-15s. And you know how easy it is to step on ants in a line. Well . . ."

Yeah. Well.

"Fish in a barrel. Ducks in a pond. Ants in a line. Just kept goin' back over 'em and over 'em and over 'em. It was like a strafe buffet: did you try the potatoes? What about the chicken? And make sure you send a couple of cluster bombs into that woman down there. Yep. You heard right. *Woman.* Women. Children. Old fuckers. All that. Wasn't just soldiers gettin' out of Kuwait. Wasn't just soldiers on that highway."

Way up the line the Unit let out a piercing whistle; let all who cared to know it was coming.

"I thought for sure that would fuck me up, knowin'—like I said, not for sure, but knowin'—I'd wiped out, I dunno, a couple hundred people. At least that. At least that many. Know what?"

"No, what?"

"Didn't fuck me up at all. In a way, it not fucking me up . . . well, I felt sorta wrong about the whole dealy. I felt . . . well, that's the thing: I didn't feel. I didn't feel, and that made me feel not right. Not . . . human. You can't kill and not feel shit. That's sick. Fuck that. I'm not sick. I wasn't about to go around not feeling human. I set about correcting that shit straight off."

He stopped talking for a third time. For a third time he went quiet and left me hanging like a kid listening to a campfire story.

The Holy Grail. I felt like I was standing just beyond the reach of the Holy Grail or that I'd climbed the highest mountain, by accident, to find a wise man sitting and waiting and ready to tell me the secret of the universe. My universe.

"How?" I asked.

"How what?" he asked.

"You said you went about correcting that; correcting how you didn't feel anything."

"Fuck yeah. Didn't want to kill people and not feel human."

"So?"

"So . . . ?" His tone asked: What is it about the painfully obvious that you do not understand?

"So, what did you do? How do you make yourself feel human?"

"Still trying to figure that out. Killed that boy in Detroit. Almost felt something. He was ten. Maybe that ain't young enough. Maybe I gotta kill 'em younger."

In zero time I iced up as if my body had just taken a massive injection of near-freezing water.

"Maybe that's it. Killed men, killed women, killed old women, killed whores. Killed any number of whores. Just can't get a feeling. Fuck that shit. I'm gonna feel something. I promise you I'm gonna keep twisting necks until I feel something."

Despite the near dark, with incredible clarity I was able to see the tramp staring at me. With the same precision I was able to measure his hands and determine they were sized just right for bare-handed slaughter. And, again, with a newfound exactitude for mental determination, I knew, in his mind, I was already dead. All that remained was for him to physicalize the act. Instinct had me groping for George and his trick before my brain even achieved the thought. All my hand felt was the floor of the boxcar, nothing more. Nothing like a goonie stick. The motion of the train had sent George rolling feet away from me. I'd been too engrossed in the tramp's—the bum's . . . the killer's story to even notice. George was near enough that I could get up and go and grab him, but I did not know if I could get up and go and grab him before the bum cut me off and adjusted my head so that I had a real nice view of my spine. The one thing that was for sure: it was no good letting the tramp in on how without George I was nothing but a hairless Sampson.

I said: "I'll give you something to feel."

All excited: "Yeah?"

"Yeah. Forget about what this side of Death feels like; the killing side. You'll never feel anything over here. I'll show you what the other side feels like." Wasn't trying to scare him. Wasn't trying to scare him by sounding tough. He was a military man. He could end my life forty-three different ways, all of them easy for him. A tough act was not going to keep Mrs. Harmon's son from dying. I had to speak to him in a language he understood. One, fortunately, that was not completely alien to me. I spoke to him in the tongue of psychosis. "I'll show you ten thousand miles of trimmed sunshine that'll come at you like birds falling from the sky. That shit tastes good. Yummy through and through."

For a few seconds, nothing.

Then: "How would you know?"

"I wouldn't give you any shit I didn't taste myself. That'd be like giving you some pussy I never fucked. And they tell me; the ones I sent over." Laughed a little. "The ones I sent over, they never shut up. C'mon. C'mon close. C'mon close, let me show you something."

For a few more seconds, nothing. The nothing dragged on into a minute. Three. Eight. The bum didn't say a word. Didn't move. The bum didn't know what to make of me except that his trying to kill me might get him some of the same. When I was sure that he was too unsure to be a danger, I casually moved for George, collected him, returned to where I'd been sitting—across from and in good view of the vet. With the added advantage of having gone many, many sleepless nights, I was able to out-awake him. He dozed. I rode wondering how Death would step to me next.

Shelby. Shelby, MT. Shelby is where the I-2 running east-west X's the north-south I-15. The main east-west BNSF line is X'd by a line running south from Great Falls to Sweetgrass in the north before it shoots into Canada. Lot of roads. Lot of lines. That made the Shelby yard a hot one. Traffic heavy. Freight. Intermodal. Unit grain trains. Some passenger rail. And colorful, too. Shelby's got color to it with the red and silver Warbonnets, the orange Pumpkins, red, silver, and blue Amtraks hauling through on regular schedules. Even all the diesel exhaust from the Units, the tractor-trailers, could only tone all the shades down, not blot them out. In an ugly world, Shelby made for a sootily brilliant oasis.

Except for a sense of foreboding and ever-present Bulls.

The foreboding I brought with me. The Bulls were in full effect when I arrived, scratching heavy—searching inside cars, searching under cars . . . scratching like they were looking for something in particular, something besides tramps and 'boes to beat for sport—and were only avoided by good skill and great luck. I had a little of both. Quick as we could, George and I left the yard, left the Bulls to their business.

Questions needed to be asked. Like a busted boomerang, I had to throw out part of a name and see what came back to me. The jungle was no good for making inquiries. The 'boes and tramps there weren't like a bunch of CCR kids I was trying to shake up with a pants-down spanking. They were train gangers. Hardcore. And in a region unfamiliar to me or not, a jungle was a jungle. In the jungles territory was staked, you stuck to yourself unless invited. Strangers were trespassers. Questions usually got answered with a shiv to the ribs. I had to find individuals who were more inclined to take inquiries, if not give responses.

A pay phone. Four-one-one. A woman, somewhere, answered my dial with "What listing?" Her voice so pretty and pure she could've earned her keep easy doing phone sex. I considered asking if she'd ever given thought to the idea.

Instead: "Salvation Army. Need a street address."

Little Miss Chesty L'Amour, or whatever I'd call her when later I touched myself to the few words she'd spoken, added a hint of attitude to her voice. She wasn't thrilled about having to read me a street address instead of just patching me into a computer that would monotone a number to me. Fuck her. I would. Later. In my mind. I'd fuck her in my head so hard she'd feel me in her life. Spiders slow-crawling over her flesh. That'll be me in your joy hole, baby.

The Sally was on Division Street.

I didn't know where Division Street was.

I detoured to a gas station to ask directions. The chick working the counter—thin, pasty—gave me a look like I'd come around asking about her daughter. I got sent for the Sally by way of vague finger-points.

I walked.

Walked.

The end of town I walked myself to was Home Guard territory: flophouses and SROs populated by the local bums. They wandered up and down the streets, sat on stoops and corners, pissed in alleyways. They were alcoholic rats trapped in a maze of urban decay. Low as train tramps were, at least they had it in them to get up the energy, make the effort, catch out and ride to somewhere even if they had nowhere in particular to be. Home Guard? They just sat on stoops and corners, pissed in alleyways.

A liquor store. A few bottles of Mad Dog set me back less than ten dollars (not technically a wine, it's listed as a wine product. You figure it out). I could barely afford the bottles, but for the work I had to do they were tools I would need.

I walked.

Walked.

Division Street.

Finally I came on the Sally; a Salvation Army store. Macy's for the poor. Bloomingdale's for those who aspired to move from destitute to indigent. Around back drunks on temp rehab unloaded used knick-knacks and thingamajigs and doodads from trucks and vans that had made collection runs. There was the occasional Volvo-driving mom who'd come around to donate little Skip or Briana's old clothes, but having made the trip was now too scared of all the poor people to get up off her leatherette seat and just drove off instead. Windows rolled up. Doors locked.

It was late in the day, but still August hot. The drunks working the trucks and vans were slick from a sweat generated by one-third labor, two-thirds DTs. It sheened their faces, soaked their clothes.

Perfect.

I loitered across the street under shade but in full view. I slid out a bottle of the MD, cracked it open—for the alchies the sound echoed same as a train jumping the rails—put the bottle to my lips, pretended to drink. Booze wasn't my poison. I was just making a show of things. Little performance was needed before first one, then another of the Home Guard spotted me. Spotted the bottle. A beat later they came buzzing over like flies to liquid shit, nonchalanting across the street as if heading my way by happenstance. Their hands wiped their brows, their tongues circled their lips. Their mouths clacked about the heat, and how it'd been hot all day, and how it was likely to be hot again tomorrow . . . Their mouths talked just to talk. Their eyes kept up a stare at the bottle.

I offered a drink. To a man they accepted. The Mad Dog was passed among them without thought of, or any care given to, the previous set of lips that had slathered the glass. Comment was reserved solely for how the goddamn Sally wants you to be goddamn sober all the goddamn time.

Life wasn't meant to be lived sober.

That sentiment got Amen'd with another hit of booze all around. And in the drinking and conversation I let slip that I was looking for work.

"Yeah?"

"Yeah."

"Gotta work. Ain't nothing free in the world," one Home Guard noted, never mind that he was taking my liquor gratis.

Another Home Guard mentioned the Sally was always taking people on.

I shook my head to the idea, made a comment about the work being too hard and drinking not allowed.

"Know a job where they pay ya ta get high?" one asked, then cracked up at his own self.

Real casual I said how I'd heard about a guy who was hiring tramps right off the rails, knew a girl who got work with him; a girl fer crissake! His name was Kessner, or Kellner . . .

The one Home Guard went back to talking about a job where you could get lifted being his wet dream.

Nobody claimed knowledge of a Koester or Kelso or Klerner. I made a point of saying if anybody did hear anything I'd be jungled up for a while. I'd be easy to find. Just look for the nigger.

Laughter. I was a likable guy. What's not to like about a guy who gives away booze?

The bottle went dry.

Real quick the Home Guard and demidrunks were no longer interested in me. I no longer had anything to take. What good was I? Back across the street they went, back to their sweaty labor like I'd never existed in the first place.

I moved on, tried the same routine at a Goody I came across. I got takers for my liquor. I got toothless grins at my nigger line. I got no information on Kleman or Kelmer or Kipman.

With nothing to show for the day, I oriented George and myself for the jungle, moving at an amble. There was no rush. All that waited was hard ground for a bed and sleep that wouldn't come for fear of what waited in my dreams. I would make my stay overnight, go fishing again in the morning with a fresh bottle for bait. I told myself I would keep trying until I turned up information or ran out of booze money. My feeling at the moment was the booze money would go first.

Near the yard: I crossed under an overpass. It was littered with scrawls and graffiti. Marked territory. A message board of the rails:

WHERE YOU AT NO KNEES  IF GOD LOVED NIGGERS WHY'D HE MAKE EM SO EASY FOR KILLIN  FTRA  SAN JOSE LONGNECK GOING TO PHOENIX. That was dated 8/12 of this year, in case anyone was looking for San Jose Longneck. THE DEVIL IS TRICKY/IF YOU'RE NOT CAREFUL HE'LL MAKE A FOOL OF YOU/DON'T BE THE DEVIL'S FOOL wrote Slo Freight Ben.

I took up a good-sized rock, tattooed my mark onto the concrete: YOU CAN'T OUTTHINK BRAIN NIGGER

I went on for the jungle.

Finding some decent real estate—with a piece of wood for a broom I cleaned the ground of garbage and shit, both animal and human—I jungled up. Among, but separated from, others, I didn't bother to join in with their drink or talk. I used the jungle only to make being found easier if any of the Home Guard should recall something about Kipling or Kilroy or . . .

With George tight at my side I lay myself down on my cardboard bed for the night. I lay from dark until light. There was maybe a twenty-minute time I could call sleep before the three-eyed child came for me.

In the early morning hours of the twenty-sixth of May in 1934 a glistening stainless steel train, slick and sleek as a silver arrow, left Denver's Union Station for a record-breaking run across the Burlington line to Chicago. For one thousand miles, across four states, newspaper reporters and photogs, radio journos lined just about every foot of the tracks. Old men and children alike stood for hours waiting to see what had never been seen before. A train like no other. The Chicago / Burlington & Quincy Zephyr.

When the Zephyr made its run America was neck deep in the depression. Ridership on the country's passenger trains had dropped to their lowest levels since the Civil War. People barely had money to eat. They had no dough for trains. Like every product, every service, the rails were desperate for a lure.

The Budds had one.

Ralph Budd, the prexy of the Chicago / Burlington & Quincy line, and Ed Budd—no relation. Or maybe a distant one depending on whose story you hear—an engineer. Ed had been cooking up a new kind of train, one built from welded stainless steel. Stainless steel was lighter than regular steel. Lighter meant it took less power to pull. Lighter meant you could add more cars to a train. Lighter meant faster. All that meant lower costs, more profit. Ralph Budd dug that. Ralph tossed Ed a big chunk of change to build a welded stainless steel train for the C / B&Q line.

And then the Budds had another big idea. Instead of building just another steam locomotive to pull their train, they were going to make the Unit an internal combustion engine. And instead of making just any engine, they were going to round the edges, give it no hard corners. What they were going to do, they were going to streamline it.

And it, the god of the westerly winds—the Zephyr—was a train like no other.

It was shiny and it was smooth. It moved at speeds upwards of 112 mph. Even small planes could not pace it. The Zephyr, all by its lonesome, was a whole new era in transportation. It was the future, now. Actual plumbing and recessed lighting and double-paned windows. Air-conditioning. Standing still, it was going places fast. And wherever the train went, people by the hundreds showed up just to ogle it as if they were glimpsing a vision of a better kind of life. Real quick the Zephyr was joined by other Streamliners. The New York / New Haven & Hartford Railroad had its Goodyear-Zeppelin Comet. Seaboard Railways' Meteor. The Super Chief and the El Capitan. The Broadway Limited. The 20th Century Limited. And just in being they changed life. After they hit the scene everything had to be streamlined. Had to be. Automobiles. Toasters. Washing machines. If it was not curved and shapely and gleaming, it was not relevant.

All things were measured against the Streamliners.

American rail had its renaissance.

The renaissance did not last.

America decided it liked cars better than trains. In '56 Ike started building the Defense Highway System—a shine the Feds and the auto companies cooked up to get the taxpayers to shell out for forty-two thousand miles of highway to drive Studebakers and De Sotos on—and America decided it liked cars better than trains and Stuckey's better than dining cars and screaming kids fighting in the back of a station wagon better than sitting upright and comfortable like Evolved Man and watching the countryside pass by your window. And fast-forward a few decades to when air travel got so cheap everybody could afford it and flying a plane got to be no better than riding a bus with wings, and trains got knocked down below Greyhounds. Other than the government-misrun Amtrak, the passenger train was pretty much dead.

But for a time . . . there was a train like no other. It is, when viewed in reflection, an insignificant thing made significant. The Zephyr put food on no one's table. It didn't truly take the hurt off anyone's suffering. But in the country's bleakest season it gave her the one thing she so very much required.

It gave her
Hope.

The nausea I normally felt from spending the night awake was, by now, merely a background sensation that I would suffer through until it faded by midmorning. My Armitron told me it was 6:20 in the a.m. when the sun forced me to stop lying awake thinking about trains that used to be, and get up and do something. I packed up my JanSport, got ready to leave the jungle and try to catch scent of Corina.

I looked up.

A Bull was heading my direction. He didn't have a gut sloshing out over his belt, so sized up to most Bulls I would describe him as being thin. Forty, maybe forty-five years of age. Hair grown out to just about but not quite where it wasn't regulation. His mustache was bushy in the cartoon walrus variety. He came at me with an ambling sort of gait. I think it was an honest-to-God mosey. Although his manner was easy, it was still unsettling. He wasn't on rail property. There wasn't much he could do to a tramp. Legally. But he had a gun. He had a sap. Technically, realistically, he could pretty much do as he pleased.

I got ready for trouble. I got ready for an inquisition and maybe some slapping around. For starters.

When the Bull arrived to me he stopped, stuck his hands in his pockets, rocked on his heels . . . had himself a good look around the jungle. When he got done with all of that he said, all he said was: "Coffee?"

Not that I didn't hear what he'd asked, but still it caught me enough by surprise that I had to respond to it with: "What?"

"Coffee. Got any?"

". . . No."

"Could go for coffee."

Never mind his lack of belligerence. I snided to him: "That's what Starbucks is for."

The Bull kept up his casual look around the jungle. Just as casual was the slight shake of his head. "That's no good for me. I've had too many cups in too many jungles. Unless it's brewed up in a can over an open fire, strong as tar . . . might as well be drinking water." He stopped looking over the jungle. He looked in my direction like he'd just then noticed me. "Got a tag?"

"Brain Nigger Charlie."

The Bull nodded as if, in considering the name, it met with his approval. He said: "Haxton." He didn't bother holding out a hand for me to shake. He wasn't being rude, or snooty; not wanting to touch flesh with a tramp. He knew a tramp didn't much want to grip paws with a Bull. He didn't bother making the gesture.

"Haxton." I repeated. "Odd name."

"My parents were odd people. You're kinda far off from the rest of the jungle. Keep to yourself pretty much?"

"Pretty much. Keep to yourself, keep out of trouble."

"Words to live by." His official company-logo'd cap came off. A handkerchief came up out from his pocket, mopped his head and brow. "Words to live by," he said again, then: "Don't see too many colored fellas on this end of the rails."

"Maybe because on this end of the rails we get called coloreds."

Haxton gave a sheepish smile that admitted fault. "No issues. African-American just feels a mouthful."

"Black'll do."

"Don't see many blacks out this way, then."

I shrugged to that. "See many anywhere?"

"Chicago. Atlanta. Plenty of col . . . blacks riding back that way."

"Been through that corridor?"

"Been all over."

I was curious. Most Bulls didn't travel beyond the direct vicinity of their yard. Without asking, but hinting: "You get around for a Bull."

"Suppose I'm what you'd call a special Special Agent. I investigate for the railroad."

"Investigate what?"

Haxton gave the jungle another indifferent review. Talking to me, but looking at something maybe a hundred yards off: "Don't get many blacks this way."

"You said."

"Don't get many Hispanic fellas either."

"Guess not."

His head came around. His eyes found me squarely. "Occasioned any, in this part of the corridor?"

Haxton was a Bull. A Bull was to a tramp what a razor blade was to a hemophiliac. And here he was not kicking ass, but asking questions and I didn't even know why. By rights my mouth should've stayed shut, and if it opened at all only to lie.

By rights.

I said, in truth: "No."

For Haxton it was like I'd said nothing at all. He didn't respond in any way other than to say, as if coming full circle: "Damn, but I could go for some joe. Some days it's hard as hell for a Bull to get brew in a jungle." A huffing breath of disappointment. The painful reality of a no-coffee morning setting in. To end the conversation, "Safe rails," Haxton offered, and started away.

He left me with no hassle or bother, only the kind words. I watched the Bull walk on a bit with that odd gait of his, and I knew if I could see my own face it would be jumbled up with some queer "what the fuck" expression same as if I was watching a carnival freak head back for its tent.

"Why?"

The Bull stopped, turned back to me.

I called again: "Why you looking for a Mexican?"

"I'm looking for a Hispanic."

Whatever. "Why?"

He took a few steps in my direction without coming all the way back to me. "Where you riding from?"

"Iowa."

"And you just now come out this way?"

"Yes."

The Bull seemed to consider things. When he'd come to whatever conclusion he'd come to, he said once more: "Safe rails," and walked on.

I found a public toilet, lathered my head with soap, and gave it a going-over with a plastic Bic shaver. Last of a packet I'd found in a

Dumpster out back of a Walgreens. It was very dull. The shave was bad. It irritated my skin. But the razor would have to make do until I could find and/or steal a new one. I had a toothbrush but no toothpaste. I took a crap, used the last of the toilet paper and the cardboard roll as well.

I was ready for the day.

Loaded with MD, I set out to make rounds at whatever soup kitchens and missions I came across. For my trouble I expected to get less than I had the day before. The kitchens and missions would be populated by true bums—men whose only job was to avoid work. The chances of them knowing anything about a guy offering labor was as unlikely as oh, say, Elle Macpherson dropping by for a bump of K and a roll in the dirt. But I was without options. I went for the kitchens.

As I walked I passed a section of rail where a couple of sedans were stopped. Standing around them were a bunch of guys in dark suits and shades. Standing, looking for something. Looking at something. Beyond them were some local cop cars, cops who kept their distance from the suited/shaded guys.

Socket Mama's warning. The Bull. Now Feds and cops in full force. A lot of badness happened on the rails with great regularity and it all went unnoticed, or at the very least un-cared-about by the civilized world. Something was happening now, and that it merited attention told me it was bad to the monumental.

Whatever. It was tangential to me. I walked on.

With all I'd ever seen on the rails, hopeless lives shuttled by freight train from one location to another, there was nothing more depressing than soup kitchens and the people who lived for its free food; for one decent meal a day and the chance to sit down and eat like a person instead of scrounging stray-dog-style through garbage in an alley. The kitchens were nothing more than a collection of men, together but alone, shuffling along a food line. Shamed by their station, they kept their heads bowed and moved in a hesitant manner as if the whole of them was a personified apology for their very existence. Suburban liberals spooned out a stewed poultice for their own upper-middle-class guilt with every ladle of whatever they slopped into the bowls that dry-drunk jittered in the shaky hands holding them.

I just about felt bad for introducing booze into this pathetic mix, introducing disease to native people. But saving souls wasn't my business. I had a lost girl to find.

I cracked open a bottle. I made my rounds.

"Keller?"

"No."

"Klinger?"

"Nah."

"Kleinman?"

"Don't know no fuckin' job-people. How about another shot of that Mad Dog?"

I finished with the mission. Wandered. Found a church. A sign outside: FOOD FOR THE SOUL. SERMON AND MEAL SERVED PROMPTLY AT NOON.

I flipped my wrist. My Armitron informed me it was 12:36.

I went to the front door of the church, pulled at it. Locked. I was never a religious man, but I couldn't recall ever coming across a church with locked doors. I went around to the side of the building, found another door. Locked same as the front. I knocked. Waited. Knocked. Waited. Pounded. Waited.

The door opened and a priest or reverend or pastor looked out. I got a smile followed by: "Yes, friend?"

I said: "Doors were locked."

"Meal service begins promptly at noon." That was delivered with enough warmth to sunburn me.

Me, snide: "So I can only get hungry at twelve?"

"No, friend. But I give a sermon at noon. The sermon is part of the service." The reverend guy must've been sixty. But he was that healthy-looking sixty usually reserved for matinee idols who refused to grow old. Lined flesh, sure, but it didn't sag. Wasn't a liver spot on him. Not one I could see. On top of that he had a hairline most guys in their twenties would date rape their mothers for.

I said: "Don't need a lecture. Just food."

My glibness didn't make him mad. He got with a disappointed look like I'd traveled a thousand miles just to hand him some bad news.

"You don't believe in our Lord? You don't believe in His divine grace? Have you never been touched by his blessings, friend?"

I hated that; hated how he called me friend and meant it, never mind me having just come knocking. I hated that he looked better than his years, healthier. More than anything I hated that this guy, apparently, obviously, had found a life of solace and contentment in simple faith when I could find none in anything.

I let my head dip, licked my lip, looked up at the man in black. "Let me tell you about God's grace: In this life I have been lied to, laughed at, kicked, slapped, cheated, beaten, and humiliated every way how. And that's when times are good. Bad times start with me wishing I was dead instead of taking what I'm being given. I've lost every decent thing I ever had, and what's left isn't worth stealing. The only reason I even bother to stick around in this life is to see what happens next. So don't come at me with your yatter about grace and blessing. And not because I don't believe in God. I believe. I just don't believe in your god. Your god sucks. I'm looking for a better one."

The reverend guy, he just turned up the warmth on his smile. "Don't know that you can, friend. But whatever it is you're looking for, I hope you find."

And he stepped from the door. Spread an arm, inviting me in.

Shit, he had such good hair.

I walked down into the basement of the church. It was more of the same from the soup kitchen: hollow men, a few women, eating in shame and silence. All the preaching in the world had done them little good, and every ladle of soup given only took their pride in return. Took their self-respect. A man who couldn't so much as sustain himself wasn't hardly a man at all. This church wasn't winning converts, it was making slaves.

With stealth, I slipped out the MD and eased my way from one likely man to the next. Even a sip at a time, the Mad Dog's life span was fractional. All I got for my question-asking was the same amount of nothing I'd come into the joint with. Once the bottle was empty I got nothing at all. I managed some food. It was mostly tasteless, and even though a giveaway I left my plate half untouched.

I could do the stamp dance again—buy a buck's worth of something at a mom-and-pop store, take the change from the food stamps and get some booze, find a new spot to ask about Corina. Thinking about the effort made me feel my lack of sleep. Picking over my options, I chose going back to the jungle and getting lifted. I'd been drug free for a couple of days and that was a couple of days too long. Burned out from my exertions and the resulting failures, it was time to correct my sober ways.

I walked.

Walked.

The street I walked was fairly lonely. A few cars passed. They paid me no attention, and I gave them none back.

Some construction. An orange sign: ROUGH ROAD AHEAD.

My ring hurt.

It did that sometimes. My wedding ring. When the weather was cold and the metal contracted around my finger. Sometimes, too, when I was bloated for whatever reason and my finger filled the band to excess. I don't know why it hurt at that moment. It just did. I wore my ring because, technically, I remained married. It hadn't been seven years since I'd split my wife. The law wasn't ready to say I was dead to the world. I figured since I was still married I might as well sport my ring.

Funny.

When Charles Harmon was still living with his wife he used to joke about the ring, call it the yoke of his oppressor. A little band of platinum and gold that iconified all that he would never do or be again. Sometimes when he was in public with Beverly, he wouldn't bother with the ring. She was his marriage. He felt no need to display any other evidence of the crime. And he never had gotten used to the physicality of the ring—the slight, noticeable weight always pulling, pulling at his hand. So, sometimes, when he was with the missus he left it off. But when he was alone, away from her, he always wore the ring. Always. Not from fidelity, but to advertise to all potential comers: Yes, I'm married. Do you care? I might not.

All potential comers seemed to care.

Or, subtly but plainly, he cared, and it was enough to scare all potential comers off. But one way or another the ring and its ever-presence even when unworn always factored into Charles's life, and Charles would have loved to have just tossed that shit. Now, Brain Nigger Charlie couldn't bring himself to part with the thing.

So I wore the thing.

Today it hurt.

I heard, behind me, the sound of a domestic engine and I knew, or sensed, that it drove trouble. I turned to see a couple of dull sedans rolling on me. They rolled ahead of me—brushing close, kicking dirt and gravel at me—stopped, blocking my way. The doors opened and altogether seven guys got out. A couple stayed near the cars—Fed plates. The rest walked for me; few black guys, few white guys. And the guy leading the pack. He was not man-sized. That is, he was under five feet seven inches, which to my way of thinking is the minimum requirement for a man's height. His hair was making a gradual exodus from his head, and making its escape in no particular pattern. There was some missing here, some there. It looked like a theater that was slowly losing its attendance. He had poor eyesight. Actually, his eyesight was probably fine as long as he wore those thick glasses he sported with the outdated frames. All that came wrapped in a dark suit that was tailored especially for him and thirty million other guys at JCPenney. It hung on him poorly. The sleeves looked long. Or maybe he was just one of those cats who had an odd body where nothing ever fit him right.

The bunch of them fanned the road. I stopped walking. Pretty obvious I wasn't going anywhere. Not until they decided otherwise.

The little guy asked: "Are you, uh, carrying any . . . do you have any identification?" He fumbled his words like they were lathered in grease.

I said: "Are you?"

Not that it was meant to, but the crack got no smiles.

The little guy said: "Well, I . . . I'm asking you if you do. And I suggest if you, uh, if you have any, you offer . . . that is if you have any identification, you present it."

"You can suggest all you want, but until you tell me who you are I don't have to do anything but stand here and stare at you. And ten more minutes of that, I'll be begging to show you what I've got."

The cars, the Fed plates. I knew who they were. But I was a lawyer. I knew my rights, too.

But the little guy, the little guy didn't seem so sure of things. He looked around at the other agents. His glasses slipped down his nose. "If you . . . if you don't present identification, we can," he pushed his glasses back up his nose, "we can, uh, remove it for you." He tried to be threatening with that. He tried very, very hard and I'll give him credit for the effort.

"You could do that, but that would violate my Fourth Amendment right protecting me against unreasonable search and seizure. Unless you can articulate before a court just cause for such a search, which I think, under the circumstances, would be found lacking. But then again, maybe you've got a signed warrant from a federal judge ordering the search of my person. Bright boy like you, you probably do. Tell you what: you just show me your warrant, and I'll let you poke around in every hole I've got."

There were seven of them to my one. Two if you count George. It was a lonely road. There were no witnesses. The little man didn't need a signed slip of paper to have his way with me. But he came off like it was day one of him being a Fed and he hadn't gotten a chance to give the manual a good reading. If I'd told him he needed Abe Lincoln's okay on things I think he would've headed off to Springfield, shovel in hand.

The little guy and I swapped some stink-eye back and forth while he figured what to do. I got bored with the whole show and leaned on George and let my pack slip from my shoulder to the ground and watched my foot make patterns in the dirt.

Finally the little guy turned and headed back to his dull car. The other Feds fell in behind him, got in after him, drove off with him.

I shook my head. I laughed. Kept on for the jungle.

By the time I got there, by the time my JanSport hit earth, my palms were salivating with a sweaty eagerness, the little man in the bad suit having delayed my high. My bullet—plastic chipped, color faded—slipped in my slick hand as I loaded it and took a sniff of K, reloaded and took another, reloaded and shot myself one more time.

I waited

I waited

The hole opened and I slid in.

I was rolling, and it came in waves. I was lifted, and it felt like

Except that the sun was peaked in the sky, making it too bright out for a most excellent high, it was a very fine trip I took—the excursion lasting somewhere between forty seconds and a lifetime.

Or maybe just half an hour.

My rib hurt. It hurt. It hurt. It hurt, in a rhythm like that. The fifth time it hurt, my eyes came open and I sobered right up and I became aware. I became aware of the two guys standing over me, one of them kicking me in the midsection.

I started to scramble for George. Before I got to him one of the guys, a reedy guy, cut with muscles, oozed an arm down at me—oozed an arm. That's how he moved; mellifluent like flowing evil. He grabbed me hard by the neck, choked me still. My head lolled and with watery eyes I looked to the other guy. The other guy wasn't a guy. The guy was a chick, and she was some whole other thing. Five and seven, about, she was tough-looking in jeans and a wife beater. But different from the Shemale I'd tussled with in Williston, she didn't come off at all dykish. She was just about pretty, never mind her hair, dyed red, buzzed short—which is what made me first think she was a he—and looking like it'd been done by a dude who normally made his living trimming hedges. Dark features were contrary to her pale skin, blue eyes. Yeah. Except that she looked like she'd be plenty happy to carve me from my flesh and fuck what remained of me, she was a real hottie.

Easing up on my neck some, just some, Liquid Evil wanted to know: "What's your name?" Mostly that was a demand rather than a question.

"Nigger," I rasped, leaving off Brain and Charlie. I had a sense lowering myself was the smart play.

"You asking about Corina?"

No hesitation, like there was nothing wrong with the fact that I was: "Yeah."

"What for?"

". . .'Cause . . ."

Impatient, fingers sinking their way back into my throat: "What for?"

I looked to Buzz Cut Girl. Just above her left eye; a tattoo. Small. Initials. Three of them. Couldn't read them right through my screen of tears, but their location fed me ideas. Things were coming plain to me now.

Answering Liquid Evil: "Fucking."

He was fast and he was strong. Liquid Evil was fast the way his hand left my throat and snake-struck my wrist, strong in the way he squeezed it until my fingers uncurled as if by his will alone. He pressed the blade of a knife—flipped open so quick while I was playing catch-up to the wrist-grabbing I missed the action altogether—into my palm. Using his strength again, he squeezed my hand closed around the blade.

My hand went warm and a little wet from a cut the blade gave my flesh. Gave it just sitting there, Liquid Evil just tightening my hand around it. If he yanked it out, if he pulled it out at speed . . .

"I'm gonna ask you a last time, nigger: why you looking for this girl?"

"I need pussy." I worked hard at my dumb act. "I ain't fucking no old shit. Hear that girl got the sweetest pussy around. You tell me where else I'm gonna find sweet pussy up in here. Serious, suh," I Sambo'd. "Hard enough to find shit, try finding sweet shit on the rails."

Liquid Evil looked at me, looked at me . . .

I looked to Buzz Cut Girl.

She looked like she wanted me dead half an hour ago.

I looked to Liquid Evil.

He looked at me, looked at me . . . It was like his eyes were a couple of truth machines computing the veracity of my answers, with the response to a lie a pull on the knife. My hand diced. The flesh split, muscle separating until it exposed bone. Tendons severed. Blood free-flowing in a volume matched only by my screams. I felt my piss pressing on the walls of my bladder and what little my colon held struggling to seep out. It was the base response to fear. It was my body trying to tell my intellect it was scared shitless. The whole of me took on a twitch, then gave an aftershock.

At the very corner of Liquid Evil's mouth there was a slight curl upward. He eased his grip on my hand, took away the knife and folded it down.

I looked at my palm. A trickling blood line ran perpendicular to my lifeline.

Liquid Evil to Buzz Cut Girl: "C'mere."

She came to him.

"Gimme the phone."

A Nokia got yanked from Buzz Cut Girl's ass pocket. A train gang bitch with a cell phone. Right in front of me she dialed and with a dull and vacant look I watched her do it, then she handed over the phone to Liquid Evil like a good little psychotic sidekick. Listening, but putting up a face that said true understanding was beyond me, I caught Liquid Evil's side of the conversation.

"Yeah . . . Nothing. Just a stupid nigger. That's what he goes by, Nigger."

Buzz Cut Girl kept up her stare at me. I could feel it without even looking her way.

Liquid Evil: "Says he wants to fuck her . . . Nah, just like I said; stupid nigger."

And then there was a long pause. I figured Liquid Evil was waiting for instructions from the other end of the line on how to handle his stupid nigger situation. He waited, looking at me, expressionless. If he had a desire one way or the other—to hurt me, to not hurt me—it didn't show. I got the feeling, for him, causing pain to another man was an empty and perfunctory act; just something that had to be done with as much regularity and as little thought as eating. Defecating.

. . . Thought I heard something.

I looked down. George, at my feet. I thought I heard him say something about grabbing him up and letting him do his trick; letting him show Liquid Evil and his girl a thing or two. I thought I heard him say . . .

"Shit, nigger's so stupid," Liquid Evil into the phone, "he don't know night from day . . .. Makes no difference. Just tell me what you want me to do."

Just tell me what you want me to do.

I hung on that, hung on razored tenterhooks. Someone, somewhere, on the far end of a cell connection was figuring my fate: I want you should let the nigger go. I want you should slit the nigger's throat. Another shake rippled through my body. My bladder and bowels got ready to purge.

Liquid Evil hung up the phone. Liquid Evil said: "You're a real stupid nigger. Ain't that just your good luck." And then he turned and Iggy Popped away from me, and Buzz Cut Girl fell in right behind him. Melted into the jungle before fading away.

And when they were gone, completely gone from my sight, I laughed a little and clutched myself and marveled, not that I was alive and untouched, but that despite the fact that I had no idea what in the hell I was doing, from this encounter I knew more about Corina and her predicament than I had just ten minutes prior never mind all the cheap liquor I had poured around Shelby. I knew where to look for her and I had a very good idea of what kind of trouble she'd purchased for herself.

I like libraries. Like to read. Reading works out the mind, keeps the brain in Brain Nigger. It is the intelligent way to kill time. Factor in the hours I can't sleep, I have much time to kill.

Libraries now, most of them anyway, have Internet access. Besides being a very handy way to check the weather in Beijing and get kiddie porn from New Zealand, there is a wealth of information to be had just beyond each http://. I checked out the public library in Shelby. Logged on. Went to the Google homepage. Buzz Cut Girl, her tattoo. Three little letters: NLR. I knew what they stood for, but before I went on I wanted to know everything I could. A well-researched Brain Nigger is a Formidable Brain Nigger.

Into the little search window I typed Nazi Low Riders, hit return. What got spat back was page after page of info. The facts on the fly: The Nazi Low Riders, a vicious neo-Nazi skinhead prison and street gang. Still formative—cops count less than five hundred confirmed members. Dwarfed by the FTRA's couple thousand gangers—they are the fastest-growing white gang in California, mostly because they're not strict race haters. They're money-motivated; heavy into the production and trafficking of methamphetamine. A big no-no with other skinhead gangs. Aryans don't do drugs, don't sell drugs. Aryans have to stay pure. That's why Aryans have no dough and have to preach hate on public-access cable.

Not the NLR.

The NLR deals and earns and they're not afraid to mix it up when they have to. In short order that's turned them into "the gang of gangs" among ignorant white trash. The NLR got cranked up when the Aryan Brotherhood—Cali's biggest prison gang—started getting heat from the correction system. The AB needed middlemen to run their drugs.

The AB recruited young skinheads at the CYA in Preston, and the YTS in Chino. When NLR recruits got paroled, they set up shop in Costa Mesa. Old money, rich, conservative Orange County, California.

If you can't be a Republican, be a skinhead.

From there they oozed north, then east riding the rails, dealing their meth, killing people when they had the occasion—a hammer attack on a black man in Lancaster, CA. A machete attack on a black teenager in Costa Mesa. Using a pipe on a Hispanic to go with that. Taking a bat to a black guy in LA. You gotta have balls to go after minorities in Los Angeles.

The NLR had balls. The NLR had smarts. They didn't always shave their domes like skinheads or dress like them or tattoo themselves up like them. They knew how to blend the way a disease knows how to lie dormant. They were young and moneyed. They were upwardly mobile home crackers.

They were as much trouble as one could hope to find on the High Line.

I clicked the page closed.

Sat.

Did another search: Five-oh-nine.

Five-oh-nine.

The first jerk of the Warbonnet dominoed along the train, passing through my flatcar and on down the line, the couplings rattling same as a mouthful of nervous teeth. I'd have rather had a boxcar for the trip. I'd found none open. The sun was still up. It was warm. An open-air ride would be livable.

Five-oh-nine.

Buzz Cut Girl had dialed the 509 area code when she made the call to whoever had veto power over my hand getting carved. Five-oh-nine, from my Google search, was a good-sized area code, but on the eastern end of it was Spokane. The bloody heart of the High Line. Buzz Cut Girl, Liquid Evil, the NLR. Yeah. Spokane was where I was headed.

My head fell back and my mouth split open just enough for me to gasp: "Shiiit." I said to Corina, I said inside myself: What were you thinking, girl? A couple of months on the rails. Eight lousy weeks. Did you get that desperate, were you that cold and hungry, you couldn't come up with any other way to keep yourself alive?

No.

She wasn't that cold or that hungry. You get cold enough and go hungry long enough they become constants; not spikes in your state of being, they *are* your state of being. They become a hurt on your flesh or a pain in your gut that you cannot distinguish from feeling normal, so you feel the hurt and pain no more. You no longer respond to it. You live with it. Corina sold out way before she arrived at such a place. It was the fear of an empty stomach and a freezing night spent in the rain, the phantom of such an existence, that made her put herself on the auction block.

Sold to the lowest bidder.

The train went from a slow roll to a steady one.

Five-oh-nine. Spokane.

Jesus.

I was fucked. Corina was already fucked, and I was heading straight west for some of the same.

The Unit gained speed to nearly 20 mph.

I thought: I should jump. Still time. Barely. Barely time to jump from the train without shattering a tibia, mangling a radius. Still time to jump and catch out in the opposite direction for New Mexico or Kansas or Florida. I should jump and catch out and . . . and abandon . . .

For a second, without even shutting my lids, I could see my baby with three eyes.

A bag, a duffel—green canvas, worn, torn—came up over the horizon of the flatcar. It reached a peak, arched downward, hit the floor of the car, slid, rolled some. A white hand reached up, grabbed at the deck, slipped away, surfaced, grabbed, held fast, got joined by another hand. The pair struggled, pulling a young boy—seventeen/eighteen, white as his hands had indicated—up onto the floor of the car. He made the climb chest high, no further. A beat later, strength gone, went from climbing to hanging on for dear life to slipping little by little: a grain of sand doing its damnedest not to fall through an hourglass.

I recalled my most recent attempt to catch out on a moving train just a few days previous. I recalled with a sharp sense memory the burn of the lactic acid in my weak and weary arms, the scorch in my lungs like the oxygen I was breathing had turned to choking smoke. Mostly I remembered how desperately I wanted there to be someone to grab my sleeve and give me the one slight pull I needed to get me into the moving car and keep me from getting sucked under, and horribly and painfully churned beneath the rolling wheels of the train. And yet, with all that memory, I did nothing more than watch the boy fight and struggle and panickedly try to figure a way to keep from falling.

The kid stopped slipping. For a second he maintained a stasis between being on the train and dropping off. Between life and probable death.

From up front: the blare of the Unit's horn. She was rolling hard now. The Hogger was letting the throttle go wide.

The kid raised a hand, threw it forward. It slammed onto the deck of the car, the impact resonated with determination. His body lifted, slithered. The muscle-shredding strain of the effort was obvious at a distance. His chest crept up onto the deck . . . his torso . . . his waist . . . the bulk of his weight at destination, the kid collapsed, his legs hanging out over the edge of the car. He lay where he fell thirty seconds into a minute, then two. Finally, his head lifted.

"Shit. Oh fuckin' shit." He did not look in my direction. I wasn't certain if he knew he wasn't alone. "Oh shit. Fuckin' shit. Almost . . . almost got killed." He paused. Took a beat. The next time his mouth opened it was to spew his guts on the flatcar's bed. The effort sapped what little strength he had left. His head descended, splash-landing in a puddle of bile and stomach juice. "Almost died," he mumbled, the words forming bubbles in the vomit. "Almost died."

"Hey," I called out.

The kid lay without moving.

"Hey!"

His head turned, hydroplaning on the slick it lay in.

"Pull your legs in before they get clipped."

The kid lay without moving.

Shit. I got up, fought the sway of the train over to the punk, grabbed a belt loop, hauled him entirely up into the car. His head came up. He had the same emerald sheen of a Chicago mick at a beer buffet four-A-Em on St. Patty's Day.

I said: "Puke on me, I'll toss you right off this bitch."

Whitey didn't get any less green, but he kept his mouth shut. His head went back down.

I sat with him for a while, disregarding my urge to move away. After a while more, I asked: "What are you doing?"

Again White Boy's head lifted, one side slathered with barf. He was making me sick. The sight of the white boy with gunk dripping out of his dirty hair was making me sick. I reached in his duffel, pulled out a shirt. Hell if I was going to give him anything of mine to clean up with. "Wipe yourself."

He managed the shirt from my hand, mopped his face.

From me again: "What are you doing?"

White Boy, stuttering: "I-I was ca-catching off—"

"Out. Catching out, you stupid fuck." Plaid shirt, nasty Levi's; he wasn't Yuppie Scum. Not hardly. Might as well have been with his ignorance of the rails. "Why are you catching out on a moving train?"

He gave me a look like the answer was obvious.

I gave him one that said: Tell me anyway.

"I didn't want the rail cops—"

Jesus. "Bulls."

"Yeah. Didn't want them to nail me."

"Then you sure as hell better learn how to catch out on a train that's rolling. Not knowing's liable to get you severed."

He sorta nodded, started to put his head back down in the vomit puddle. I grabbed him, pulled him clear of his own mess, let him sink down into a weary sleep.

I lay down as well. Not to sleep. Just to rest. The rock of the car, the ambient of the trucks over the track; I didn't care. I would fight The Drift to my dying day. I fired up the Silvertone, and there was old Art Bell going on about the aliens and the black copters and cattle mutilation and how he was putting himself at risk just talking about such things even though he talked about such things four hours a night, five nights a week.

We all had our crosses to bear. We all had our missions in life.

Never been there. Didn't matter. I knew for a fact Spokane was one of the hardest yards on the line. With the slop of train gangs mixed among the tramps trying to catch out for all points, the Bulls watched the yard and watched it well. Watched it harsh. They got their hands on you, they made damn sure you didn't give thought to trespassing their property but one time in your life. They beat it into you. They beat all other ideas out of you. Knowing this, I was ready to jump from the car short of the yard and make the rest of the way on foot.

The kid, White Boy, lay passed very much out, and didn't look as if he'd be waking prior to hitting the yard. So what? Let him sleep. He'd learn better than to stay down into Spokane. He'd learn better than to do a lot of stupid things. I'd learned.

Sure, I'd learned. But I had Chocolate Walt to teach me.

What was that? What was that I was feeling? Was five years so long that the emotion that churned inside me should seem so strange? Was I so far from humanity I couldn't recall it?

And just like that I was nudging at White Boy's ribs with George Plimpton. George asked what the fuck I was doing? For a second I thought he did.

I said to White Boy: "Hey."

"Huuuuuh?"

"Hey. Get up."

"We in Spokane?"

"No. Get up."

"I'm going to Spokane."

My hand reached down. My fingers knotted themselves in the soily mop White Boy wore on top of his head.

As I yanked him from the deck of the car: "Ahhhhh!"

"Grab your duffel. We're jumping off."

"What?"

"We're jumping."

"You said . . . you said not to board a moving train."

"I said learn how to. And we're not catching one. This bitch slows, we're jumping."

Whitey confusedly gathered his duffel. I couldn't tell if he was spaced from his near-death experience catching out, dazed from just waking, or if vapidity was, for him, a natural constant.

Up front: the Unit broke. The whole of the train slowed. I looked up the rails, sized the oncoming earth for a good place to land. Land without snapping too many bones.

A patch of dirt approaching. To White Boy: "Ready?"

The only thing he looked ready for was more puking.

Again my hand shot out, this time grabbing him by the shirt. Me, George, my pack: we all took air. Ready or not, White Boy took a ride with us.

The ground was soft. Fairly so. We landed. Skidded. Tumbled. Slid to a stop. George I held fast. My pack I had to collect. Only then did I check to see if the White Boy was alive or dead. He had a cut on his palm. Nothing bad. Other than that, he was suitable. Anyway, he carried on about his hand some. I let him. When he was done, he asked: "Now what?"

"Now we go make a jungle."

"There isn't one near the yard?"

"I'm not jungling in Spokane with a bunch of peckerwoods. You want to, you want to get beat in the head or fucked in the rear, go on with yourself. Me? I like being alive with a nonbleeding ass."

I waited while White Boy looked around the dark, took up a hard but spunkless stare at the dirt he stood on . . . finally he owned up to the reality that his best bet was to stick by me.

He said: "I'll go with you."

I started walking.

White Boy fell in behind me.

I stopped walking. I said: "Don't walk behind me."

"What?"

"You want to walk beside me, okay. In front, that's okay too. What you don't do is walk behind a man."

White Boy gave a fool's nod, pulled up next to me. I got back to walking.

He asked: "Can I ask your name?"

"Brain Nigger Charlie."

"Thanks for looking out for me, Charlie."

"Brain Nigger Charlie."

White Boy opened his mouth to repeat after me, but shut up without saying anything. His sensibility could not bring him to say the oh-so-horrible N word. Least, he couldn't say it in my presence.

"It's all right. That's my name. All of it. Nigger too."

"It's . . . it doesn't . . ."

"It doesn't what? Doesn't sound right? What sounds right; Brain Person of Color Charlie?"

White Boy gave a little smile to that and for a second I didn't feel so hard toward him.

"My name's Steel Rail Steve."

Steel Rail . . . ? Whatever softness I'd felt for White Boy went rock hard again. "You give yourself that tag?"

"Yeah."

"You don't tag yourself. You earn a tag, and there is no way you earned a tag like that."

"It sounds good."

"King of England sounds good, but you're not getting called that either, and if you did it doesn't mean you get to fuck the queen."

"I wasn't—"

"You think I came up with Brain Nigger Charlie on my own? That out there," I pointed off at all the land beyond us, all the country I'd traveled through, "that's what gave me my tag."

White Boy took on all kinds of hurt, me not appreciating the name that, no doubt, he'd practiced in the mirror time after time before first catching out. ". . . Well, what's a good tag for me?"

No hesitation. No thought needed. "Dumbass."

"I don't think . . . I don't like—"

"Stupid Dumbass. That's your tag."

"I don't got to take that. Just 'cause you call me—"

"Stupid Bitch Dumbass."

Not that Stupid Bitch Dumbass was happy about his name, but he shut up, thinking, rightly, the more he protested the more I'd christen him.

We walked on, parallel to the yard, Stupid Bitch Dumbass looking down at his feet, me looking past the chain-link fence and stretch of land that separated us from the rails.

Inside: A hubbub going on. The Bulls going delirious with themselves, their Fords zipping around, lights flashing. Why, what for; don't know. But how happy they must have been to be able to turn on their strobes and play like men. Oh, the stories they would tell over some iced-up PBRs at O'Malley's while trying to drunk-fuck recently divorced Mrs. Kowalski: "I'm not saying every day on the job is a walk in the park. The other day I had to use my lights." I did wonder, though, what the hell was a light-level crisis for a rail rent-a-cop in Spokane?

Stupid Bitch Dumbass was watching me watch the Bulls. He asked: "What are they doing?"

"Nothing."

"Don't look like nothing."

"Not our concern. You want to stay here and catch the show, it's on you, but choose now because I'm going on and if you come running up behind me I'll likely kill you."

With kind of an "oh, c'mon" laugh from Stupid Bitch Dumbass: "You wouldn't—"

"I will end your life and not even think about it." Truth or not, it sounded good. I walked on. Stupid Bitch Dumbass walked with me stride for stride.

We rolled on an industrial park, warehouses and light plants shut up for the day. It was far enough from the yard, I figured, I hoped, to avoid the wrong element. The wrong element being any element that might want to kill me.

Night was making itself felt. I hurt for rest. The search for Corina—days old, no longer—was wearing on me. Not so much physically, but the drain on my brain seemed to burn an equal number of calories as hard labor. No matter. I had things to do, and when had sleep ever been any good for me?

To Stupid Bitch Dumbass: "Stay here."

"Where you going?"

"I'm coming back."

Stupid Bitch Dumbass's face got all frowny and sad.

"What?"

". . . You coming back?"

"What did I say?"

"You said—"

"I said I was coming back," I said again. Again it didn't take. Stupid Bitch Dumbass was worried about being left alone, and he would worry all the while I was gone. An activity; that's what he needed. "Find us something to eat."

". . . Find?"

Lord, was he earning his name. "Stupid Bitch Dumbass, how long you been on the rails?"

"A month. Less."

"Less than a month. What have you been doing for food?"

"Begging."

I made a big show of looking around. "Don't see too many people hanging out to beg from. You?"

". . . No."

"So maybe you ought to start learning to figuring out other ways to live."

". . . Yeah."

"Start diving."

The only thing Stupid Bitch Dumbass did was stare at me.

"Garbage cans: whatever you find that isn't too rotten, that's mostly maggot free, keep it. Find a can, big one, some clean water. We'll make a fire, make stew."

"Look for food?" Stupid Bitch Dumbass was still back on that. "In the garbage?"

"If there's someplace else you can think of to find your eats . . ."

"I don't . . . I don't want to dig in the garbage."

The kid must've done a pretty good job begging that he had yet to get familiar with trash piles. I could see how. There was something so pathetic about him it just caused you care. People must've been stumbling all over themselves to give him their spare change. But being weak, dependent, was going to help him zero. It was only meeting someone like Chocolate Walt, hard but with a heart, that had earned me my current length of years.

"Do it, or go hungry." I picked up my pack, started off.

"You're coming back, right?"

"Yeah."

"You can leave your pack."

"Yeaaaaah," I laughed.

He was what I was looking for. Young. White. Grungy, dressing down by choice rather than circumstance. And he was holding. Dealing. Conspicuous with his poor attempts at being inconspicuous: spiked across from a dance club near Gonzaga University talking up Trance couples that slinked in and out with glitter and glow sticks, going through the routine of shaking hands, fumbling with his pockets, shaking hands again as deals were done, exchanges made.

Painfully conspicuous.

Had he been moving anything harder than vitamins, had he been anything other than a privileged white kid who wanted to make textbook money some other way than flipping burgers, cops would have been up his small intestine a long, long time ago. But he wasn't and he wasn't, so he was walking free, and he was what I was looking for.

Not knowing how he would take my approach—the approach of a grubby, middle-aged black man outside a campus dance club—I eased for him. When I got within hearing distance I asked, softly: "K?"

The boy said nothing.

"K?" I asked again.

The kid looked me over. Nah, I didn't look like a cop. But I didn't look the customary customer.

"K?"

He shook his head no.

"E?"

A nod. "How many?"

"One."

A laugh. Dismissive. "Right." No doubt he was not used to such low-volume sales.

I flashed a twenty—a goddamn twenty-dollar bill; the largest, the last piece of my non-food-stamp fortune—said: "All I can afford." The truth by a long chalk. I let the twenty hang out there.

The kid eyed it.

The door to the club opened.

From inside I could hear the pounding of the Trance and Techno: Hybrid. Gouryella. A little ATB. Some Alice DJ. I knew the sounds, the scene, but had never rolled in the middle of it. I had heard—well, hell, who hadn't—that E was a whole other thing deep in the throb of Eurobeat and wrapped in the stink of sweaty young bodies pressed close, pressed tight, generating a heat and humidity all their own. The writhe of shirtless, shaved men, and women—eyes irisless—who are desire embodied, their fuckability primped high, glimpsed between the strobe of colored lights and modified senses and moving like a single organism in some cousin to dance one step removed from ritualistic copulation. God bless those who owned their sexuality, who showed and shook and teased with it. To hell with those, sex free, without the ability to arouse, who stood coldly by and tsk-tsked and would never know the sweet release that comes with letting go of higher thought and giving over to base instinct: You want to touch me? Touch me. You want to put your tongue on me? Put it there. You want to get so revved you can find love, rare among intimates, plentiful around strangers? Crank the Industrial and I will love you until all the serotonin is wrung out of my brain. That, all of that, is the terminus of human pleasure. It's the pot of gold at the end of the sybaritic rainbow. I got hard for a taste. Christ, I lusted after it—tongue licking moist dry lips, dried out from sick, insatiable hunger for the high of highs.

The door to the club closed.

That twenty just kept hanging from my hand.

The kid gave a "what the hell" shrug. He took the bill, put it in his pocket. It did a presto-chango, reappeared as an E tab. A Versace. He made a motion to shake.

A white college kid shaking hands with a black 'bo outside a dance club. No, we weren't apparent. Jesus. I wanted to tell the punk: The cops—who aren't here—don't care. But I played his game, made him feel big-time wheeler-dealer. I shook his hand, took the tab.

Right there I downed the tab. No water. Dry-swallowed.

I asked: "Deal much?"

"College ain't cheap."

"I'm looking for a guy. Supplier. Don't know his name. Koester. Keller."

That just got a stare.

"I'm not a cop."

"Right. Yeah. So what? You looking to get a hook-up, why should I help? I don't need someone else selling on my corner."

"Not looking to sell. I'm looking for information."

"Fuck that."

"Four-hundred-level English is paying off."

"Fuck you."

"I'm not asking for anything that's going to get you heat, just common knowledge. Who moves heavy around here?"

Nothing.

"C'mon. And I'm not talking vitamins. Serious weight."

The boy considered things. It was a slow night. What else did he have to do besides talk with a curious black guy? "I'm just telling you common knowledge shit, right?"

I nodded.

"The freight trainers."

"FTRA?"

"They move everything. The E, the K, the meth."

FTRA weren't the initials tattooed above Buzz Cut Girl's eye. What was tattooed there was: "NLR? What about them? They're heavy into meth."

"No!" A hard head-shake went with that. "Maybe they move meth everywhere else, but no fucking way is anybody around here moving the Nazis' shit. FTRA are wacked enough, right? They put out the word: anyone moves the Nazis' shit, expect to get put down."

"But they're trying to get territory; the NLR."

"You writing an article?"

"Yeah. I'm Upton Sinclair."

"Who?"

Jesus. Fucking. Christ.

I was going to say something, but he beat me with: "You're pretty smart for a homeless guy."

"Went to college. Had big plans."

"What happened?"

"Sold drugs to earn my keep. And I'm not homeless. I'm a hobo, or at worst a tramp. Don't insult. The NLR . . . ?"

"They've got a lab around. Somewhere. But they keep it hid 'cause if the FTRA got on them they'd tear the place up. The Nazis are trying to get mules. Not easy. Like I said, the FTRA put out the word on that."

Thinking out loud more than talking to the boy: "But somebody would mule for the Nazis if they were desperate enough."

"Right, like I'm that desperate."

"Who's heading up the NLR? He got a name?"

"Sure he does, but I don't know it."

"You must've heard something."

The boy started getting nervous. We were circling things he knew better than to talk about.

"I'm just asking for a name."

A paranoid look around, then: "Kessler."

"He travel with a thin guy and a chick, they do his strong-arm for him?"

The boy hedged, the space around us got another paranoid scan. "Know what I am?"

"A lazy white kid."

"Got a mouth for a . . . a hobo."

"It's all I got, so I make the most of it."

He appreciated that, gave a smile, a little nod. "Riiight," and went on with: "I'm an econ major. I'm an econ major in Spokane, Washington. Those two together add up to less than they do separate. So all I'm trying to do is move a little E, make a little bread, graduate out of here, get myself to Wall St. and earn my first million before I turn twenty-three. I think you can see how getting caught up between the Nazi Low Riders and a bunch of maniac train bums might make all that difficult."

Fair enough. Having what I needed, I started back the way I came.

"Hey, man!" The boy calling after me. "I deserve something for all that."

A college boy moving drugs in NLR and FTRA territory. Yeah. He deserved something for that. Sooner or later he'd get it.

I calculated that the chances of Dumbass finding us any edible food was about 42% less than the chance I'd return to find, oh, say, Elle Macpherson camped out in our mini-jungle.

Maybe 60%.

Walking my way back, a little convenience-store-slash-grill found me with its strong and good smell of fried eats, and as I got closer, I could hear the sizzle of the food which was volumed by my hunger. Hot, nonrotted food. I would have none. My means would afford me a couple of Slim Jims and a freshening of my Little Debbie products supply. Nothing more.

I entered the store-slash-grill.

A middle-aged woman worked the counter. She was Asian. Not from Japan or Korea or China. Not Vietnam. She was from some other country over there where the people were, apparently, fat and brown and their faces were mostly flat. It was probably a poor country where nobody had much of anything. Probably it was a big deal to make it to America. Probably once they were here they got treated like shit for being from *over there* and not speaking our language particularly well. And no matter how long she lived here, no matter how often she voted or regularly paid taxes, she would always be looked down on, pretty much hated, for not actually being born in this country, even though coming to this country and doing good in this country is what this country is all about. In spite of that, she seemed to have down the number one requirement for being an American: she didn't like black people. The instant I took step one through the door she tossed me a scowl and her hand made motions below the counter that resembled a grope for a gun. Course, maybe that had nothing to do with the fact that I was black. Maybe it was just me myself that repulsed her. When I was middle class and acceptable and of my right mind, I used to watch the deranged homeless people who pushed their shopping carts along busy Ventura Boulevard, or danced in the middle of busy Ventura Boulevard, and I wondered if they knew they were insane. Or is it when you're nuts you have no way of knowing that you're nuts and the nutty things you do seem perfectly normal to you. Maybe now that I was lightly coated with a crispy-crunchy crust of craziness, though I felt like I was just walking into the convenience-store-slash-grill, I was really spastically howling my way into the convenience-store-slash-grill trailing a tail of fresh-brewed saliva.

Didn't know. Couldn't tell. Couldn't worry about it. I was going loony. I knew that. How I looked while I was doing it wasn't important.

The woman chattered something in her native tongue to a guy—fat like her, brown like her. Flat-faced like her—stocking the shelves with a soup that was not Campbell's. He looked at me, chattered something back, then faked ignoring me while keeping one eye in my direction at all times.

Fine. Semi-ignore me. You live in your world, I'll hang out in mine. Just let me grab some Slim Jims and maybe some Snickers bars, a couple of Little Debbie fruit pies first.

"Hey."

Usually, usually being the five years since I'd transformed from Charles Harmon into Brain Nigger Charlie, in a store or a shop, on any property that was private, when a voice said to me from behind, "Hey," next up was grabbing hands—empty of gentleness, loaded with roughness—and a quick toss to the pavement outside.

Usually.

This voice, this "Hey," was pleasant and amicable, "Howdy" friendly. This "Hey" was free of trouble.

I turned.

At the counter at the grill, sitting, eating, was the Bull; the one who'd talked to me back in the Shelby jungle. "Hey."

Didn't know what to say. My experience conversing with Bulls was limited. Limited, pretty much, to the Bull who was talking to me now.

Again: "Hey."

I said: "Hey."

"Coffee?"

Asking? Offering? I didn't know what his meaning was. Didn't matter. If he was asking, I couldn't afford whatever the going rate for a cup was. If he was offering, I wanted his charity about as much as I wanted to kill time with a Bull in the first place.

But the food smelled good. At least, different from jungle cooking, it didn't smell bad, which gave it the illusion of smelling good.

"C'mon over," the Bull circled a hand in his direction, "and set some."

Set some. Buddy Ebsen does railroad hack. But his countrification seemed as much a part of him as the thick hair that weeded his forearms, as his fingernails that grew in varying degrees of short, long, and scraggly. And if he wanted me to "set some" it made me think I hadn't yet arrived at the spastic and howling level of dementia.

The food smelled good.

I moved for the counter. Sat. Kept a stool space between myself and . . . what was his name?

"Saw you come in, and I said: 'Is that old Brain Nigger Charlie?' "

He had no problem saying my name. Wasn't that he got the usual white man's kick out of a gratis opportunity to say nigger. Far as he cared, Brain Nigger Charlie was my name. My name is what he called me.

What was his name?

"Got a good look at you, and, yep. It's Brain Nigger Charlie; right here. Can't say that was expected."

"Why's that? Didn't figure you'd see a nigger this deep into the High Line."

I meant to hand him a little verbal spanking, but he dodged it. He dodged it with the truth. "Yes," he said. "That, and you just don't expect to see people as regular as you would if you were working, say, an office job. Guess, anyway." To the guy behind the counter: "Coffee." To me: "Cream, sugar?"

I shook my head. "Some tea, maybe." Like sunshine at midnight, like Siegfried and Roy being anything less than flamboyant, a Bull putting out for a tramp just didn't happen.

The guy behind the counter, white guy, poured me some hot

water, dropped a Lipton's on the counter. The look on his face: pissed. Bad enough he had to work for a couple of Asians, now he was serving black bums. He wasn't going to be any less pissed when he saw the tip I wasn't going to leave him.

The Bull pushed his plate away from him and slightly toward me. On it was a smallish steak, country-fried, picked-over mashed potatoes, corn niblets. Half eaten, going cold. It looked good. Anything looked good when it came on porcelain instead of out of the garbage.

I asked: "You guess? Never had an office job?"

"Oh, heck, no," he said, and said as if he'd rather take a bullet than work a desk. "Old Haxton here . . ."

Haxton was his name. I started to ask myself how do you forget a name like Haxton, but ended up asking how do you *get* a name like Haxton?

"He's never worked anything but the rails."

"I used to. Work an office, I mean." And there I was, without even thinking about it, engaging the Bull. For whatever reason, against logic, I found Haxton easy for talking. One reason, maybe, is because I told him I worked an office job and he took it in stride. No raised eyebrows or guffaws given in editorial of my statement. The black tramp used to work an office, then the black tramp used to work an office.

All Haxton had to say to that was: "Gave it up?"

I shrugged. "Gave it up. Gave up on it. It gave up on me. Dealer's choice."

"Mind if I ask where you're headed?"

"Keeping an eye on me?"

"Reason I should?"

"I used to work an office job."

"Uh-huh."

"Used to make six figures a year. Five days a week I was in a suit and tie. With all that, I'd go into a Macy's or Saks and the hired white help who couldn't afford to live in my garage would follow me around because they thought the nigger was going to steal something I could just pay for fifty times over. So a white guy asks me where I'm headed, yeah, I'm guessing he's eyeing me."

"Those people who gave you a hard time; they were bigots."

"Yeah."

"They had it in for all black people."

"Yeah."

"And that makes them ignorant, if not just stupid."

"You've got being obvious down to a habit."

"Now you've got it for all whites."

I said nothing.

"What does that make you?"

I said nothing.

"So, again, if you don't mind, where you heading?"

"Don't know."

"Just tramping?"

"Hoboing this time," sure that Haxton would know the difference. "Doing work. Favor for a friend."

"Some favor to get you up on the High Line." He didn't get any more curious about my chore than that. Wasn't sure if he didn't care, or if he figured whatever my business, most likely it was illegal and better he shouldn't know the particulars.

Haxton's plate kept up its vigil between us, the steak taking a bath in its own coagulating grease. I wanted to chow on it bad, but not so bad I'd dig into another man's mostly eaten food and make myself look like the bum that I was. Not in front of a Bull. I don't care how decent he was being to me.

Haxton: "High Line's not much friendly toward minorities."

Minorities. His PCness was killing me. "Not many places are," I said.

"Maybe, but most places aren't unfriendly to the point you get your head stoved in with a goonie stick."

I nodded to his truth. I asked: "When I saw you before, you asked me about a Mex; if I'd seen him riding."

"Hispanic fella."

"What'd you want to know for?"

"There's been some killing on the rails."

"Always is. If I had a food stamp for every—"

"This time it's real bad. There've been some stabbings, all of 'em hell of vicious. The bodies were mutilated. The victims had their scrotums amputated."

The clinical way Haxton described the crimes added to their chill. Real quick my thoughts went to: "Any of them girls?"

"No. Least, of the bodies that were found none of them were girls."

Corina was still alive. Maybe.

I asked: "The Mexican did it?"

"Don't know that he's Mexican."

"Hispanic. Whatever."

"There's a witness to one of the killings. He claims there were two perpetrators. Young males. One Caucasian, the other fella Hispanic-looking. Figure, around these parts, it's easier to track the Hispanic."

"That why you're out here; your company's got you looking into things?"

"A body was found on company property, just inside a yard."

I shrugged. "Dead train bums. Who cares?"

"Nobody. Most times. 'Cept one of the victims wasn't a train bum. He was a college boy catching out between semesters, looking for thrills."

"Yuppie Scum," I said. My eyes went back to the plate. My tongue took a lap around my lips. My stomach got into an argument with my brain over dignity vs. digging in.

"Any rate, his old man runs an insurance company or some such. He's got enough money he can make a stink to the right people about his boy getting murdered, never mind he had no business on the rails in the first place. Now the Feds are all into things."

Federal investigators, like I figured: the plain car. The dark suits, sunglasses. The little guy with his big bad attitude. "Yeah. Saw them. And if that's what the government's sending, they're not real serious about closing out this one."

Shifting his ass to one side, Haxton dug his wallet from his back pocket. From his wallet got taken a business card. Plain. Basic. White with black letters: HAXTON BOOLE. Below that: BURLINGTON NORTHERN SANTA FE SECURITY. Then a couple of numbers; office, cell.

He said: "If you should have an opportunity to hear anything, if you happen to see anything or anyone, maybe you want to give me a call."

I gave a laugh. "I'm not your Huggy Bear."

Haxton tilted his head, signifying nonunderstanding.

"Huggy Bear. *Starsky & Hutch.*"

From Haxton, more head-tilting.

"C'mon. The TV show."

"Don't know it. Recall it, but never was much for television."

"Huggy Bear was a pimp, and Starsky and Hutch, they were cops, and they used to go to Huggy for information."

Elbows on the counter, Haxton folded his hands and used them for a chin-perch. From that position he gave thought to the Starsky and Hutch mythology, and then pronounced: "That doesn't make good sense; going to a panderer for information. I've never known one to do anything other than slap his women and take their money."

"It was just a character, man. He was a good pimp."

"A good—"

"Hey, you're a Bull coming to me for information. How much sense is that?"

"All the sense in the world if the information you want is on train tramps and railroad killers."

Sense.

I asked: "What's in it for me?"

"You do good."

I "yeah, right"-ed that with: "That's why you're putting in the hours, riding all over; 'cause you're bucking for Pope? Police are on this, the Feds, what do you care about who's shanking tramps except what it'll do for your career? And don't give me any of that homespun country shit. You're in this for what you can get out of it."

Haxton kept his head on his hands. He looked across the counter to a refrigerated display case. Inside the case were four different kinds of pies, three of them missing just one slice and the fourth, a cherryish-looking pie, nearly all gone. Locked inside the case, crawling on the glass: a fly. He kept crawling around, crawling around, slowed by the cold air, looking for a way out. I'm sure at the time, going for the pies seemed a good idea. Except that flies didn't have ideas because they didn't have higher brain functions. They just lived by instinct, and that made them stupid.

Haxton said: "When I was fourteen I got my first rail job. Underage. Scissor-Bill. Know what that is?"

"Brakey."

Impressed: "You know something about working rails?"

"I like libraries."

"So, I'm a Brakeman: running over moving trains, jumping cars and tying 'em down. You're wrestling trains before you've even had your first woman, well, that'll make you feel all of a man. By the time I was twenty I figured I knew all there was to know about kicking and switching, lacing up air hoses, swapping out knuckles. I got cocky. At twenty-two I got careless, got my left foot crushed between the rails and some steel wheels.

That explained his mosey. It wasn't a mosey. It was a fucked-up foot.

"Since then I've been a Special Agent. Don't have to be able to jump trains for this job. Anyway, since then, for going near thirty years I've been in a yard giving every piece of equipment from Unit to Crummy my full respect, and I'm still too young to quit things. I could. I could if I did something like bring in a railroad killer. This insurance man has put up a good amount of reward for that." He looked from the dying fly over to me. "Sure. Like you said: I'm in this for what I can get out of it."

I respected that. Truth. I respected Haxton.

From his wallet Haxton counted out some bills and left them on the counter. As he got to his feet, "Safe rails," he said.

"Safe rails."

And he left, doing his mosey away from me. His plate of food remained. I pulled it closer. I took his fork, scooped it into the room-temp potatoes and corn, shoveled it into my mouth. Shoveled in another forkful, picked up the knife and got ready to cut away some of that steak. The white guy behind the counter bused the plate, me still holding the knife and fork, and left me his contempt.

I got up, walked past the Asian woman and the Asian man, not buying any Slim Jims or Snickers or Little Debbie products. I'd get them somewhere else. Hell if I'd give this bunch my business.

The Asian woman said something to the Asian man in their Asian language as her eyes marched me from the store-slash-grill. The Asian man didn't miss a beat stocking the shelves, but eyed me all the way out the door.

There were two of them. Two guys with Stupid Bitch Dumbass. I could see them plainly at a distance. I was too far and it was too dark to read their faces, but body language made the situation clear—two guys standing over a crouched and self-clutching Stupid Bitch Dumbass. Ninety minutes I'd been gone. If even. Ninety minutes. Just enough time for the boy to buy himself trouble. Dumbass.

I kept walking for the scene, made noise, did some whistling so I wouldn't startle the unknown quantity. Acting relaxed with myself, I displayed none of the worry I carried. I hoped my casualness would give them concern—lack of fear translating into self-confidence. I got close enough to read the two men: both white. Both young. Barely thirty. One had a slight beard. One didn't. Their distinctions pretty much ended there. I didn't think they were hoboes, or tramps. They had no packs. Most likely they were only Home Guard just begging food. If that's all they wanted there would be no trouble. If they wanted something else, well, me and George were ready for that too.

Moving close to Stupid Bitch Dumbass, keeping distance between myself and the Home Guard, I set down my bag of groceries. Small bag. Taking out a Slim Jim, I tossed it to Stupid Bitch Dumbass. It hit him in the shoulder and fell to the ground without him even making a try for it. "Eat up." Far as I cared, the way I acted, the other two weren't there.

Stupid Bitch Dumbass picked up the Slim Jim. Sweaty fingers slipped over the plastic wrap, kept him from opening it. He just held on to the spiced jerky stick the way a Buddhist monk clutches incense while praying.

One of the Home Guard, I didn't look to see which, asked: "Got food?"

"You see us eating."

I was eating. Dumbass was just doing his monk act.

"We'll take some." Not a request. A demand.

"Got anything to trade?"

"No." That came from the other Home Guard.

"Got nothing, you get nothing."

"How about we just take some." Not a question. A statement.

I turned my head, finally giving them a whit of my attention. I did it slow, milking all the drama there was to be had from the beat. Spreading my gaze between the two of them: "How about you try?"

The Home Guard with the beard said to that: "Think the two of you are any good against the two of us? This one's nothing but a bitch."

Dumbass he was talking about. Obviously. And he was right about that.

I said: "You're right about that. What you're wrong about: it's not just two of us."

The Home Guard kept looking at me like I was packed to the eyeballs with Grade A shit. Then, real subtle, they looked around, looked for the other "us" I was talking about.

I double-clutched George Plimpton.

I said: "You want to start some shit, let's get some shit started. It doesn't make us," the *us* got underlined and emphasized, "any difference. Otherwise take yourselves out of here so me and my partners can do some eating."

The Home Guard stood around thinking, considering things. The more they thought and considered, the less likely trouble became. The rule I knew was that violence, when it occurred, was almost always instant and hot and in the moment. Once someone gave thought to force, the idea faded as reasons against it grew, chief among them being you were as likely to get your ass kicked as kick ass. That notion was coming to the Home Guard. They watched us eat. Watched me eat. Stupid Bitch Dumbass was still holding his wrapped Slim Jim, the only alteration was he had one end in his mouth and was sucking on the plastic.

Home Guard watched us . . .

"Oughta slit your throat," one said, convictionless.

"Want another Slim Jim?" I said to Stupid Bitch Dumbass, who hadn't even opened his first.

"Oughta." They stood around a bit more, but the more they stood, the more stupid they came off, and they knew it, and pretty soon they just walked away, one of them saying a final time and for the record: "Oughta."

Once the Home Guard had wandered Stupid Bitch Dumbass sort of fell over, and for a beat I thought he might puke again—the one activity in which he excelled. I was glad he hadn't eaten the Slim Jim. I'd have been pissed to hell if he'd puked up food I'd just bought.

"I thought . . ." his voice was weak and raspy, dry like he'd spent the last half hour too scared to swallow. "Thought they were going to kill me."

"Probably they were."

"Geeezuz."

I dug in my pack, got out Lady K, took a hit. Took another. I took it because I needed some calming down. I took it because I was jangled. I took it because the sky was more black than blue. I took the K because I was an addict, and that's what addicts do.

"Probably they would've killed you for a finale."

"Shiiit."

"But they would've gone through a catalogue of sick and nasty before they got there."

Slobbery: "Whyyu tryinta scare meeeee!"

"I'm not trying to scare you. I'm trying to school you on the way things are. You're living a world where people take; your food, your shoes, your sex. Your life isn't anything more special to them. So when it's time for shit to get taken, shit will be taken. Weeping and crying and carrying on isn't going to change that reality one bit. Only going to make you look like a girl. Only going to make them that much rougher about the whole deal. They're going to take and you're going to give, so why bother with all the bitchness? You chose to be out here on the rails. You get what comes with it."

It was about then that Stupid Bitch Dumbass's brain finally realized his hand was holding on to a Slim Jim. For a minute he just fumbled it around like a monkey would a stick. He opened the Slim Jim.

Ate the Slim Jim. Some of it. His stomach was in no mood for consumption so he quit trying two bites in.

Stupid Bitch Dumbass looked at me, asked: "Why you out here?"

"I should be staying at the Four Seasons?"

"Not here. Not right here. In general, why you here?"

"Got nowhere else to be."

"But why?"

"This is where my life dumped me."

"But—"

"Jesus, what the fuck?"

". . . Aren't you trying to find something?"

"Something?"

"Aren't you looking for some kind of . . . you know. Something." That was as articulate as Stupid Bitch Dumbass could get. Anyway, I understood his meaning.

I said: "I'm here. If there was someplace else I could be, some other way I could live, then I'd be there and I'd be living that way. There isn't. I'm not. I'm not looking for anything." I was insistent with that. "I'm just trying to get by."

"I thought maybe you were . . . you hear people do this, ride the rails because . . ." A pause, slight, like he had to confirm things with himself, then: "I'm looking for . . . you know. Answers."

"To?"

"I don't know, you know? That's the messed-up part. I just know the way I was living wasn't the answer. I was in college . . . junior college," a little ashamed, "and I was studying automotive sciences—"

I kind of laughed and Stupid Bitch Dumbass laughed a little with me.

"Yeah, I know. Big talk for being a grease monkey. But I was good with cars, you know? I mean, you're sixteen in Cincinnati, there's nothing to do but mess with cars anyway. So I was in college, junior college, living at home still and I had a friend, his dad owned a garage, and I was working there on the weekends. He tells—my friend's dad—he tells me soon as I graduate I can start working full time. And . . . and that was it right there. That was all the more I ever had going on. I didn't even have a girl, you know? I never even had a girl all the way through high school. One time I went out with this one girl who was on the prom court. Wasn't queen or anything, but she was on the court and I was like skying to be going out with a girl that was that good, you know? That's something. Right?"

"Sure," I said with little or no conviction.

"But it was just one date, and I didn't even get a kiss, let alone feel her up. Guess I shouldn't've told you that. Guess it makes me come off like a loser."

I sort of shrugged.

"It don't matter, you know? I know I'm a loser. Always have been, I don't know, different."

"Different how?"

"Different . . . I don't know how. I'm just not like everybody else. It's like I got something inside me that's ripe and I got this funk of not-the-sameness. I didn't have no girlfriend like I said, you know? Didn't matter how nice I was, or, you know, I'd do corny shit like send them flowers. They didn't want nothing to do with me. And other guys, they'd treat their girls like crap, and they'd keep coming back around for more."

"Hell with 'em. Straight to hell. They're just women. A man without a woman is like a bird without a—"

"But it was everybody. I didn't have a lot of friends, and the ones I did have . . . they were always busting on me. I mean, that shit was . . . they're supposed to be my friends, right? But every time we hung out the jokes about Steve doing this stupid or Steve doing that stupid or how Steve can't get laid would start right up." He stopped. Looked at me. "I don't mean for it to keep coming around to me not getting any, but what else is there?"

His age, having somebody; what else is there? Any age, having somebody, not being alone and lonely and miserable and feeling disparate; what else is there?

Stupid Bitch Dumbass: "I was always . . . I was different, like I said. People, I swear, they smelled it coming off me. They'd look at me, catch a whiff, then screw up their faces in disgust 'cause I'm so not goddamn normal."

The thing about all that which struck me the most was how

descriptive it was said; that as mealymouthed as Stupid Bitch Dumbass was, he could orate with such clarity on his disease of dissimilarity. It was pretty obvious he had spent a good while in study on that aspect of himself. And for a kid all of eighteen or nineteen to spend that much time trying to figure why he was queer . . . it was pretty sad.

Charles Harmon could relate. When he was younger, in high school, when he was just about the only black kid among fifteen hundred whites, he knew what it was like to be terminally different. Never out-and-out hated or despised because of his race. Proper liberal suburban kids were open-minded. But so many times there were the jokes about watermelon and barbecue chicken, and after summer vacation the other kids would gleefully run to Charles and press their flesh to his, smile and chirp: "Look, Charles. I'm darker than you!"

Charles tolerated them.

Brain Nigger Charlie hoped every last one of them was dead of cancer.

"So, one day," Stupid Bitch Dumbass going on, "I get up, you know, and I'm eating cornflakes in my parents' house and I'm getting ready to head off to JC to study auto repair and I'm thinking about how to kill another weekend 'cause I don't have anybody to hang out with and I'm watching TV, and there's this real good-looking chick giving the news and I'm watching her thinking that's one more woman I could never get with and I start wondering: what the fuck is wrong with me? What the fuck is wrong with my life? And then, and I swear to Christ this is how it happened, I'm staring at the strawberries floating in the milk and cornflakes . . . I'm looking at them floating and I think: maybe I'm not the one who's all . . . whatever, you know? Maybe I'm okay, but it's the rest of the world that's all fucked up. But how am I going to know that from Cincinnati; living with my parents, living my whole life in looking distance of where I was born?" Stupid Bitch Dumbass gave another go at eating his Slim Jim. This time he made a good job of things, finished it off.

In the meanwhile I said nothing. I knew Stupid Bitch Dumbass had a lot to get out, and as I had no other way to occupy me, I'd give him the time to do it. I tossed him another Slim Jim.

As he opened it: "All of a sudden I felt . . . I felt like I was in a teeny tiny box, getting smaller by the second, that was crushing the life out of me. A box that would just end up being my coffin one day. There's got to be something more than a city in Ohio. There's got to be more than all the nothing I had, and all the nobody I was. I can have things. Right? I just gotta, you know. I just gotta go out and find 'em. So that's when I decided it was time for me to catch off. Catch out. Sorry."

I didn't say anything to that. Stupid Bitch Dumbass was learning terminology. That's all that mattered.

"That's why I'm here. That's why I'm on the rails. Not, you know, for an ass-fucking. You know?"

I knew.

Having shared himself with me, Dumbass asked, again: "So, what are you looking for?"

Questions. Personal questions. I did not ride the rails to get asked pointless introspective questions from slow white boys who were lost in the world.

And yet

And yet

No. Fuck that. Kid wants to cry himself to sleep, let him if it makes him miss mommy less. But Brain Nigger Charlie's got nothing to weep over.

I said: "I'm here because I'm here. That's all there is." I fell back onto the ground and looked up into the black of space. I was done talking.

Stupid Bitch Dumbass slept. I avoided sleep, the hauntings that waited for me with a couple of kisses from Lady E. Within one-half of an hour I got a familiar tingle in the lower part of my legs, and not more than fifteen minutes after that I was clutching at my thighs with an anxious energy that demanded to be expunged from my body. I dug in my pack and dug out a page torn from the Sunday *Times Magazine*. An ad. A girl modeling a swimsuit. A swimsuit kind of outfit. Pink in color. Liz Claiborne. The model was young and sweet and smiling. She was not pencil thin, but she was certainly not heavy. She had great tits. Real. She was my woman. She was as much woman, all the more woman, I'd had over the last few years. There had been others like her. The snotty rich girl from the fashion ad in a *Vanity Fair.* Don't even recall what she was selling, I just remember she was begging to be taken down a peg with some rough sex. There was that smiling twenty-something that was in *Entertainment Weekly.* She, too, had been trying to get me to buy what I didn't need. She, too, just got my sex for her trouble. There was that one girl with the tight, flat stomach, tan skin, muscles, on the cover of that fitness magazine I'd dug from the garbage while looking for edibles. She had stayed with me a long, long time. Edges torn, creases and crinkles obscuring most of her goodness, I kept her until she was more rag than picture. But a woman like that, lean and strong and so wonderful, so easy to cum to, was hard to come by. There were times when I missed her dearly, but day by day the image of her slipped from my mind and begged to be replaced. This girl, this girl modeling a swimsuit kind of outfit, young and sweet and white and smiling—she was my woman now. And now—me on E and her in all her silent, one-dimensional glory—she was all the woman I needed. I unhitched my pants and reached between my legs, excitable to my own touch. Then me and the girl in the swimsuit lived a couple of fantasies before I landed on one that involved putting something in her mouth other than a part of my body and it took me to orgasm. Right after that I wasn't so interested in her anymore. I folded her up . . . first I flipped the jizz off my hand and wiped what was left—a generation of Brain Nigger Charlies—on my shirt, thanked Liz Claiborne Girl for her kind attentions and told her that I loved her and would never forget her the way I had Hard Body Chick, and then I folded her up and returned her to my pack.

I uncellophaned another Slim Jim, lay back, took the picture of Corina from my chest pocket. I wondered if she was lying back looking at the stars at that moment. I wondered if she was, as I was, eating some food that cost her less than a couple of quarters. I wondered if she was sitting wondering if anyone was wondering about her. Mostly I wondered how in the hell I was going to find her.

I put the picture of Corina back in my chest pocket. I lay awake until dawn.

Blondie got old.

I thought of her one night when my Silvertone pulled a song of hers out of the endless invisibility where radio music traveled.

Her name was not Blondie. Blondie was the name of the band. But she fronted it. She was blonde. Everyone thought of her as Blondie. And years ago she was all a teenage boy could want: sexy and pouty and free-spirited in a New Wave way back when razor ties and parachute pants and sports coats with their sleeves pushed to the elbows were the extreme of cool. For a time Blondie—Blondie the band and the blonde girl—could not do wrong. Hit after hit after hit after hit. Magazine covers. Fluff-pieced in the starfucker rags daily.

And then she went away, slipped away from my, from our collective consciousness. That was okay. I was focused on other things. Getting out of high school. Getting into college. Getting over in life. And razor ties and parachute pants and sports coats with their sleeves pushed to the elbows were, by then, extremely uncool.

Then, one day, years on, I saw a picture of Blondie. The band was attempting a comeback. Has-been rock stars were always attempting comebacks. And old prizefighters were always trying to climb into the ring one last time when they were too punch drunk to call it a life.

Fine. They're entitled.

Except

Blondie had gotten old.

No longer tight and trim and beautiful, she was soft and heavy. The bags under her eyes were stuffed full with her years. The lines on her face obvious even with the gentle light of studio photography. She looked worn and tired, and worst of all the seemingly boundless sex appeal I remember her spewing had been drained away. Gone. Sex is what she'd traded on. She had nothing left to barter with.

Who am I to blame her for following nature's laws? We all get old. We all lose what little appeal we own.

But

Not all of us are icons of our generation. Most of us will never be the ingredient of mass sexual fantasy. So how dare she? How dare she show her aged face and rob me of my memories of her, remind me that the past is slipping away at an exponentially increasing rate and all that's waiting in the future is fading memories of better days I never had in the first place?

Morning.

August. No matter. Clear, bright everywhere else. Here, Spokane, the sky was more cloudy than sunny. The difference between night and day was a subtlety of hue. The hours and hours of dark and a little less dark reset my body clock in a most fucked-up manner; made me dizzy. Literally. Made me nauseous. And it was wet. It was not raining, but no matter that it was August there was dampness all around. You could smell the water in the too cool air the way you smell a thunderstorm in summer, threatening constantly but keeping its distance. The wet clung tight; a handmade suit soaking you little by little each minute of every hour until you were moist to the core. I did not like Washington. The dank and the chill and the night-for-day made me want to lie down and veg when there was much to be done. A patch of land should not be able to affect you so. There is something not right about such a place. I did not care for Spokane and I would be glad to be done with it.

In the meantime, as I waited to catch scent of Corina, I felt I should do something for Stupid Bitch Dumbass. More rightly, all his blathering about being different and unaccepted guilted me into wanting to do something for him. Something being, teach him in the same manner Chocolate Walt had taught me. Stupid Bitch Dumbass would not be traveling and jungling with me forever. I hoped. And as he was now, alone, his survival skills were just sufficient enough to get him killed. So I took him around for a couple of days. I taught him how not to have to stand on a street corner, palm out, depending on the charity of strangers; to take advantage of assistance the government provided for people like us: food stamps. Glorious food stamps. The requirements for getting them: be underpaid, or unemployed, or on welfare, or too old or sick to work. Or be homeless. You got no home, you're an automatic qualifier. Tramps and 'boes didn't generally have homes. So you go to a food stamp office, fill out an application. Thirty days later you start getting your stamps. Plead destitution, get 'em in seven. That easy. But you can't use stamps for booze or drugs. So you do the stamp dance: do the alchemy to change government aid into money. Cash money. Take the money and get what you need. A lot of work, yeah, from getting the stamps to turning them into spendable green. But not as much work as Joe and Jane Taxpayer had to do to feed the machine that paid for my stamps that I swapped for cash that I used to buy the K and E that kept me high. Thing is: you can only get food stamps for three months in a thirty-six-month period from any one state. But there are a lot of states in the Union. The great thing about being a tramp or 'bo, it's easy to get to one you haven't bilked in a while.

I taught Stupid Bitch Dumbass how to Dumpster-dive.

No.

Not how to dive. Digging through the garbage for things to eat is a short lesson and one learned easily. I taught him *where* to dive: the trash containers out back of fast food joints. The government, God bless it again, has rules about how long restaurant food can be left standing. Daily, Whoppers and Big Macs and Jumbo Jacks and Chalupas got tossed out because they were two minutes or ten minutes or forty-three seconds past freshness. Too spoiled for the general public. A feast for 'boes and tramps and Home Guard alike. We found a KFC off a main drag. Slightly isolated. Good. We had it to ourselves. Stupid Bitch Dumbass and I went diving and surfaced with biscuits and mashed potatoes still warm, potato wedges, cole slaw—which I didn't eat and would not trust under the best of circumstances—and for a trophy, a bucket nearly full of Extra Crispy. We ate some right there by the Dumpster before the manager chased us off. What the hell were us bums doing eating his good thrown-away food? Fuck him. Yeah, he could chase us away, but he's the one who would be a manager of a Kentucky Fried Chicken until his dying day.

I took Stupid Bitch Dumbass out tagging. We went round to some underpasses where we could leave our marks. I kept us clear of the rail yards. No need to invite trouble. Still, even on the outer edges of train territory there were plenty of tags by 'boes and tramps to be found. TODAY I DRINK UNTIL I DIE    I WILL FIND YOU GRACE. In a message dated 8/23 Slo Freight Ben wrote, again, THE DEVIL IS TRICKY/IF YOU'RE NOT CAREFUL HE'LL MAKE A FOOL OF YOU/DON'T BE THE DEVIL'S FOOL. THE DEVIL IS NOTHING BUT A FALLEN ANGEL C of Love wrote back. FTRA marked their territory, and, finally, the Chief wanted everyone to know YOU CAN ALL KISS MY ASS AND WHEN I SEE YOU, I'LL KILL YOU. With a rock I scratched: YOU CAN'T OUTTHINK BRAIN NIGGER, and dated it so everyone would know just when it was Brain Nigger Charlie braved the High Line. Stupid Bitch Dumbass kind of liked that. I gave him the rock, told him to leave his mark. He held it for a bit, screwed his feet around as he thought. He said he didn't really want to write anything, felt bad about having to make reference to the fact that he was a stupid dumbass. And a bitch.

I told him look at it this way: years on, when he had a better tag, he would ride this way, see his old mark, and have a laugh at what a stupid dumbass he used to be. And a bitch.

He nodded like that wasn't such a bad way of considering things. He fumbled the rock in his hand for a minute or so, then scratched: DUMBASS AIN'T AS STUPID AS YOU THINK.

I thought that was pretty good. I told him so.

Stupid Bitch Dumbass tossed away the rock and we started from the underpass.

I stopped, suddenly caught up in loose thought. I went back to tags, read through them. To myself: "Jesus . . ."

"Brain Nigger? Brain Nigger!" Stupid Bitch Dumbass called.

That girl back in Williston, the CCR girl . . . What did she say? She'd told me . . .

"Brain Nigger?"

I gave the tags another looking-over, headed back to Stupid Bitch Dumbass and walked on. He fell in a couple of steps behind me. I yelled at him for that. He apologized and paced me by my side.

One thing I did not do was introduce Stupid Bitch Dumbass to Lady E or Lady K. They were mine and they were precious. No way in hell I was going to let them cheat on me with this kid.

I like libraries. I like to read. Reading works out the mind, keeps the brain in Brain Nigger. It is the intelligent way to kill time. Factor in the hours I can't sleep, I have much time to kill. I had time to kill with Stupid Bitch Dumbass and I figured a good way to do it would be to introduce him to the wonder of complimentary education. I tried to get him to read about rail travel—thinking he should know of his world—or to check out papers from across the country or, hell, for that matter, around the world. All that nearly bored the white off him until he found out the library stocked *Playboys*, which were free for the reading, and got real interested in navigating the Internet until I told him that the computers had filters that kept them from logging onto porn sites. After that, Stupid Bitch Dumbass tired of the library and wanted to leave. I made him stick around while I read the *Christian Science Monitor*. Not that I wanted to read the *Christian Science Monitor*, but I wanted to make him sit on his ass for a while because I was in that kind of mood. Then the *Christian Science Monitor* started to fatigue me more than I could stand, and I realized I wasn't punishing Stupid Bitch Dumbass as much as I was just punishing myself. I left, took Stupid Bitch Dumbass with me.

Two guys. Two guys hanging on a corner across from some kind of factory. Lunchtime. Asian immigrant labor flooded out to buy food of suspect quality from Julios working a roach coach. The Asians lined the sidewalk. Squatting. Eating. Looking like refugees trying to stay one step ahead of Charlie.

Most of them did that; bought food, ate.

Some gravitated to a bunch of the ugliest whores—their skank literally defying description other than to say it could be whiffed from across the street; an odor of human fluids absorbed from filthy mattresses of cheap motels—cut some quick deals, and took them around a corner for a quick S&F.

And some of the Asians floated to the two guys on the corner and swapped what little money they had, earned for what hard work they did, to buy drugs. The exchanges, cash for drugs, were open and obvious, and obviously no one cared—not the Asians who needed a boost to get them through the day, not the dealers, not the management of the factory who didn't give a good goddamn if their little yellow men got lifted and made a shitty product as long as they did it for no-green-card / below-minimum-wage rates.

Two guys. Two guys hanging on a corner dealing. I would've passed them, me and Stupid Bitch Dumbass heading back for our jungle, without thought, except the two guys were the same two guys, the same two Home Guard—one with a slight beard, one without—I'd returned to our jungle to find hovering over Stupid Bitch Dumbass just days prior.

All the real estate in Spokane, and a couple of meth-pushing bums just happened to be at my jungle?

And real quick I got real angry. Angry for being played like a small-town fool. But anger wasn't going to do me any good. I was nearing a situation that would require navigation using logic with a capital B for Brain Nigger–style. Logic told me I needed to get me and Stupid Bitch Dumbass out of there before we got spotted. Logic said—"What?"

Stupid Bitch Dumbass: "I didn't say anything."

I wasn't talking to him. I was talking to George. I could've sworn George had just told me to

But reason was telling me to

And then I could've sworn George told me to tell reason to lick my middle finger.

Well, okay, George. If you say so.

I gave a little hysterical laugh at myself. Yes. Definitely. Insanity had just stamped my passport.

To Dumbass: "Get out of here."

"Get out . . . ?"

"Go back to the jungle." A quick thought: after . . . after whatever was going to happen was done happening people were likely to come looking for me. No good being where we were; where the Home Guard knew to find us. I thought a beat. "That KFC; remember it?"

"Yeah."

"Back behind the parking lot, that field; go there. Jungle there."

"Why we gotta—"

"Don't be a dumbass. Not now! Just do what I say." I gave my pack to Stupid Bitch Dumbass.

I gave my pack to Stupid Bitch Dumbass?

The anger I owned, with George's inciting, was slapping the shit out of logic.

I said again: "Do what I say. Go there, stay there."

"What are you gonna—"

"Go! And keep out of sight." One more thing: "And don't you run off with my shit and make me come hunt you. Be there when I get there."

Stupid Bitch Dumbass looked like a scared little puppy dog as he started down the street alone. Started, stopped, turned and looked back, then started off again. I waited until he was completely gone. Not so that Stupid Bitch Dumbass could avoid getting caught up in what was coming, but so that he didn't see me engaging in an action when I was clueless as to what that action should be. Real quick I got the sweats and my stomach felt like expelling its sparse contents. My anger had not diminished, but I questioned my own ability to execute George's plan for dealing with the two men on the corner. George and I knew violence. We were intimate with it. But the violence we engaged in was, almost to an incident, in reaction to violence perpetrated against us. That was about to change. A line, fine as it was, was about to be crossed.

I waited. I waited for the lunch hour, more like a lunch half hour—boss man wasn't about to let his hired help dillydally all day—to end. The Asians trudged back to the slave labor they waged in the name of capitalism. The two guys on the corner were left mostly alone; the Mexicans with their roach coach gone off, the whores vanished to find new tricks or cash out to their pimps.

George wanted to know if I was ready for this shit?

He felt good in my hand; hard and heavy.

Yeah. I was ready.

And then George was all over the first of the Home Guard, the one with no beard. Racing across the street for them, lifting, swinging George; all that I don't even remember. I just remember the vibration that ran hand to shoulder when George said hello to the bearded guy's head. Down he went discarded-rag-doll-style; limp and mostly lifeless. It's what happens when you crack a guy's skull, spill some blood and rattle his brains. The sound of George connecting with the Home Guard's head: a ripe melon wrapped in a wet towel getting split open. It was low and soft and sick. And beautiful. The crescendo of a symphony. A high note I instantly loved and would never forget.

George picked the rib cage to go at on Home Guard numero dos; the guy who'd been all threatening and big mouthed in the dark the night he'd come around. George whapped him, whapped him a couple of times, then went for the spine when the guy doubled over. That sent him down to his knees, so George came low, arched upward, clipped the guy in the face—that symphony played again—and sent him skipping away, down to his back. Wasn't enough to knock him senseless. Just enough to make him do a spasm dance on the ground. I let him get it all out. Then me and him had some talking to do.

I said: "Call him!"

"Wha . . . ?" came out of his mouth in a long, red seep along with a couple of teeth George had busted right from his gums.

I turned to the other Home Guard, the one who went down with one hit to the head. I swung George, catching the guy across the midsection. I swung George again. There was a crack. A busted rib. Maybe. Probably. In response to the beating and the breaking the guy's body did nothing but lie right where it was. Fine. I didn't need him to do anything in particular except accept a demonstration of what kind of violence noncompliance bought.

Back to the other HG, again: "Call him."

This time no dumb questions asked back. This time a cell phone got dug out of his pocket.

A Home Guard with a cell phone. Yeah, I was on the right track.

Shaky fingers punched numbers, started to, stopped, then hit a programmed number on speed dial. Panic, fear clearing just enough for the Home Guard to remember the number he was calling was *the* number.

I looked around some. Down the street was a Mobil station. I barked to the Home Guard: "That gas station; you tell him to meet us there. You tell him Brain Nigger Charlie's looking for him."

Following my directive, afraid to do otherwise, Home Guard bled into his phone.

". . . Water . . ."

Wasn't feeling angry anymore. At least, I was back to feeling more stupid than angry.

". . . Please . . ."

Most of my ire I'd burned off on the two Home Guard. One I'd left unconscious on the street. The other I'd dragged by the hair over to a Mobil station where we'd wait for his boss. Kessler. Having been played by Kessler; that's what made me feel stupid.

". . . Just a little . . ."

Business at the station was slow despite the fair amount of traffic that rolled by on the street. It was Spokane. Lots of Greenies driving their Hondas and Toyotas, trying to grab bragging rights for best mileage. The attendant didn't even bother to give us an eyeing in particular. Gas stations were meccas for bums looking to wipe windows for change. Prostitute themselves for food. Mostly me and the Home Guard went undisturbed as we waited. Well, honestly, Home Guard was disturbing the hell out of me.

"Just want a little water."

I looked to him lying down at my feet. His mouth was caked over with blood. More kept pouring out.

I was going to spray some water from the water hose at the little air/water station into his face to shut him up. It cost a quarter. Hell if I was about to burn twenty-five good cents on Home Guard. George told him to pipe down and that did an equally good job of making him go quiet.

We'd been waiting nearly a half an hour. A Mercedes had pulled into the station and I thought it was Kessler's but it wasn't. The only other high-end car to stop was a Saab, and I knew that wasn't his. There was a Camaro. That was white trash. Maybe Kessler reveled in his white trashiness. The owner was white trash, but she was a white trash mom with her two white trash kids; a girl wearing a T-shirt singing the praises of some heavy metal band, and a baby wearing nothing but diapers. Soiled.

I could've used a bump of something. Anything. But Stupid Bitch Dumbass had my pack, had my ladies. Anyway, I needed to be straight, straight as I could be, for whatever was coming.

I waited on. Fifteen, twenty minutes more.

And then she sailed into the station. With a wheelbase of nearly one hundred twenty-seven inches, it was quite possibly the largest piece of automotive crap ever to get defecated out of the good city of Detroit: a 1972 Imperial LeBaron sedan. Four-forty big-block V-8. TorqueFlite transmission. Vinyl roof. No doubt: this was Kessler.

The Imperial parked. The front doors opened. Liquid Evil and Buzz Cut Girl got out.

The back door opened. Peter Frampton got out of the car. Not Peter Frampton. A guy who looked like Peter Frampton. Not "now" Peter Frampton; weak eyes wearing spectacles and male-pattern-baldness-thinned hair. This guy looked like "then" Peter Frampton. The *Frampton Comes Alive* Peter Frampton I rocked to when the rest of the young black kids in Jack and Jill were grooving to the Sylvers, the Commodores. This guy had the Frampton glowing golden locks, open shirt revealing smooth milk-white flesh pulled taught over a lean body. And he had Peter Frampton's sweet face. Sweet. Pleasant-looking. That this sweet face was the one which whispered nastiness in the ear of Liquid Evil made him seem all the more creepy, in the manner of a smiling perv hanging around the girls' locker room at a grade school.

The package Kessler came wrapped in—long hair and tattoo free—didn't much make him look like a skinhead. But NLR were only loosely skinheads; skinheads because when you're white and in a gang you were either a skinhead or a biker. Mostly they were just nasty fucks who dealt drugs. Kessler got himself about four or five yards from me. Stopped. Looked at his bloodied-up boy sitting on the ground. Kessler's expression changed little. Just a little. Just enough to register his disgust; for me to know he had low-to-no tolerance for foot soldiers who didn't have it in them to keep tabs on a bum—a coon bum—without getting the holy hell beat out of them. Kessler's face told me this foot soldier wasn't long for the world.

Then, Kessler turned his attention to me.

He said: "Brain Nigger Charlie."

I said: "Kessler." That's all I said. I wanted to add something snide; something smart and clever. Something Bond would say to Blofeld. Wanted to. Didn't. Frightened by the reality of facing down a collection of genuine badasses, my breath came in stuttering spurts and put sly quips beyond me. Trying to weave verbal gold would just make me sound like I felt: little-girl scared.

Kessler wanted to know: "Where's Morgan?"

Morgan must've been his other boy.

I shrugged.

That subtle mutation eclipsed his face again. Another Home Guard bites the dust.

Me, playing at tough guy: "Gotta do better."

Kessler sort of nodded. I think he did. His head moved some. Mostly, if he was impressed by my performance it didn't show. "You wanted something?"

Getting right to things; simple, direct: "Where's Corina?"

Kessler didn't say anything to that.

"C'mon, man. I go asking around about her, then your little circus act shows up," I jerked my head at Liquid Evil and his girl, "do their routine, like they're going to cut me. I go dumb, but they know better. So, you have them play me with your phone number, bait me out here, then you've got this creep," this time my head pointed toward the mumbling bleeding guy on the ground, "eyeballing me not two seconds after my feet touch ground. You're watching me for a reason. The only thing you and me have in common is Corina. Where is she?"

Kessler swept back his hair, let it get lifted and tossed by the wind. Like that, blond and sexy, he was an Aryan poster child. Rockin' for the Reich. Hitler Youth by the shore. He was true NLR, true to their Orange County Calif. heritage. His little SoCal drawl went well with the package. "Man, if I," he said, "knew where the bitch was, would I be wasting my time on you?"

"Why are you looking for her?"

"Why you think?"

The mumbling / bleeding Home Guard mumbled: "I'm bleeding," then to prove it, mouth-bled onto the parking lot asphalt.

To Kessler: "If I'm guessing, I'm guessing you're looking for her because she tramped on your heart, stole your manhood, and left you a sick, turned-out faggot."

Kessler stared off somewhere. Anyway, he didn't look at me. "I ain't a bum, dude. I don't got time to play. You're the one smacking around my crew. You're the one called me out here like you're somebody. You wanna dialogue, let's dialogue. Otherwise I got shit to do that don't include niggers."

"I don't feel so . . ." From the ground below us, more mumbling. "I got blood in my stomach. I'm sick, man. Just want some water. Help me . . ."

Me, Kessler, the redhead, and Liquid Evil: we all couldn't care less and did just that.

Kessler, his attitude, his look; everything about him was starting to edge me up. My edge got me angry again, got my heart and lungs pumping hard but steady. "Corina's got something of yours, and if it's yours it couldn't be much. Money. Drugs. A little of both."

"The girl was riding the rails." Kessler talked right past me. Ignored my jabs. They meant nothing to him. Neither did I. Pointed: "Man, that's some stupid shit. She ain't flying in an airplane, she ain't even rolling in some shitty wheels. She's riding the goddamn rails like it's the Middle Ages or some shit. By the time she gets around my way she's all wore out and hungry, going on about how she needs dough to get by. I tell her she can fuck for her food, but she doesn't want any of that."

Good girl, I praised to Corina.

"Let me ask you something: you ever hear anything so stupid; a bitch, pussy clean, and she don't want to use it?"

My mind jumped ahead in the conversation: Kessler saying he didn't care Corina didn't want to give up her sex. Kessler saying he took Corina's sex. My mind jumped on a bit more: Kessler lying dead on the ground, me and a bloody George Plimpton standing over him.

Kessler: "I'm like: cool. Bitch don't wanna do things the easy way— "

"Ever get tired of saying 'bitch'?"

"Let *the bitch* work for her keep. I let *the bitch* do some runs for me."

"Run drugs."

Kessler shrugged, not confirming anything, not denying anything. Not saying anything, as if, for a split second, he thought maybe I was wearing a wire. "I let her work, let her travel for me. Then one day the bitch don't show where she's supposed to show. The bitch disappeared with my product."

"How much?"

Finally, an expression from Kessler. A smile. "What are you gonna do, bum? You gonna pay for my shit?" I'd read Kessler wrong. It wasn't a smile he was giving me. It was a cold laugh, and he sent it whipping my way like a throwing knife. "What are you gonna do? You gonna shine my shoes, bum? You gonna lick my car bright? You think that's gonna even things up? Bum, you couldn't give me what that bitch owes if your life was riding on it. Your ass is, like, borderline, so you might wanna keep clear of things. The little bitch's already paid me back, now it's time to send some payback her way."

I disconnected with that. "She paid you back how?"

Home Guard: "Help me . . . Kessler, man . . ." a bloody hand reached up and out. "Least get me some meds."

Kessler gave some kind of a look to Liquid Evil. Next thing, Liquid Evil poured himself on Home Guard, snatched up his head by his hair, collided Home Guard's face with his fist. A couple of times. Home Guard fell back, his head smacked ground with an audible thunk. It was the last sound Home Guard would make for a good long while.

Liquid Evil looked to Kessler.

Kessler looked to me. He continued as if he'd never been interrupted. As if the violence that had just happened hadn't. "So, like, if you got anything to tell me about Corina, maybe you wanna give it up now while you're still in condition to be cooperative."

"I got nothing to tell you."

Kessler let himself slink to one side as if taking up a pose for a *Rolling Stone* cover shot. "You don't know nothing, or you got nothing to tell, 'cause there is a difference."

I shrugged. I said: "Adds up to the same. You lost some drugs to her, that's the price of doing business. I'm here to tell you I'm taking her off the High Line, and that's a concept you need to learn to accept."

Kessler smiled. He smiled at Liquid Evil. Liquid Evil caught the smile the way dry brush catches fire, then he tossed it to Buzz Cut Girl. They were all smiling. Lots and lots of ivory that George wanted desperately to whack from their faces. I had to hold him back. I honest-to-God had to hold him back. I was very much starting to get with the feeling that George . . . I know this is queer, but I was starting to think that George had a mind of his own.

"You gotta be, like," Kessler said, "one insane fucking nigger bum; standing there talking to me like that. Way it is you already earned yourself a serious ass-kicking. You wanna get yourself turned into a stain, I'm good with that."

I co-opted the Lowriders' smiles and threw it back at them. "And you must be high on yourself. I know about the NLR. You all walk and talk like little boys who ate a big breakfast, but," looking down at knocked-out Home Guard, "you all are nothing but frightened mice, and you got cats-in-heat all around you. Bloods and Crips'll kill you for calling yourself skinheads. Skinheads'll kill you for smearing their Aryan image by selling drugs. The FTRA'll kill you for trying to claim their territory. You're just a low-rent dealer who's got to get runaway girls to push his shit 'cause he's too scared to do the job himself. You're nothing. You're less than that."

"You talking about me, dude? I'm nothing? You're fifteen feet away and you smell like human rust."

I liked that line, and I laughed to it. Still, far as I cared, reality was: "I can wash my stink clean. There's nothing in the world you can do about yourself."

That put out Kessler's smile. It was replaced by a sheen of frost that iced its way over his face. "Call yourself a smart nigger. Brain nigger. You're not. You're *just* a nigger."

George was bucking me in my hand.

"You're just a nigger 'cause you don't get shit. I ain't hiding out from nothing, ain't dodging nobody, man. I'm here for a reason. Cali is sick with meth. Everybody's running that shit: nigger gangs, spic gangs, biker gangs . . . Might as well sell that shit at a 7-Eleven. But up here, no niggers to worry about 'cause except for you the niggers are at least smart enough to stay away. I don't worry about the Aryans 'cause the Aryans are nothing but white shit. Talking about how they're gonna take things over; run the government. Not a one of them that don't live in a trailer park and pump gas for a living. Know what I got? I got mules running my shit all up and down the High Line, and I got no problem letting little girls do my work. Little girls most times don't get a second look from the cops. Little girls most times are too scared to fuck with you. Most times. And when they do, little girls are easy to make examples out of. See, runaway little girls end up dead in a ditch and nobody gives a fuck."

She's dead.

In one instant I confirmed with myself what I'd believed since I'd first caught out from Britt: Corina is dead. The only news was that this was the man who had killed her. And for a second I felt a loss that went beyond a hobo looking for a girl in the middle of nowhere as a favor for a friend. In the split second I knew that Corina was gone nothing mattered anymore. Just like that, not one single thing seemed to have any importance. If I lived, if I died; suddenly there seemed no consequence to either. So let's just end things now. Let's just me and Kessler and Buzz Cut Girl and LE all go out together. Like Slim Pickens riding that nuke right on into Mother Russia, let's all go down toge—

But then logic, logic . . . logic came back to me after being run off by George for so long. Logic said if Corina was dead, Kessler wouldn't've wasted so much as a minute watching my tail. He was still looking for her. She was still alive. This moment did not end my search. This moment made my search all the more urgent.

To Kessler: "You think nobody cares about the girl? You see me standing here. I made it this far up the High Line, I'll make it back. With Corina. Like I said: you can accept that, or you can take the trouble that comes with getting in my way."

"You really think you're a tough nigger bum." Kessler's tongue slid over his teeth.

"Come on over. Come see how tough I am."

"Just 'cause there're people around you think I'm not gonna stomp your ass?"

"I think you're not going to do anything because all your heads together don't have the brains to find Corina. The best you're going to be able to do is try and keep up with me. I'm all you've got."

Kessler thought; the first time since our little powwow convened that he'd given due consideration to anything I had to say. In near appreciation: "Man, that's good thinking. It was. But, know what; you're such a goddamn smartass nigger, fuck Corina. I'm good to see you dead."

Dead.

He moved.

One word. A word like a trigger pulled: Go. Do. Kill. One word. Dead. And at the word Liquid Evil moved for me. His hand flipped, flashed the blade of the knife he'd been palming. It kicked light and screamed murder, bloody murder! It was all very skilled, fluid and fast. But from the first, from the moment Kessler had hit the parking lot and stepped from his Imperial, I'd kept an eye on Liquid Evil. He was Kessler's messenger. When violence came it would come from him. I'd seen the knife he'd been stealthing. I knew it was meant for me. When he moved I moved with him.

George Plimpton was up, angry. Doing work. George was a badass. George was a head smasher. And though some tried, George Plimpton was not to be trifled with.

George swung out, arched down and signed his name across LE's skull with a deep red gash running ear to jaw. Liquid E's head meteored for the ground. Where the head goes, the body follows.

Buzz Cut Girl looked to her man, took her eyes off me. Concern. How sweet. I let her have all of George right across her tits. Her response was the only sound I'd so far heard from her. It came like the ugly noise deer make when pickups clip them hopping roads in the dark of night. The blow stumbled her back, hands clutching chest, feet caught up in Liquid Evil's body. She tripped down. Flesh smacked flesh. Bone smacked asphalt.

In an eternal instant I had time to dig my handiwork. The peckerwood and his featherwood rolling on the pavement. Home Guard still stretched out and silent. And looking at all that, I felt how I'd never felt about violence before in all my time on the rails. I felt good.

Then instinct arrived, joined the party thrown by rage, boycotted by intellect. Instinct told me to get over myself, jerked my head, got me looking to Kessler.

Kessler, his eyes; they lavaed hate.

Instinct told me to run.

I ran. Where to, I didn't know. Didn't matter. Run, instinct told me. Get out of there before Kessler pulled a gun, before Liquid Evil and his girl got up, grabbed knives, and whittled the black off you. Eventually I'd lose them, make my way back to Stupid Bitch Dumbass and our KFC jungle. Eventually. For now, run.

I did that.

I ran all out, ran as fast as my demilame leg would carry me, George churning air in my hand. I didn't look back. The one thing I'd ever learned from the Bible is: don't look back. All looking back would do is slow you down or let you see the bullet that was coming your way. My major concentration was on heading forward, dodging what people were on the street, skipping through traffic as I sprinted red lights. I hadn't even gone a half of a quarter of a mile when my legs started to burn and my chest overheated from extreme lung use. I figured Kessler, or Kessler via his stooges, had to be on my ass. Figured that, but couldn't look back. Didn't hear a car, so maybe I was clear of them.

Don't look back

Whipped around a corner.

Still didn't hear Kessler's wheels following me. But then, I couldn't hear anything over my own huffing, over my own breath racing in and out of me blast-furnace loud. So maybe he was right behind me, so maybe he was just then taking aim at my head.

Don't look back!

But maybe I still had a second to put the dodge on him and save my skin.

So look back!

I did. I twisted and looked behind me and saw a few pissed people giving me the eye, wanting to know what I was doing tearing up the street, one guy picking himself up off the ground to where I'd knocked him. What I didn't see was Kessler. He hadn't followed me, or if he had I'd lost him.

Fuck you, I smiled at his last known location. You can't beat me, and you can't catch me. I'll tell Corina you said "hey" when I find her.

I heard the scream of rubber on road; locked tires. I turned back around, looked, saw the grille of a Chevy Caprice. I felt it clip my legs. Sort of. Mostly I felt a sense of weightlessness as I took air and flew away from the car. Definitely I felt the street as I tumbled over it, slid to a stop, leaving a skid mark of clothes and flesh behind me. But I felt okay. That is to say, I felt a whole lot of pain over ninety percent of my body—the parts of me that weren't bruised and banged starting to go warm, then hot with hurt from the quick friction—but the pain said I was still alive and I was okay with that. Then, I thought, the pain was probably the by-product of several broken bones I would never properly recover from, leave me a quad for life wishing the car had finished what it started.

Never should have looked back. Listen to the Bible.

"Don't move!" A guy in a dull brownish uniform, gun out, barking at me. "Don't you move!"

I didn't move, except for my eyes that looked past him to his car, the car that had nailed me: a sheriff's RMP.

"Don't move!"

This guy'd just hit me with his squad, launched me through the air, and sent me skipping across the ground. Don't move? No shit.

I was in a box. Physically. Mentally. Literally, figuratively, I was in a box. I was center of the perpendicular lines of my search for Corina, Kessler, his crew, and the local sheriff's deputy who'd hit me with his car, scooped me up off the pavement, and brought me into a substation with handcuffs and without compassion.

That was the other box; the physical box. "The Box." The interrogation room cops put suspects in to sweat or sweet-talk or pummel confessions out of. No one was doing any of that to me. I was left alone with a table bolted to the floor, a couple of wood chairs—maple or oak, whichever was cheaper. Mostly they were worn and old, splattered with something. Paint. Blood—and wall, wall, wall, and wall of gray cinder block. Its monotony relieved only by a straight-from-cop-show two-way mirror, so old the reflective material had worn down and I could see through it from my side. That was okay. No need to hide things. Everybody knew, from watching *L&O* and *NYPD Blue* and *Homicide* and a thousand other TV detective programs that the other side of the mirror is where the cops sat and eyeballed suspects. No one was watching. It was just me and a substantial amount of quiet.

I was not under arrest.

I was being detained.

I was being detained because some good citizen, some self-appointed high chief of the Conscience Squad, had nine-one-one'd about a ruckus going on at a gas station to the boys in blue, and I got picked up by the boys in brown. I had, my luck, run—for real—into the law. The law picked me up off the street, brought me in. No one fingered me as having anything to do with anything, but my lack of government-issued identification didn't earn me any pleasantries.

Can I go to the hospital?

Don't have to. You're fine.

Can I make a phone call?

Don't need to. You're not under arrest. Just being detained.

How about a lawyer?

Don't need one. You're not under arrest. Just being detained.

Detained, why?

That's when I got left alone.

Good luck I didn't have any drugs on me. Stupid Bitch Dumbass had those. Along with my pack. If that bastard steals them . . .

Better luck if the boys in brown, the boys who now had control of George Plimpton, didn't figure out his trick. If they figured the trick I could be in for some serious . . . but they wouldn't. To them, to the world at large who didn't know him well, George was just a walking stick. Nothing else. Nothing more. So the deputy sheriffs wouldn't do a thing. All I had to do was ride them out until they got tired of baby-sitting a—

The door opened, the door to The Box. Along with two others, in he came. *He* being the funny little guy in the dark jacket, dark pants. Him, and two of his boys—also in dark jackets, dark pants, and with—stereotypically—dark glasses. They came in alongside the same sheriff's deputy that had first smacked me with his car, then sat me in The Box and left me alone when my question-asking about my civil rights had become too problematic.

"That's him." The deputy pointed at me with his chin. Useless gesture. There was no other "him" in the room. "Some trouble up at a gas station. Picked him up. Far as I can tell he's just a train bum."

The Fed nodded, said "Thank you" in the littlest of voices.

The deputy started for the door.

"How about that phone call?"

The deputy stopped and turned and looked at me, then looked to the Fed. "He's been asking for a phone call."

The popular belief perpetrated by those TV cop shows is that people have a constitutional right to a phone call. They don't. I tried to reason with the FBI guy: "I'd like to notify someone as to where I am." As if it mattered. As if he cared.

The Fed smiled back at me and said across what I couldn't help but notice was a very well-manicured set of teeth: " 'As to where.' Well, you, uh . . . you certainly are well-spoken."

"Here's something for you: to black people 'well-spoken' is a pejorative. I get the call, or no?"

In his usual, halting way, the guy stumbled through his answer. "I . . . suppose. Although, I mean, who would . . . you're a . . . well, you're homeless. Who would you call?"

That was an answer I hadn't thought of, as, previously, no one had taken my request seriously. And as I actually put thought to it, well, I didn't have anybody to call.

Except

I dug around in a pocket. In a couple of them. I found Haxton's card. What the hell, right? I was his Huggy Bear, and didn't Hutch always help Huggy out? Maybe it was Starsky.

I held the card up and the Fed took it, squinted at it, handed it to the deputy, said "Thank you" again in his little voice like he didn't want to disturb anybody with his words of parting.

The deputy left.

From the Fed: "I would say something like: 'And so we meet again,' but I'm afraid, heh, it would make me sound a little cartoonish."

"You did just say it, and you don't need to say a thing to come off like a cartoon."

He adjusted the left side of his jacket, which made the right side hang wrong. The Fed said: "I guess we should probably start with your name."

I ignored him, looked to the two other Feds; the big boys who backed up the little one. They flanked him in near-perfect forty-five-degree angles. I imagined, at the academy, they excelled at formations. That, and they were probably head of the class in window dressing. Beyond said skills, they were good for nothing. Except giving me trouble. Trouble always shows up when you mix the law with the underclass. I kept an eye on those two, said to the littlest Fed: "I guess you didn't hear me before when I pointed out you need to properly identify yourself before I'm required to do shit." I looked over at the worn-out two-way mirror. There was nothing new to see, but paying attention to it made it real clear I wasn't paying attention to the Fed.

And he let me do that for a little bit. When the act got old and he got tired of my putting it on, he slipped a hand inside his coat pocket and pulled out a little bifold made of cheap plastic meant to look like leather but fooling no one. In the bifold was a laminate with what, I supposed, was the official Federal Bureau of Investigation emblem and a picture and some printing that ID'd the Fed as Smikle, Mathais. Mathais Smikle. Backward. Forward. Any way you said it, it was a name that danced off the tongue with all the grace of a blind guy in leg braces.

"You serious with that? Man, your parents must have hated you."

I think, from somewhere, I could hear George laughing: go get 'em, Tiger.

Mathais Smikle closed up the bifold, put it back where it came from. "So, that's that. I showed you mine, so, you can show me yours."

He laughed a little.

He laughed alone.

"Brain Nigger Charlie."

"Well, I find that a little . . . that you were actually given the name Brain Nigger Charlie is a little—"

"You've got a name like Mathais Smikle," I got tired of waiting for him to work his way through a sentence, "and you're cracking on me?"

Mathais Smikle pulled the empty chair from the table. It gave a loud shutter as it scraped along the floor. He sat. He crossed his legs. Right over left. Not in the way where the ankle of the right leg rests on the thigh of the left. He crossed them the girl way; one leg completely draped over the other. It made his right pant leg ride up some, showed stringy-haired flesh above his sock. It made him look stupid all the way around.

He said, sounding as stupid as he looked: "Well, Mr. . . . can I call you . . . uh, Charlie, I would, I'd urge you, at this point, I think it would be in your best interest to cooperate fully and completely in our investigation."

The other two Feds, they floated wide around the table and came up behind me. Intimidation time. Tough guy posturing. It was FBI one-oh-one as professored by Efrem Zimbalist Jr.

"Am I under arrest?"

"I wouldn't say . . . technically speaking, you're not at this—"

"Then I've got nothing to say."

"I just want to ask you some questions."

"Ask them to my lawyer."

Smikle kinda giggled. "You are . . . you're an indigent transient, and . . . am I actually supposed to believe that even though you're homeless . . ."

Christ. This guy couldn't sneeze without making it into an essay.

"You are homeless, but you . . . you have legal representation?"

"I represent myself."

"You were a lawyer?" Again with his giggle.

I didn't like that. This cat, laughing at me?

To his question I answered: "Still am. Never been disbarred."

"If you're, if you're a lawyer, then I see no reason I can't just speak with you."

"I'll advise myself not to answer."

I liked my own glibness. I smiled.

Smikle sat for a few seconds. Squirmed in his chair. Uncomfortable. Uncomfortable with playing at being a federal agent. "Charlie," he said, "and I . . . I think that must be some part of your real name—do you, are you, uh, do you know why you're being detained?"

"Some kind of something at a gas station." Offer nothing, any lawyer would tell you. Never offer anything.

"No, Charlie. You're not being . . . not for some kind of something. There have been a series of murders in the Pacific Northwest. Several . . . I guess you call them train bums. Several of them have been killed."

"Good of you to care."

"It's my job."

"So, if you weren't getting paid you wouldn't care."

Smikle thought on that, confused, then let it go. "I'm here because . . . the reason I'm here, I specialize in psychological forensics. The criminal mind. The bureau is known for its specialists."

"That explains things."

"Explains . . . ?"

"I was wondering how a dope like you got to run around and play cop. You're just a shrink with a badge. They probably only let you out of the office every other leap year, and then only to work on nonsense like tramps getting shanked. My apologies for expecting anything out of you."

Somewhere, George snickered.

I think Smikle was a little hurt by my jibe. I think. Hard to tell. Mostly his face was expressionless. Expressionless besides his permanent look of befuddlement.

Smikle, defending himself: "First of all, I get out of my office . . . I routinely do fieldwork. I've worked on very, several, high-profile cases. And this one, this case, is certainly . . . not all of the victims of the violence were train bums."

"The insurance kid."

Smikle paused, looked at me, face still empty as a church collection plate in Beverly Hills.

He said: "The insurance kid. His name, actually, was Randolph Fitzgerald, the boy was. The Third. Randolph Fitzgerald the Third. You wouldn't think a man who works in insurance could gain enough political . . . uh, connections to . . . but I suppose, Charlie, when enough soft money is pressed into the right hands . . . Apparently, Randolph Fitzgerald . . . the Second," he giggled, "was able to do just that. And so, I find myself traveling the so-called High Line looking for a . . . a killer. Who would've thought?" Smikle smiled some, dipped his head in mannered embarrassment. "But, I, uh, heh, I go on, don't I?"

"Yeah. You do."

"You know something? You . . . you have a very smart mouth."

"I get that a lot. But I'm a smart guy. That's where the brain part of my name comes from. Guess where I get the nigger part."

More befuddlement from Smikle. I was starting to think the whole world was confusing to him.

At the two-way mirror, movement. The sheriff's deputy. He was watching. Watching like a baseball fan who'd worked his way down from the nosebleed seats to the lower boxes. He was getting his kicks on the cheap.

Seeing him reminded me that there were two other Feds in the room. So quiet, their presence had slipped from me. I looked to my right, left. They stood just behind me, flanking each side. Stood. Not sat, or slouched, or leaned against the wall. They stood. Stood ready for action. Ready to do something. It came to me I didn't like the idea of Feds at my back ready to earn their pay.

"Do you know," Smikle. I turned back to him, "and this is interesting. Well, I think it's . . . Most serial killers have an above-average IQ?"

Didn't know. Didn't know, didn't care.

"The organized serial killer . . . there are three classifications of serial killer; organized, disorganized, and mixed. The organized killer—the ones who meticulously plan their crimes, are able to avoid detection—is smarter than the general population." With his whole hand he moved his glasses back up to a proper position on his nose. "They feel they are better than most people. They're usually very bored with their circumstances and are looking for a, well, a challenge they think matches their intellect. Like . . . taunting the police and criminal investigators."

I did not want this.

I did not want this in a great way.

I did not want to be in The Box. I did not want a seminar on psychos. I wanted to pee. I was not in a good mood.

I said: "What am I doing here? You don't care about what happened back at that gas station, then why are you holding on to me?"

"There have been some killings."

"I know."

"Serial murders. Probably committed by someone—"

"I know! You made your speech!"

Again: "Probably committed by someone with a great deal of intelligence . . . Brain Nigger Charlie."

A beat.

From the moment Mathais Smikle had sat down and started talking, the obvious had passed me by. Now, a semitruck loaded with realization turned the corner and plowed over me. Mathais Smikle liked me for the murders.

"I didn't kill anybody." That shot out of me in a blurt.

"Did I say you killed anyone?"

"Head games aren't going to buy you anything. I used to be a lawyer," I threatened.

Smikle, a slight grin, a "fuck you" grin: "Still are. You haven't been disbarred yet. As an aside: did you know that Theodore Bundy was a lawyer? Was. Well then, would you like to tell me about the killings?"

"I don't know anything."

"You don't know anything about the insurance kid?"

"I just heard about him."

"His identity hasn't been reported in the media."

"It's the rails. People talk."

"A body was found in Shelby, Montana. You were in Shelby, Montana."

"Lot of people are in Shelby. You were. You do the job?" My mouth wasn't getting any less feisty. Right then, a feisty mouth couldn't've been any less helpful.

"The killer is dark-skinned. My skin's not dark. Yours, on the other hand . . ."

There was something I was noticing. I was noticing Smikle wasn't stumbling over his words anymore. I was noticing, too, never mind his coat that didn't fit, his too big glasses, he was no longer coming off as a funny little man.

"The guy you're looking for's not black."

"He's not?"

"He's Mexican, or something."

"And you know that how?"

"People—"

"Talk," Smikle finished for me.

Offer nothing, I'd counseled myself. Never offer a thing. All along I'd been offering Smikle the rope he needed to knit me a noose.

I said: "That's not common knowledge, the guy you're looking for's Hispanic?"

"It's not common. Just as it's not common for people of color to ride the so-called High Line."

Indignation got me up out of my seat. I thought it would serve to redirect the conversation. "Because I'm black all of a sudden—" A hand took me where my shoulder met my neck—one of the Feds behind me—jammed me back into the chair. The wood groaned from my weight, I grunted from the pain of the Fed's hard grip, his message wordless but clear: Get your ass down, keep it down.

Yeah. Okay. We're cool. But all getting my ass slapped against the seat of the chair did was crank up my need to pee.

I took a couple of breaths, chilled myself, tried to be reasonable. "Look, I've got no knife," I said, thinking of George Plimpton. "Those vics were stabbed."

"Were they?"

"Stabbed and mutilated. Yeah. You told me that."

"I don't remember saying so."

Hadn't he? Didn't he tell me that? I was confused. My bladder was ripping. Felt like it was. It made me squirm, made my butt cheeks dance across the chair. "I gotta—"

"All you have to do is sit there."

"And there were two of them."

"Were there?"

"Fuck you, man!" I grabbed at my crotch, the outburst having made me spritz a little. I should've just pissed there, pissed down my leg and onto the floor. Should've. Pissing down my own leg rides low on the meter of filthy things I've done to me. Should've just pissed. Would've, but I wasn't about to give Smikle the glee of watching me degrade myself. Nah. I would hold it in and eventually get to a urinal and relieve myself same as any other normal nontramp human being. Eventually I would get myself to a urinal. I clutched my crotch harder. I ranted on. "There were two of them. A Hispanic, and the other was a white kid."

"You were traveling with someone."

Fuck.

"We have a witness who can place you with a young Caucasian boy."

"He isn't a—"

"So, then, you are traveling with someone?"

Fuck.

Smikle was having all the pleasure a man could. Everything I'd given him he was now handing back to me. "I imagine he's the kind of boy a man could find himself becoming, uh," that giggle again, "physical with if he didn't have a female companion."

"I gotta pee."

"Maybe you do that sometimes; when you can't find a woman, you sometimes have relations with a boy. And then you hate yourself for it. And you hate the boys. And you kill the boys. And you cut off their penises as both an expression of your rage as well as your need to convert the boys into the girls you desire. Does that sound familiar, Charlie?"

Did it sound familiar? Did I fuck men, then chop off their dicks as punishment for not being women? For a second the pain I felt from the shredding of my bladder by the urine that bloated it took a backseat to disbelief. "Is that what you came up with? Is that your genius theory? Christ, you really think you're a bright guy, don't you? You got your public school education and your state college degree and you were able to take all that and get a cop job with a government-sized paycheck. Smart as you think you are, your bosses decide the only thing you can handle are rail bums getting killed, and you can't even get this one right. God, it's got to be awful to wake up in the morning and know you're you; an ugly little man living an ugly little life. I'll tell you something, Smikle, I wouldn't trade all my nothing for any of what you have."

That said, my bladder went back to reminding me, in the strongest possible terms, I had to pee.

Smikle sat looking at me, expression remaining sum zero. If he'd felt any sting from my deconstruction of him, he displayed it not at all. He sat, a blank, then from his hip Smikle pulled his gun. The metal of the barrel scraped the leather of his holster. The sound of it bounced off the walls of The Box. He lay the gun on the table, the end of the barrel, the eye of the weapon, casually looking in my direction.

I didn't like that; him pulling his piece. He didn't strike me as the kind of guy who knew how to use a gun. Properly. That made him having one all the more dangerous.

So what, right? The gun didn't mean anything. A Fed shoot a guy in cold blood, in a sheriff's substation with a deputy watching? I looked toward the two-way mirror. Yeah, the deputy was still watching. So the gun didn't mean anything. It was for show. It was theater. Right?

From the table: a thud. My head jumped back around. Smikle was holding a piece of machined metal. Middle-finger long. Small but heavy. A sap. A sap not even covered in leather. It was meant to hurt when it hit. He lifted it from the table, let it loll around in a lazy circle, let gravity bring it back down to the tabletop. Thud. A loud thud. A loud thud without even putting any effort behind the action. Made you wonder what that sap could do to bone, to a skull, if a guy put a little elbow grease into things.

Smikle put the sap down parallel to the gun, a space between them. Choices. His. My poison to be picked. Smikle wanted a confession out of me, and I believed he would earn it any way he could.

"This is not—" I started.

Smikle cut me off with: "This is not what? Not fair? Not right? Right. Rights are just a state of mind, Charlie; a convention of man. What's wrong and what's right are dependent on the circumstances. The Nazis tried to exterminate the Jews. Millions were killed. That was wrong. A war was fought to stop the Nazis. Millions were killed. That was right. Right and wrong on the, uh, grandest scale, to be sure, but I'm certain you understand my meaning."

The only thing I got was that the tenor of his talk made him sound insane.

The gun, or the sap.

Something else I was noticing: Never mind Smikle was tiny and cheap-looking. I'd been fucking with somebody I should not have been fucking with.

"The point I'm trying to make is that right and wrong are decided after the fact. And the fact is, you're here, now, and there are things I need to know." Smikle, hand to the gun. The gun came up off the table, slid back into his holster. "Technically, what stands between the things I need to know and my knowing those things are your, heh, rights. You have a right to legal representation." Smikle didoed his actions with the sap. It went from the table back to his belt. "A right not to say anything which may incriminate yourself. Our society grants those rights, and anyone who is a member of our society is obligated such rights. But you, Charlie, have chosen not be part of our society, or to abide by our laws. So tell me, why should our laws abide by you?"

From under his jacket Smikle produced a box. A little black box. Looked like a box, contoured, with two metal studs on one end. The box had a red button. Smikle pressed it. The studs popped with a bluish energy that snapped at me like the foaming jaws of a mad dog.

One of the agents behind me pushed me back down into my chair. I didn't even know I'd gotten up. And as I came back down all my wiseassness, my smartassness flowed from me as does blood from a throat-slit calf that's been strung up after the slaughter. Witless, all I was left with, all I could muster, and weakly, was: "I didn't kill anybody."

"Perhaps. Perhaps you did not. Perhaps you, as you say, know nothing of these killings."

The little box did more snapping with its metal teeth.

Teeth or

One of the agents behind me kept me in my chair. Never mind my growing panic, the flailing and jerking around that went with it, he wrangled me rodeo-style and kept me from going anywhere.

"You say that; you say you know nothing. You say. Let's be sure of things."

Fangs of a snake.

Across the table, faster than I would've given the little guy credit for, Smikle thrust the stun gun at me. And just like fangs of a snake, those studs bit into me, electricity their venom. A jolt of it ran the length of me, shoved my eyes back in my head. Every muscle I owned snapped tight, went sequoia stiff. Stiff like the dead. My tongue slapped around inside my mouth, yanked open and screaming a new language constructed of a single word: AAAAGGAAAHHHRRAH!

With all that, there was one other thing: from the cuticles of my toenails to the outer layer of skin that covered my head, I felt pure, undiluted, utter pain.

I was crying.

When I regained a sense of myself, my surroundings, I was sitting in a chair in the reception area of the sheriff's substation clutching my body, bawling the way a lonely girl cries on a Saturday night.

I was hurting.

My body felt as if it had been intricately, completely stitched with a frozen thread, and every slight move caused the thread to snap and pop within me, breaking off icy shards that tore me bloody from the inside out. The pain caused me to move against myself. The movement broke off more shards. I was locked in a bitter, self-punishing cycle of herky-jerks and total agony.

I lifted my head. Gravity ran snot from my nose into my mouth. I opened my eyes, looked around. Tears prism'd the world, little rainbows danced at the corners of my vision.

Fucking rainbows.

I cried more, then gave looking around another shot.

Haxton.

Haxton was there in the substation. A shimmering Haxton was talking to a diffused Smikle. I tried to listen. I actually had to *try* to listen, had to mentally throw the switch that would connect the circuit which would reactivate my auditory sense. When I did that a pack of Africanized killer bees swarmed my inner ear. I jammed my palms up against them, tried to smother the noise. Had to move to do that. Movement caused the thread in my body to snap. The snapping brought pain. The pain brought crying.

I cried.

After a while the pain went down. The bees thinned out. Some. I looked up. Haxton was still talking to Smikle. Heated. Animated. I gave listening another try, dialing those two in amounting to tuning a distant signal on an old crystal set. It was no good for all my effort. I quit trying. I sank into myself, did all I could to remain still, not break any more of the frozen thread inside me.

I realized my crotch felt warm and wet. I'd peed myself. Smikle had made me pee myself. That . . . bastard had made me humiliate myself, then he left me to sit, weak, jittery, and soiled. I wanted to kill him. I wanted to get up off that chair and twist his neck. But I couldn't. I couldn't find the rage to fuel the strength to pick me up, cross the room, and end his life. I was so beaten down, so whipped. I'd talked tough, and all my tough talk got was me turned inside out.

Napalm sloshed across my back. A hand. Haxton's. Rubbing me. Comforting me. Killing me.

"Get off me!"

"It's all right, Brain Nigger. It's me. It's Hax—"

"Get off!" I weighed the pain the motion of pushing Haxton away would cause against the hurt his hand waxing across my back generated. I made my choice. I shoved Haxton aside, growled at him: "It . . . hurts."

He got my meaning.

"Just sit there, Brain Nigger. Just sit there until you get right."

As if. As if I had other options.

While I sat, Haxton explained: "Got the call from the sheriff, or deputy, or whoever. Told me you'd been picked up and all; that the Feds were talking to you. Figured there might be trouble. Didn't figure there'd be this kind."

Talk. Talk.

"I came down, told them you were working for me; you were a company investigator riding the rails. Got some BS paperwork together to show them. They didn't much believe it, but after what they done to you, well, they weren't much going to challenge it. I could make things as bad for them as they could for me."

Talk. Talk.

All his talking, all his words were like a flowery scent that lured those mutated killer bees back into my head. "Shut up!" I screamed at

Haxton through clenched teeth, making my face burn beneath its flesh. "Shut up!"

Haxton shut up.

We sat some. How long I don't know. In my state I could not judge. Pain and agony have a way of slowing time for their enjoyment.

From the corner of my eye: Smikle leaving the substation with his boys.

Leaving.

Walking past me.

Walking past me without even looking in my direction—rubbish he'd tossed aside that no longer rated so much as a glance. That action, Smikle's *non*action of denying my very existence, was an insult I could not carry. At Smikle's back I screamed: "You bastard! You goddamn bastard! Look! Look at me!"

Smikle kept walking.

Blubbering now: "Look at me! Don't you not look at me, you fucking . . ."

Smikle was gone.

"You goddamn . . ." I let it go there. My impotent fury; I let it go. From the time I'd first set out on the rails, degradation had kept close company. But the cruelties done to me were done by people at whom I could lash back. At first I didn't know how. I learned. I learned to defend myself. I learned to protect myself. Then I was introduced to George Plimpton and I learned to give as good as I got. I learned to hurt as badly as I'd been hurt, and that made me an equal to all.

But now

Now there was nothing I could do—not one thing—about the little man with his magic box that brought pain. My torture ended only because some other man, some man I knew barely in passing, had chosen to take it upon himself to fend for me. Otherwise I was helpless, powerless to strike back; an invalid good only for squirming when kicked. Smikle had shown me a certain truth: for all my big words, for all my talk about being a brain nigger, I was, as he said when he put that blue flame to my body, a nonentity. I was nothing, and the shame of things, the reality of my lack of any significant substance represented by Smikle's casual stroll, unpunished, from acts he'd done . . . that was a hurt that tore me through and through.

I cried.

Eventually a sheriff's deputy came over, I thought to offer a tissue or something to wipe my tears and snot with. He told me I had to leave. He told that to me. Not to Haxton. Haxton was a citizen. Haxton could've camped out till the Second Coming if he cared to.

"C'mon," Haxton said to me. "Let's go."

I stood. I put a toddler's effort into the simple act of walking. I took a spastic step, put a shaky hand to a wall to steady myself, stopped, rested, went through all that again. I netted myself five feet of traveling distance.

Then I remembered and said to Haxton: "My walking stick . . ."

Haxton crossed to one of the deputies. Words got passed around. Pretty soon George was back in my possession, his trick, his secret, apparently still known only to me. I had to grip George a couple of times before he felt comfortable in my hand. There was something queer about him. Something that seemed to say, to taunt: Not so tough without me.

No. I wasn't.

I leaned on George, took a spastic step, put a shaky hand to the wall . . .

Outside.

Haxton kept pace with me, moving easily in contrast to my great effort. He was trying to be a good guy and look out for me. He was annoying me.

"Go on," I shooed.

"Let me give you a lift somewhere."

"I don't—"

"Not going to get anywhere walking. Not like you are."

I did not want to be around him. I did not want to be near Haxton for one more second. Having saved me, he only served to remind me of everything I wasn't. "Go away!"

"I'll give you a ride."

I looked down at myself. I looked at the dark patch of urine that stained me from crotch to lower thigh. "I pissed myself, man! You want this in your car?"

He shrugged. "It's a rental. Not much of one."

I could not take it. His every decent word felt like a shameful slap. "Why you doin' this to me!" Back to crying. "Why you . . . why are you being good to me?"

"One thing; what they did to you, nobody should do that to a person."

A person. A person.

"And right now you're in a state. You look like you could use a—"

"You want me to go ride the rails and find things out for you, that what you want? You just doing this so I can owe you? Owing somebody's what got me out here first off."

"I envy you."

It was getting cooler. We were on the edge of the changing of the seasons. Summer into fall. The brisk air was given sound by the rustle of the dying leaves it carried.

"You envy . . ." No more crying. I was laughing now. "Piss your pants. Go on if you want. Let me . . . how about this; we'll go find a light socket you can stick your finger in; get you a little of what Smikle gave me." I should've thanked Haxton. After everything, it was good to laugh.

He said, again: "I envy you. I envy most men who ride the rails; the ones who aren't bums, aren't in train gangs."

"I don't see the envy part."

"My job I don't have to tell you anything about. You know what I do. Every once in a while it passes for exciting. Guess if you call busting guys stealing out of freight cars exciting. Rest of the time it's just work. I've got a wife. She's very pretty. I think so. Especially for having three kids. Even at that, she's no . . ."

"She's no, oh, say, Elle Macpherson."

Haxton smiled some, said: "No. She isn't. I've got a mortgage and some car payments I face down every thirty days with the rest of the bills. I've got decent memories, a little guilt, all the shouldas and if onlys you collect in forty-four years of living. I've got all that. But you've got freedom, Brain Nigger. Go where you want, do what you want. See a train, catch out, ride to wherever. End of the day, you ask me what I think any fella really wants, it's not a fancier car or bigger house or a younger woman to look in his direction when he's feeling old. I think a man wants his freedom. Freedom to travel the world or sit on his ass just as equally."

I said: "Do you know how you get Freedom? Capital F Freedom? You get it by walking away from every single thing in your life. You know what the price of Freedom is? Spending the rest of your life wishing you could get every single thing back. Maybe your wife, for all your love, maybe she's like . . . maybe she's a flower fading out of season. Same with your kids. Your love for them is a deadweight of responsibility that nearly crushes you. And your job is nothing but a mile of broken glass you wake up every morning to crawl over. I know. I looked at my life the same way. Not great. Not bad. Terminally mediocre. Maybe that's the worst kind of life. A great life is nothing but cocaine and whores. A shitty one ends with a gun in your mouth. But a mediocre life just keeps snailing on one dreadful day into the next, doesn't it?"

Haxton looked down at his feet. At his foot and a half.

"Mediocre as it is—mediocre, average, middle rate . . . Look at me, Haxton. Haxton, look at me."

He looked.

"Christ, man, I'm a fucking addict. I need drugs to get me through the day, I need them to keep me from sleeping at night. I . . ." I hefted up George. "I've got a stick that's started ordering me around!"

*You bet your black ass I do. Somebody's got to run this circus*, George said to me and me alone. I don't know why he called my ass black. It is, yeah, but no need to get racial about things.

To Haxton: "You want to trade what you have for this; to be me?"

Haxton took a moment in answering, said, mumbled: "Grass is always greener . . ."

"You got grass. I wish I had the dirt to grow some on."

Haxton was visibly disappointed a train tramp's life wasn't all he thought it would be. I felt bad; dispelling him of the one good myth that he wore like a blinder to get him through his daily grind. I'd shackled him back up in the chains of reality, and for that I believed I owed him something. A glimpse, at least, at all the things he thought he wanted.

"You want to feel some Freedom?" I asked him.

"What?"

"Freedom, you want to feel some capital F Freedom?"

No hesitation: "Yes."

"I'll show you." That is, I'd show him if Stupid Bitch Dumbass hadn't crossed me and stolen my pack.

Haxton's rental was a Corolla, which seemed very much not him. I figured he should be driving an old Tahoe, or Jimmy, which in fact, he told me, is what he did drive back in Seattle where he lived. Once in the car, discreetly, Haxton rolled down a window, my palate of stinks too much for him at close quarters. I gave him a break and did the same with my window.

By description and vague direction he was able to find his way to the KFC, to the field across from it. I did not even have to wonder about Stupid Bitch Dumbass. There he was, waiting, anxious but patient—old dog faithful. And I was actually, for a beat, glad to see him. Not just because I had trusted him with what passed for my estate. I was glad to see him . . . I can't say for certain why. My reasons, the emotions that generated them, were obscure to the point of being barely memorable, like high school Spanish learned years ago that I was now vaguely able to recall and could no longer decipher. Like the name of my third girlfriend. I was, I suppose, at base, just happy to see what amounted to a friendly face; another soul not trying to electrocute me. Still, even with that—

"Brain Nigger! Where you been? Jesus, I been here for, you know, like . . . I don't know how long for."

"Dumbass—"

"Didn't know what happened to you, was gonna go back and look for you, but, you know, you told me to stay here, so I stayed."

"Dumbass—"

"I stayed, then you didn't show up, and I thought I should go get you, but I didn't go. I mean, obviously I didn't, but, you know, I wanted to. I wanted to go and—"

"Stupid Bitch Dumbass, shut up! Give me my pack."

He looked a little sad for a second. I didn't care. He handed me my pack and I rooted around in it.

Stupid Bitch Dumbass eyed Haxton, nervous in his ignorance of the situation. Haxton swapped Dumbass's stare with some full-drawl "hey, how are you" niceties that did nothing to dial down Dumbass's edge.

My radio, still there . . . My food stamps . . . Train book . . . Liz Claiborne Girl . . . Found what I was looking for.

To Haxton: "Let's go." I kept my pack. Stupid Bitch Dumbass had proven trustworthy once. Why push things if I didn't have to? But me leaving with my pack only put extra ants in Stupid Bitch Dumbass's pants.

"Where you going?"

"Stay here!"

"But you just got—"

"Stay here!"

"You don't want to leave your pack?"

"No, I don't."

"You're not gonna leave me, are you? You're not—"

Like I was trying to make the deaf hear: "Dumbass, stay here!" To Haxton: "C'mon. Let's go."

I led the way back to the Corolla, my pain dissipating. My motor skills returning.

Once inside, once seated again, Haxton wanted to know: "Where we headed?"

"Just drive some. Look for a place that's empty, boarded up."

"Have to be boarded up?"

"If it's dark, it's better."

"You don't want to go clean up some?" Haxton was easy with that so as not to offend. Reeking like I did, there was little offense to be taken. I wasn't sure if he was asking the question out of concern for my hygiene, or if he just couldn't take the smell anymore. I could deal with it. I'd worn my own filth plenty.

"No. Drive."

Haxton fired up all four cylinders of the Corolla. The engine purred like an asthmatic cat. He drove.

We rode around, rode around . . . Rode around looking for an abandoned building or empty duplex or shuttered store. We drove looking for a deserted place where, in the middle of what would come next, Haxton and I could go unbothered. We rolled by a few likely places, run-down places, shitty places. But they were places with signs of life—the doors half pried, the smell of food cooked over squatter's fires. Free and empty space was at a premium. We rolled on.

I told Haxton to stop at a mini-mart, told him to buy a couple of bottles of water. Those would be real good later. Especially for him.

We rode around, rode around . . . An old, small movie house, fossilized in the era of the mutiplex. Shuttered down, boarded up. We did a drive-by, looked it over. It would take some breaking and entering to gain access. Good. It would be just us.

Haxton parked. I got out of the car. Haxton sat.

"C'mon," I said.

Haxton sat, not sure of things, at the edge of a pool, unwilling, unable, to make the dive.

"Haxton, c'mon."

Haxton sat . . . Haxton got up and followed.

We tried a door, but a heavy chain looping the handles was unbreakable, unmovable or removable. The same with a thick board pounded across a window. Same with another window. A third window; boarded too, but in a lazy manner. Some pulling from both of us got the board yanked free. Some punching got the windowpane smashed. We got inside an office with a door that needed just a little coaxing to break from its hinges. The theater was ours.

Inside, in the dark, was a relic of a grand place—the molding hand-etched, red velvet seats . . . seats once red with velvet, now zebra'd with water stains and dirt. Wraiths of dust held a ball, danced in the fractured light, swirled in air stiff from months of being sealed in and uncirculated. The carpeted floor held a collection of rat pellets. But the theater was mostly dark and completely empty. It was perfect for our needs.

I went into the bathroom. There was a mirror already spiderwebbed. I broke it out, carefully, took a sizable piece back into the theater, set it on the stage before the silver screen that was actually white and mostly torn. From my pocket I took Lady K; white powder in a bullet.

"Got a credit card?"

Haxton took out his wallet, took out a Discover card. Member since '89.

"Cocaine?" Haxton asked.

"Hell, no. Coke is garbage; tweaks you with a weak high, then crashes you hard. Hard. People are always killing themselves on that crap for a reason. I've got enough ways to die without me trying to help myself."

"So, what is it?"

"K. Special K. Ketamine. It's a cat tranquilizer."

"What does it do?" He was halting with his speech, still on the edge of that pool, still not real sure about making the dive.

"It takes you places. It helps you see things you otherwise wouldn't. Mostly, it just makes you feel good. That's what it does." I was talking to talk, talking to keep Haxton from asking silly questions while I was doing chores—screwing off the top of the bullet, dumping some K, refining it with Haxton's Discover card; chopping it, sifting it into two lines on the broken mirror. Cut, clean, ready to inhale.

Handing back the credit card: "Got a dollar?"

Haxton slotted the card, checked his wallet's innards. Embarrassed: "Got a ten and two fives. A five do?"

Will a five do? You gotta dig this guy. "A five'll do real good."

I took the five, rolled the five, tubed it, put it to my nose, and leaned for the mirror and the white powder rows.

"Hey." Haxton's hand on my shoulder, pulling me back. "This isn't . . ." He looked uneasy about what he was going to ask. He looked serious about it, too. "There won't be any homosexual activities going on, will there?"

Yeah. You gotta dig this guy. "No. Nothing like that. I'm just going to show you some Freedom. Capital F. I'm just going to show you what it's like when all of you lets go."

I went back to the glass. I sniffed, ran the rolled bill over a line, felt the powder smack the back of my sinuses, drip and burn its way along my throat. A hit, good and stiff. In a moment I would get some tingle, feel myself sink as if my soul was losing traction inside my own body.

Haxton was hesitant.

"It's just like doing a little weed, only . . . only it's more than that. You're going to tell me you've never done a little weed?"

Haxton was hesitant.

"It's all right," I said. "You may hate this. End of the day, no good in the world comes from taking drugs. But you'll feel something you . . . you never felt before." I went sluggish, my eyelids collapsed. I turned my head and turned my head and the world floated all around me. "You'll feel . . . nothing." I let some of nothing come.

Through my now tiny eyes I saw Haxton take up the bill, position it in his nose. He bent to the mirror . . . faltered, straightened . . .

Dive, man. Just dive.

He bent to the mirror, vacuumed the line. To his virgin flesh the K was harsh, and I could tell it razored his inside as it bled through his passages. He held his broiling face, tried to sink his fingers into his cavities and douse the fire.

"Drink water," I mumbled.

He cracked open one of the bottles and drank deep. "Goddamn!" Water spilled from his mouth. He took another swig.

". . . Careful . . . Gonna need that lataaah . . ."

Again: "Goddamn. Godaaa . . ." He slowed. A machine with its batteries running low. From where he sat he bent forward, kowtowed until his head smacked the stage. Not hard. Not too hard. Just hard enough to make noise. He rolled, made it onto his back. His slits-for-eyes looked up at a spot two miles beyond the ceiling. He was deep in the hole.

Knowing that, knowing Haxton was safely on his journey, I set my mind free.

I was high. I was tweaked just enough that ideas and concepts slipped free of where they had been jammed up by rationality and conventionality. I saw things. Beyond psychotropic hallucinations, I saw things.

Haxton told me about his trip. First, after a good forty minutes' ride, he drank a bottle of water. Drank most of it. Gargled, rinsed his nose with some. Then he told me about his trip. It involved America West Airlines and a flight that he may have taken two years ago, or sometime tomorrow. He was his own father, and he forgave himself for something he'd never done. Then, somewhere between two countries he'd never heard of but had been to five times, he saw a girl of light who crystallized into the chick he'd always wanted to do in high school but never could because dolphins don't swim backward. From there it was a slow glide back to a squalid, run-down movie house where a black tramp waited for him to come in for a landing.

"And?" I asked.

"And?" he asked back.

"How was it?"

Haxton thought about that some; thought about my question, thought about how "it" was. "It was," he started, stopped, thought more. "It was . . . good. It was . . ."

"I know." And I did. More than just how a good high felt, I knew that it was beyond description—accurate description—with bare words. How do you describe the consistency of a cloud? How do you describe the color white? And when you've got that figured out, how do you describe them to someone who's never had the gift of sight? You can't. A trip is an experience. You can have the experience. You can not have the experience. There was no middle ground of explaining it.

And then, from me, for Haxton, regret: "Sorry."

"You're . . ."

"I'm sorry. I'm sorry I did that to you."

"You didn't do anything. I wanted it. At least, I wanted to try. And I'm glad for it." Haxton couldn't stop playing with his nose. K would be caking it up, drying it out for hours to come. "It was like you said: it was freedom. For the first time, I know what freedom is."

"And now that you know, now that you've felt what it's like for every thought, every concern, every deadweight you carry to melt and pour from you . . . once you've felt freedom, do you think you can stand the feeling of normal again?"

Nothing from Haxton but a slight, sad look in his eyes.

From me, once more: "Sorry."

"What was that stuff?"

"K. Told you."

"But what was it?"

"Ketamine hydrochloride. Animal tranq. Blocks the nerve paths without depressing respiratory or circulatory functions. Very safe. Very reliable. Least, as hallucinogenic psychotropic drugs go. As long as you keep the dose around one to one-point-five milligrams per pound. Keep it in that range, the effects are awesome. That much you know."

". . . Yeah. I know."

"That high you were feeling, that's the K-hole. The drug actually induces an NDE; near-death experience. There are five phases: feelings of peace and joy, detachment from the body, travel through a dark tunnel, a bright light, and entering the light."

"You saying I died?"

"No. Just felt like you did. Either way, now you know what God looks like."

"Jesus, you know your stuff. You deal drugs?"

Shook my head. "Just like libraries."

"What was yours like, your . . ."

"My high?"

"Yes."

"I don't get high. Not normally. Not much. Not that I don't want to, but I've been doing it too long. My body's built up tough flesh to a couple of lines."

"Then why do you do it at all?"

"Mostly it keeps me from sleeping."

Haxton laughed. Not at me, but he couldn't help but find what I was saying queer. "Why in the hell don't you want to sleep?"

I didn't feel like explaining the blue-cheek-eyed baby. Didn't know that I could.

I said: "It's overrated, and gets in the way of me being tired all the time."

Don't know if Haxton bought that. Doubt if he cared.

We sat for a while, tired from our trips, and let ourselves sober up.

I asked: "Tell me about the murders."

"Murders . . . ?" Haxton was still a little lifted, still a little slow in the head. It'd be hours before he returned to baseline.

"The killings on the rails."

"Hispanic fella, like I said. That's the only ID there is, anyway."

"But there were two of them. A Hispanic and a white boy."

"Yeah, but, in these . . ." he had to steady his mind, "in these parts a white fella doesn't amount to much as a description."

"How many killings all together?"

"Why you asking all this?"

"You wanted my help. If I'm going to go out there and ask things, I've got to know what I'm asking about."

Haxton eyed me. Through a lingering K-haze he gave me a thorough examining. But his X rays were weak. Dulled by drugs, they were unable to penetrate my deceptions.

Maybe.

Or maybe he had trust for me, and that's what softened his edge. Sort of made me feel bad about lying to him. Sort of, it did. But I was where I was—the Pacific Northwest, the High Line, the corridors of racist hate—for a reason. The reason didn't involve being sensitive to a Bull's feelings.

He said: "Four bodies. One in Harve, Shelby, Glasgow, and here in Spokane."

"All the same killer?"

"Looks that way. They'd all, like I'd said—"

"Had their balls hacked off."

"Didn't say it that way, but, yeah." He paused. "Thought you didn't want to help me."

"So, now I do."

"You going around asking questions; you know that can get you some hot water. Inside the law and out."

"I know."

"I'm not looking for anything for helping you out with the federal boys."

Haxton had hauled my dirty black hide out of an electric fire. He didn't know me, he didn't owe me, but he'd stuck his neck out for me and just passed it off as a favor one guy does for another, like helping him move or paying for his first whore. For that he wasn't looking for anything in return. I wished he'd shut up. All his talk didn't make deceit any easier to perpetrate.

"Want some truth? I don't want to help you as much as I know helping you get this killer is going to do damage to Smikle. How's that going to look; a railroad cop beating a Fed to a killer? It's going to look like hell, and making Smikle look like hell is all I'm living for right now. There's going to be another killing."

"How do you know?"

How did I know? "The guy's a serial killer. Crazies like that don't just quit to quit. They quit when they finally get stopped. So there's going to be another killing. Just stands to reason. You hear about it, you let me know. I mean, I hope to God I get something for you before that, but if another body turns up you let me know, okay?"

Again some eye from Haxton. Same as before, it burned hot for just a second before cooling off. "Yeah. I'll do that."

We sat more, hydrated more. Sobered up as much as the lingering sway of Lady K would allow. Finished with all that, we got up and got out of the theater, went out into the light. The light of day. The rude, harsh sunlight was the severe downside to doing drugs at any other time than night. Darkness made getting juiced fun, sexy. Light just made the whole activity unseemly and repugnant.

Haxton drove me back to the field across from the KFC.

Stupid Bitch Dumbass was waiting.

Haxton: "Thank you."

"Can't make any promises, but if I hear anythi—"

"I don't mean for doing what you can about the killer. I meant for showing me . . . for letting me be . . ." Haxton mumbled the last word of the sentence, "free," as if the concept of it was too embarrassing to be spoken aloud even to the sole witness to his liberation.

Fine. Let's never speak of it. Let's pretend it never happened; experiencing the greatest feeling a living person can know.

I got out of the car.

Haxton drove off.

For whatever reason, my ring was hurting me.

I like libraries. I like to read. Reading works out the mind, keeps the brain in Brain Nigger. It is the intelligent way to kill time. Factor in the hours I can't sleep, I have much time to kill. Besides the books, I like libraries. Libraries are bum friendly. For the librarians, the staff, it helps assuage their liberal guilt for them to feel as though they're doing good deeds. They let us bums and tramps sit and read like maybe if we sat and read enough we might actually be able to read our way to a better life.

I like libraries, too, because they have good bathrooms. Big, usually. Usually clean. Pretty clean as public toilets go. Public was the key word. One of the few entitlements a bum had was to be able to freely use the library bathroom of his choice. You could relieve yourself, wash in the sink, and get yourself as fresh as someone who catches trains and sleeps in the out-of-doors is likely to get.

I was in a bathroom of the Spokane Public Library. I had gone to the library for other reasons, but was taking advantage of the bathroom; relieving myself, washing myself. A janitor, a black guy, was cleaning up. He gave me some stink-eye, a few quiet "tsk, tsk" shakes of his head. Maybe the white librarians could endure me, but far as brother-man janitor mopping piss off the floor cared I was bringing the rest of the race down. Humiliating black folk I'd never met, never would meet, just by being me. He soaked his mop in his tin bucket. Got up some more piss off the floor. On his cleaning cart was a radio. The radio was tuned to a pop station. A song ended and blended into "Oh, Sherrie." The intro played, that bit of chorus done with a high-octave electric piano in the style that was popular back when the song itself was a tolerable bit of bubblegum.

. . . And all of a sudden, I wasn't in a bathroom of the Spokane

Public Library. I was back in the summer just after my freshman year of college. I was back at my old high school at a track meet. It was warm and sunny, the air accented with the unmistakable smell of fresh-cut grass. And all the kids still in high school, only a year or two younger than me, thought I was a man-stud because I'd made my college track team. A couple of the girls—so raw and appealing as they balanced on the rail dividing youth and womanhood in the way that is exclusive to a girl of seventeen—fawned at me just because I was a college boy and a track star, even if I wasn't really a track star, but just a guy who'd been allowed to run on the team because, what the hell, I was a walk-on and wasn't costing the university anything in scholarships. And there was this one girl—a girl, but plenty of girl; a little plump but in the right places—she came over to me bursting with unconversant sexuality that demanded to be educa—

And some guy at a urinal started singing along with the radio as the lyrics to the song kicked in, singing off-key and out of tune. And all of a sudden it was no longer warm and sunny. I was no longer at my old high school, at a track meet being approached by five feet five inches of flesh-wrapped desire. All of a sudden I was just in the bathroom of a public library in Spokane washing in a sink, getting a stare-down from a janitor.

I finished my business and left.

I like libraries. I like to read. Reading works out . . . ahhhh, you know all that already.

Anyway, I was on the prowl for info, and the info I was looking for put a bit of a scare into me. My last visit with Lady K, my trip, had opened my mind and let disparate and unconnected facts flow together to form an alternate reality that I now had to—*had to*—explore; had to prove true or false.

Microfiche. The local paper. I dug through it, scanned, scanned . . . found a story on a body that turned up shived in the back and with its balls hacked off. Harve paper. A piece on a body found shived in the back, balls hacked off. The Shelby paper had the same kind of story, only it ran a second article bigger than the first when it turned out the shived and deballed body was Insurance Kid. A third story followed that one. Bigger still. More play. More media milking of gory details and sordid facts to boost circulation otherwise dragged down by the boring news of the state of worldwide financial markets and international conflict. Now we got exact information on where the body was found and what a ball-less corpse looks like. A quote from the still grieving mother, a vow for justice from the resolute father. A line or two about the dead kid from a former classmate—pulled up from under an overturned stone by some intrepid reporter—who sorta knew the vic. Sorta. There was a witness, too. Two people involved, young, one Hispanic, the other white.

Fourth story. Mention of a body found in Glasgow. Now the Feds are getting into things. The murders are linked and there's a chronology. Second vic found was the first kill. Insurance Kid was murder #3. The freshest body was in Spokane. The killer—the killers—are working the rails. A couple of quotes from Smikle, typical bits on how the FBI's on the case and how they've got things under control and how they're not going to rest until they track these dangerous killers—who they wouldn't give a damn about for killing train bums except that they also killed a rich kid—to the ends of the earth.

Killing train bums.

Train bums to the rest of the world. In my world, train gangers.

The alternate reality melded with mine.

Fucking libraries.

I headed out.

A librarian—lily white. Liberal white—flashed ivory my direction. "Please come back. You're welcome anytime."

On my way through the door I gave her the finger.

"What are you doing?"

I was reading Corina's letters. I was trying to make emotional contact with a girl I'd never met through words on pages and postcards scratched with loneliness and fear as much as ink. I was trying to remind myself of my mission. I was trying to reinforce the reason why I was where I was. Especially now that I knew how bad the "why" was.

All that was internal. But that I was reading letters was obvious. Stupid Bitch Dumbass didn't need to ask me: "What are you doing?"

I clocked Corina's trajectory from happy kid to scared young woman:

*I'm doing things I know I shouldn't, Unc, but I got to do to live.*

*I know you wouldn't want me to, but I just got to do to live.*

Right.

Do to live. Scared girl. Broke girl. Hungry girl. What's a girl like that got to do to live? Get with a guy like Kessler. But then you cross a guy like Kessler. Then what do you have to do to survive? What'd Kessler say? She drew first blood.

"Charlie, what are you—"

"Dumbass, shut up!"

"I only want to know what you're—"

"I'm trying to figure a few things."

"Figure what?"

"Things, Dumbass. Don't worry about it."

"I was just—"

"I don't care what you were 'just.' You want to just do something, just shut the hell up and—"

"StopitStopitStopitStopit!"

Steel wheels dragging over rails; that was the same shrill wail Stupid Bitch Dumbass's voice made. Just like it. And just like an ice pick driven into your brain, then twisted around for good measure; that's how his voice hit me. The tears in his eyes slammed my already raw guilt like a sledgehammer on a game toe.

"Stop it! Stop treating me like . . . like . . ."

He was crying too much to talk. He cried, and cried, and I watched him cry. I watched this kid that I had been slapping around since the day we crossed finally snap and I felt . . . I felt like shit. Jesus, that I could feel anything was a miracle.

I let him cry more, let him get most of it out. Then, I said: "I don't mean to—"

"You do it anyway. Mean to, or not, you fuck!" He cried some more. Cried. Finally he settled up some, cooled off. He was done sobbing and heaving, but he was still in the middle of a breakdown. "I know I'm a dumbass, okay? You don't gotta tell me every two seconds. And I wouldn't even be here except for you. You're the one, you know, who scared the hell out of me, made me too scared to go anywhere. Otherwise I'd be—"

"You'd be dead." Stupid Bitch Dumbass could be as weepy-cryie at me as he wanted, but some facts had to be told true. "I don't treat you like a dumbass to treat you like a dumbass. I treat you like I do—"

"This is gonna be good," he slobbered at me. "Go'won. Toss some of your fucked-up logic my way."

"You can't take what little I give you—"

"Morning till night you ride me."

"I talk at you; I say shit. I ever touch you? I ever try to beat you, rape you, try to make you do things you'd rather kill yourself than do? I ever come at you in the middle of the night with a goonie stick looking to turn your brains into soup? No. Not even close. So if you can't take what I give you, how good are you going to be out there, alone, when things get hectic for real? You going to be anything more than dead?"

"Like you give a fuck about anybody but yourself."

I let him have that shot. It was slight. I deserved it.

He took another: "I don't think you ever cared about nothing but Brain Nigger Charlie in your whole life. You hate everybody and you hate everything. You can't open your mouth without a slur or put-down coming out. You know why?"

"No, I don't. How about you te—"

" 'Cause when you're busy hating everybody else, it makes you forget how much you hate yourself."

And that time Stupid Bitch Dumbass hit bone.

I sat for a second, stunned still by the precision application of words from a boy who could see me so clearly no matter I could see him as nothing more than stupid. A dumbass.

He said: "I'm sorry."

I stayed quiet.

He said, again: "I'm sorry. I know you're mostly trying to help me, but, you know, you just keep pushing me, pushing me . . ."

I stayed quiet.

Then, I started confessing shit. And I listened to what I was saying: "You asked me what I was looking for out here; why I was traveling the rails."

"Yeah."

"I believe . . . in his whole life I believe a man really only has two things he ever has to do. He has to be a provider to his wife, a father to his children. A man marries a woman, he makes a promise to her before God to be with her forever. A man has a child with a woman, he makes a commitment to raise a family. Owning buildings and having money is nothing next to being a husband and father. You tell me what's a guy's worth if he can't do as he was intended? He's worth nothing . . . I couldn't do like I was meant to, Dumbass." Shame made me look to my finger that meandered in a random path along the ground, meandered around a little crater punched in the dirt by a tear that fell to the earth from my crying eyes. "I grabbed onto the first excuse I could find, a drunk man's dream, and threw everything away." After five years, after how many lies about the whys and ways of my being, I'd owned up to truth. Truth hurt. "I do hate myself, Dumbass. For what I did . . . for what I didn't do. That's why I'm here."

"To punish yourself?"

"There's a girl, she's in trouble. Serious and bad. I have to find her."

Dumbass: "Know where this girl—"

"Corina."

"Know where she is?"

"Yeah. Sort of."

"Where?"

"That's the 'sort of' part. I have to wait."

"For?"

"Some blood to spill."

Dumbass gave me the curious look of a monkey trying to figure out math.

"All I know for certain is that she crossed a drug dealer. Least, he thinks so. How the rest of it works, I'm not sure. Not exactly. Except I know there's going to be more blood. Might end up being mine. Doesn't matter. I'll do whatever it takes to find her." I ran the back of my hand across my eyes, pressed it to my nose, and blew snot from a nostril. "I have to."

"I don't . . . finding some girl; what's that got to do with you?"

"There's something like two hundred thousand miles of working rail in America."

"That's a lot." Stupid Bitch Dumbass. Prince of the obvious.

"Yeah. That's a lot. I've traveled a good chunk of it and seen nothing but the worst of all there is. But now, with this girl, I've finally found what I was looking for: I've been looking for a way to *not* be out here anymore, to not be living like I am. I've been looking to make up for the promise I never kept to my wife, my kid. I'm . . ." searching, searching for the way to express what I felt, "if I could prove that I'm not worthless, that I'm still a person. Not just a nigger . . ."

"Prove to who?"

To the only one who mattered: "To me."

Stupid Bitch Dumbass nodded a couple of times, said: "Thank you for telling me all that."

It was queer. It was an odd indicator of where my life was: someone thanking me for telling them about my quixotic task that might very well kill me. Between Haxton and Stupid Bitch Dumbass I was being hit with more genuine human interaction than in all the years I'd been on the rails totaled up. And the only way I knew how to deal with it was to avoid it.

I got up from where I sat, crossed the field, and took a piss.

Wait.

All there was to do was

Wait.

Wait for someone to die. Wait for a body to turn up with a rigored finger pointing me the way to go. Most times, being a tramp, waiting is easy and effortless. As you have nothing to do, as there is never a deadline of importance approaching, the whole of your life is a steady flow of one empty moment into the next. There is no anticipation to counterbalance the sheer boredom of your existence. Everything is maintained at an even commonality.

But now

Now I was a kid on Christmas Eve waiting for morning to come, or waiting for the last bell to ring out the school year. I was a guy who couldn't move until Death struck. My days were spent accordingly: filling my time with distractions. I found a cemetery, found a lonely headstone that looked as if it had been unvisited in years, and buried some plastic-wrapped food stamps. Not many, but if I ever found myself lost in Spokane it may be future salvation I was planting.

That took .0002 percent of one day.

With the KFC Dumpster so close, it eliminated the need to hunt for food. Five years on the rails, I never would've thought I'd wish for sustenance to be a little more scarce. Chasing off some Home Guard who tried to raid "our" luncheonette killed five minutes one afternoon, Stupid Bitch Dumbass putting on a good front of menace. I was so proud of him I told him I was going to drop the "Bitch" from his name.

Don't recall ever seeing the kid so happy.

I was thinking it might be a good time to introduce Stupid Dumbass to the wonders of a goonie stick, his own George Plimpton. Maybe make a graduation present out of it. Congrats. Now, go forth and bash a few heads. It was a thought. Thinking occupied time.

I sat outside the rail yard, clocked trains as they departed for all points, and marked them in my rail book. I wanted to be armed and ready when it came time to light out.

The one thing that did fill my waiting and filled it well was fear. Every day in Spokane was twenty-four more hours Kessler or his minions—Liquid Evil, Buzz Cut Girl—had to spot me, hunt me, kill me. One time I'd squirreled away from him. And even with all the badassness my fractured psyche had been displaying and George had been encouraging, I didn't believe for a moment I was rough enough to survive a second skirmish. I knew for a fact my fortune was not that good. And the fear of an eventual encounter, the fear of that fair-skinned and lean and even handsome man, unseen, but his threat well felt—a constant crawl over my flesh—made the passing of minutes all the slower, all the more torturous. There was nothing to be done about it. No way to speed up the leisurely business of biding time for someone to be murdered. All I could do was pray to the patron saint of incognizance to go another day unrecognized and unfound by Nazi Low Riders.

I was heard, and I was blessed. Except that I was a black tramp trying to navigate an Aryan world, I went day to day unnoticed. Did all I could to not get noticed. Avoid trouble.

Mostly I avoided trouble.

Sometimes mixing things up is unavoidable. It is nearly impossible when you are borderline insane and you start taking orders from your goonie stick.

One time: me and George out walking, minding my own, keeping to the side streets and alleys, I came on a couple of Home Guard using some deserted space to avoid detection as well. Their needs different from mine. I needed to stay alive. They needed peace and quiet to beat the life from some third hapless bum. They were deep into things. They'd already pounded him to the ground. Hands only. No goonie sticks, no boards or pipes. These were guys who wanted to enjoy the unfiltered physical sensation of a pummeling well done. These were guys I should've just left to their chore. Wasn't my food they were stealing. Wasn't my ass they were trying to fuck. What did it matter to me? Was it any business of mine?

Didn't. Wasn't.

George disagreed. For whatever reason, George seemed to feel it was imperative for us to wade into the situation and bash some heads regardless of the fact we didn't know whose heads we were bashing, or why.

I thought—I knew—to do such a thing was stupid and then some.

But George implored me. When that only converted me halfway, he played on my festering need to feel like the badass that, in truth, I wasn't.

Sure I wasn't. I wasn't because I would stand around thinking, mostly in an irrational manner, when there were asses to be kicked.

George. He knew all the buttons to push. He pushed them good.

I did not like going insane. I did not care for having a tricky piece of wood dictate my actions. But, fact, other than my ladies, that piece of wood was the only faithful thing I'd known in five years. If, even in my dementia, it asked a simple favor like handing a beat down to some unknown men, could I refuse?

No.

I hefted George. I went and let him do work.

It was over, he was done with the job, in a matter of seconds; one guy limping away, arm dangling from where George had shattered his elbow. The other clutching his face, talking—screaming—about how George had put out his eye. Mostly, I think, he was only blinded by blood running from a gash George had seared across his forehead. I think. After that it was just me and the vic; the bum rolling around on the ground, holding himself, dodging blows that were no longer coming.

"Hey," I said. "Hey, it's all right. They're gone."

The bum stayed balled up.

"I chased them off. They're gone."

Slow, the bum loosened his grip on himself. With the same kind of slow his head lifted off the ground. He looked at me. He looked at me. He said: "I don't need no help from no nigger." That came with blood that waterfalled from torn gums over a busted lip down his chin, over his neck where it got soaked up by a black bandanna. A black bandanna that was, I knew, pissed on by several men before this guy was forced . . . Not forced. Before he *elected* to wear it days straight while it stank and fermented and gestated disease. But he would have kept it on because if he'd taken it off he wouldn't've passed his final initiation—after being jumped, after having jumped some poor civvy, after having stolen a few things or sold a few drugs. If he hadn't done all that, he wouldn't have had the distinct honor of being yet another peckerwood member of the Freight Train Riders of America. This guy belonged to the biggest band of degenerates, psychos, and killers on the rails; the original dope-dealing, throat-slitting, badass, racist white fuck train gang. And I'd just saved his life.

In my hand George busted up over the irony of it all.

"Shit," I said at the FTRA guy, smiling some because I couldn't help but laugh a little along with George, "Should have let them finish what they started."

"Didn't ask for your help, nigger."

"How are you going to ask for anything when you're busy having a couple of guys kick you in the face, or were you planning on appealing to their conscience through your nonviolent passive resistance?"

"That some kind of joke?"

Apparently sarcasm was not big in the Pacific Northwest train gang circles. "No, it's a very, very serious question that I always hoped I'd be able to ask of some act-tough WT when he didn't have a couple of his friends around to back his big talk."

The FTRA guy tried to get up. Weak, hurting, all he could do was flop around—a turtle on its back—then abandon the effort in a bad attempt to make it seem as if lying in the dirt was his original intent.

He said, mostly in pure hate, partly in an effort to distract me from his inability to stand: "You sure are one smart-talkin' nigger."

"Hey, here's a tip for you: if you're trying to make me bust out in tears by calling me nigger over and over and over, it's going to take a couple of months and some harsher talk. Breaking niggers down by calling us niggers went out with sharkskin suits and tail fins, which is to say, for an ignorant little cracker such as yourself, a long time ago. You can also forget about coon, jig, jungle bunny, spook, spade, moolie, eggplant, Tom, and boy."

"Think you're such a smart nigger."

"You don't hear real good."

FTRA Guy started to pull himself up to his feet. Tried to.

"Keep talking like you're talking, all you're going to do is piss off George."

"Who the fuck is George?"

George poked FTRA Guy square in the chest, dead in the sternum, sent his ass back down to the ground.

"Now, knock that 'nigger' shit off. From where I stand, which is over you with a goonie stick, you're the lower form of life. What's your name, cracker?"

"Fuck off."

George whacked FTRA Guy across the knee. The noise of George hitting bone bounced down the alley, chased by the sound of FTRA Guy yelping.

I said: "Be polite. What's your name?"

"Fuck o—"

One more time George had at FTRA Guy's knee. Again, FTRA Guy squealed accordingly.

"You got two knees, I got all day. Beating on a white guy? That's the kind of thing brothers jerk themselves to at night. Why not be good to yourself; admit the nigger's got the better of you. What's your name?"

FTRA Guy sat rubbing his knee, his mouth a faucet spewing bloody saliva, but still acting defiant. He milked the moment for all it was worth, glared at me in silence. Finally, his little show over, he mumbled something in my direction.

"What?"

"Grady."

"Grady? That doesn't sound like any kind of a train name I ever heard. That's your tag; Grady?"

He went back to his little defiant shtick.

Subtle, but obvious, I twisted George in my grip.

"Rat Dog Grady."

"Rat Dog Grady. That is one fine tag. You're both a rat and a dog. That one must've come real easy to whoever tagged you." I was having the time of my life. This ride was an E ticket all the way. "So, let me ask you something, Rat Dog—can I call you Rat Dog? Ratty?"

Rat Dog spat blood at my pant leg.

George slapped Rat Dog across the face.

I kept talking. "Here's what I want to ask you: how's a guy like you end up getting turned into a back-alley bitch by a couple of Home Guard?"

George had reopened the spigot on Rat Dog's blood flow. It poured steady from his mouth. Couple of teeth came with the mix. "What do you care?"

"Don't. I don't care at all. But I've got hours and hours to fill, so I might as well do a little learning about your kind. I'm like a kid on a field trip to the white trash museum. I'm not that interested, but I'm here, so I might as well make the best of it. And on top of that, George likes you."

George perked up in my grip.

Rat Dog flinched.

"So, what's your story? You try to roll those guys a couple of days ago when you were with your boys, feeling like a man. Maybe you thought you'd take their moonshine, or Kmart credit card, or whatever it is white trash is big on stealing. Except, today you get caught solo, and you get shown off as the little girl you are."

"Fuck you."

"Really need to work on your vocabulary, Rat Dog. A man is only as much as he's able to present himself." All of a sudden I was Henry Higgins to the trailer park set. "Why were they beating on you?"

"Those fuckers were moving meth. Moving meth in our territory." Rat Dog reached down into the soup made by the ground's dirt and his dripping blood. He picked something up. Looked like an incisor. If it was, it wasn't any use to him anymore. He tossed it. "Me, some of my boys, we found the lab, busted it up."

"Then they found you, gave you some of the same."

"Fuckers were asking for it. You don't move meth in FTRA territory."

I laughed some.

"What's so goddamn funny, shine?"

"You talk tough . . ."

"Not just talk."

"You talk tough, but you got train gangs moving junk right under your noses."

"And you just know all our shit."

"You telling me I'm wrong? The NLR's cutting in on your turf, and you-all are too weak to stop them."

Rat Dog looked up. His eyes were alive with hate. It wasn't for me. Mostly it wasn't. "What do you know about—"

"Enough. Enough to know that Nazi Kessler's got a trade in these parts, and if you think you're going to stop him, you're wrong. Neither one of you are geniuses, but he's got you beat by a long chalk."

"All that fucker does is hide out in his lab, lets other people do his heavy lifting for him. Tell you right now he can't keep hid forever. You better believe we find him, we gonna turn him out."

"Sure you are. It's not the good old days, Rat Dung; the FTRA the only game in town. You all ganging up and beating the shit out of tramps and 'boes just because you could; just because nobody else gave a fuck about them or you or the rails. Now you've got real competition; motherfuckers whose asses are bad. And you're gunning for Kessler and his crew? Look at you: taking a beating from a couple of lowly Home Guard, me of all people having your back. Some advice: you better get your act together before you get yourself extinct. Got to learn to expect the unexpected. Hell, I didn't expect to save an FTRA's ass today."

Rat Dog sat with the thought for a bit. "Never expected to get my ass saved by a nigger."

I kind of smiled. For a second I thought he was saying—without saying—thank you. Then Rat Dog looked at me like he wanted to cut my throat with his fingernails.

I shot back: "Yeah, well, between those two things, I don't know how you're going to tell the rest of your Girlie Train Riders of America how you spent your day."

"Think you're so smart."

"I am."

"Think you're . . . Let me tell you something: Kessler is dead aboveground. Dead same as anybody that fucks with the FTRA, white and nigger alike. Cross us and there ain't nothing but a goonie stick and a bad night of blood waiting for 'em. You tell Kessler that."

"I got nothing to do with him. And I'd be plenty happy to see him dead."

"I'm the motherfucker to do it."

That was funny to me. "Right. If this is as bad as you can get . . ."

"How about you stick around, meet a few of my brothers, see how bad things can get."

Yeah. There was that. Over the last couple of weeks I'd been grace-of-God lucky enough to keep up a dodge on Kessler. But standing around trading lines with an FTRA member would surely drain the last of my good fortune from the kismet bank. Sooner or later Rat Dog's brothers would come looking for him. Sooner or later they would show, ready to beat heads. In circumstance after circumstance George had proven himself tough, but I didn't know and could pass on finding out if he was FTRA tough.

Trying not to give him the pleasure of knowing he was right, that I'd overstayed my welcome, I smiled, said: "Think I've done my good deed for the day. Safe rails, Rat Dog." I started away. "Careful for any Girl Scouts out wilding."

"Hey!"

I stopped, turned.

"Why'd you do it?"

I looked at him, not getting his meaning.

"You helped me. What the hell you do that for?"

I got his meaning. "Your whole life you go around hating niggers, now a nigger does you some good and your little brain's about to fry itself trying to figure out why. That it? You thinking, maybe, God in all His sick humor put me here to save your life; show you the light and the error of your ignorant, clodhopper, nigger-hating ways?" I gave my head one little dismissive shake. "Fuck that. God doesn't give a fuck about cats like you and me. Dumb luck put me here. The craziness in my head told me to get into things instead of walking away. Chance made a nigger save your life. Accidents are about the only thing you can count on. Accept it before you really go insane."

I left Rat Dog sitting in the alley. Sitting, bleeding, thinking about concepts that were far beyond him. I went back to my little jungle.

Waiting there with Stupid Dumbass was Haxton.

Someone was dead. I knew it before Haxton said: "They found a body."

"Where?"

"Pullman. About a hundred miles south of here."

I asked: "Man or girl?"

Haxton's X rays were all over me, wanting to know why, again, I was asking if it was a girl. "Man," he said.

"Shanked, cut up, same as the others?"

Haxton nodded. "Just beyond rail property. Means I can't do anything officially. But I'm going down, gonna take a look-see. No doubt those federal boys'll be there. Figure if we leave now we ought to be able to—"

"I'm not going."

A beat.

Haxton: "You said—"

"Don't matter what I said. I'm saying now I'm not going."

Haxton hit me with a look. Not X rays this time. This time just a hard, cold stare. "You said you would help me. You promised me."

"Jesus. You sound like I broke our prom date. Whoever's dead in Pullman is dead. Me being down there does nothing. I got your cell number. I'll ask around while I'm riding. I hear anything, I'll call. Collect."

Hard. Cold. Stare.

"I don't feel like doing the work. What do you want from a bum?"

Nothing. Haxton didn't want one more thing from me. He turned, did his gimp-footed walk for his Corolla, got in, and drove off. For Pullman, I guessed.

I watched him go. Watched him head down the street, race a yellow light, disappear around a corner.

Gone.

I moved. I went for my pack, my rail book. Flipping through the pages; had I clocked a train for Pullman?

"Charlie . . . ?"

Dumbass. Ignore him. Had I clocked a train for . . . ? Found it. There was a line that fed down to Walla Walla that would take me right through. A local freight that—thank God—pulled daily from the yard at 4:00 p.m. My Armitron told me it was ten after three. I could make it.

"What are you doing, Charlie?"

"Found her."

"Found . . . ?"

"Corina." I packed up. Cardboard, clothes I'd left out to dry. The ends of my empire. I was ready to roll. "The girl I was looking for. She's in Pullman. If we bust ass I think we can get to her before the law does. Definitely before Kessler."

Kessler. Witless. Arrogant.

In my head I laughed in his face as I moved across the field at a clip. In my head I told him what a stupid fuck he was.

"C'mon," I yelled back at Dumbass.

In my head I told Kessler you can't outthink Bra—

And inside my head, a burst of light traveled from my occipital lobe to my frontal. It scorched the fields of my mind with a wave of pain from a blow to the skull that was unrivaled even by the hurt I felt when my face took the ground full force, left me there numb and epileptic. The only part of me that functioned was visceral. It rolled me onto my back to lift George Plimpton and set him swinging in my defense. George refused me. He sat on his ass like he weighed ten thousand pounds. I regained control of my vision, looked: Stupid Dumbass, his foot pressed down on George, keeping him held against the ground. Stupid Dumbass, gun in his grip. Little gun. Cheap gun. A Saturday night special no good for anything but putting one or three or six bullets into me, any combination of which would meet the minimum standard required for ending my life.

Stupid Dumbass showered hate on me. "You fucking nigger!" A sweet, sweet smile of revenge on his face. "You goddamn nigger, crying like a bitch over your fucking nigger family! Who's a dumbass now?" His rant was reaching fever pitch. "Who's a fucking dumbass now!" He was ready to kill, his cheap little gun ready to send me to the other side of being.

I said it.

I said a prayer good and loud.

I said a prayer of salvation.

I said: "Save me, George Plimpton."

And George did his trick. A twist. There was the sound of metal scraping metal as I separated George's innards from his body. I pulled, I swung. Sharpened steel bit air, shrieked with joy. Sharpened steel bit flesh, tore bone.

Stupid Dumbass kept pointing his arm at me. He pointed his arm at me as his right hand lifted, spun in the air, flipping a rooster tail of blood behind it. Still gripping the gun. The hand dropped, thudded on the ground, rolled in the dirt. Still gripping the gun.

Stupid Dumbass kept pointing his arm at me. I took a facial of piping warm blood from his fresh-made stump. Then, in a long, slow beat, Dumbass's brain allowed reality to process. I had cut off his hand. That's when the screaming began. A long, freakish cry that came from his gaping mouth pried wide by pure pain, lubricated by a frothy spittle that allowed the noise to run on a continual loop. It went on and on until the lack of air in his lungs thankfully, mercifully, snuffed out the horrid sound. When the screaming stopped, the babbling started.

"MyhandmyJesusohChristohfucking . . .!"

Dumbass went down on his knees. With his left hand, his good hand, his remaining attached hand, he chased after his right. With a frantic clumsiness he got it out of the dirt. With a crazed, desperate unacceptance of the situation he tried to graft it back onto his arm. It would not take. It wouldn't have even if he weren't trying to put it on upside down.

He looked at me, drool pouring from his mouth, blood pouring from his stump.

"Youyou. . .whatthefuckdidgoddammyouwhatdidyoudo!?"

"I chopped off your hand." For spite: "You know?"

". . . You cut off my fucking hand!"

"You were going to shoot me. If it's me taking a bullet or you getting hacked . . . You see how that's no choice."

Stupid Dumbass gave up the effort of reattachment. His right hand slid from his left. Bizarre sight. And still the hand clutched that gun.

For Dumbass, more pressing: the blood free-flowing from his stump. Life flowing from his body. "I'm dying." Already his voice was slowing, going soft, weak. "Charlie . . ." No more "nigger, fucking nigger" from him. It was Charlie. We were again on a first-name basis. "Do something, Charlie."

My CNS went back online. I roughed it up to my feet. I regained my vision. I could see clearly. "You've been pimping me for Kessler since first you 'just happened to' catch out on the same flatcar I did. Those Home Guard weren't looking for me, they were talking to you. These last weeks, I thought I put the dodge on Kessler. But he hasn't found me 'cause he hasn't been looking for me. You've been his eyes all along, haven't you?"

"Christ, Charlie . . ."

"Haven't you!"

"Goddamn it, I'm dying! I'm . . . fuck. Please . . . please do something."

I did nothing.

Dumbass squeezed his stump under his left armpit, tried to stop the bleeding. His shirt was saturated in an instant. "Do something!"

I did nothing.

I . . . couldn't just do nothing. But there was very little of anything to be done. I did not know first aid, except what I'd seen on TV medical shows. I knew with heart attacks you pounded the chest. With bad bleeding you made a tourniquet. I went to Stupid Dumbass, took hold of his shirt. Stupid Dumbass sat, vegged. I tried to rip a strip of cloth like they do on the TV medical shows. Shirts don't tear as neatly as they do on the TV medical shows. I didn't tear loose a strip, I just tore the shirt. Coming up with a better idea, what should've been my first idea,

I took off Stupid Dumbass's belt, put it around his forearm, and pulled it tight.

Stupid Dumbass's head floated around, looked at my handiwork. ". . . Still bleeding . . ."

I pulled the belt tighter.

"It won't stop." Stupid Dumbass got some panic back into him. "It won't stop bleeding."

I said to Stupid Dumbass, without malice, but with cold truth: "All bleeding stops eventually."

"I don't want to die, Charlie." Stupid Dumbass moved his head in a smooth, slow fashion, angling his face in my approximate direction. His eyes were soft, hardly more than symbolic and functionless ornaments. "Not like this, I don't want to."

I felt no sympathy. I felt no anger either. What I felt was born from a misguided moment of trust that had grown into an overwhelming sense of compassion. From the very first, if I did not hold a natural suspicion of Stupid Dumbass, I should have shown no complacency toward him. He was sent for me, yeah, but I invited him into my life. He was meant to kill me, but I'm the one who showed him my throat. I had trusted, and this is what happens when you trust.

I said: "I'll get you to a hospital."

"I'm bleeding out. I can feel it . . . Half gone already."

"A doctor'll—"

"I'm dying!" He was sharp with that, burning off what little life he had left. "It's slow and . . . and it hurts, and I don't want to go like this . . . You owe me."

That, I did not even begin to get. "For trying to empty my head, I owe—"

"For whatever. For . . . just if you ever gave any kind of a fuck about me . . . End things. Please . . ."

He was talking about . . .

"End things, Charlie."

Do it.

The surreal got even more unreal. George got into the conversation.

Do it, he told me. Finish what's started.

I looked at George in my hand, at the red that streaked the silver steel of his trick. I had to admit he looked good like that. He looked badass. And every drop of blood that ran his length chorused the same thing: Do it.

A question from George to me: What is he to you; Stupid *Bitch* Dumbass, this kid, this . . . this punk who smiled while he lied, played the simpleton while bamboozling you; let you be his boss's errand boy and find the girl he was looking for. You let him make a black-skinned monkey of you.

Goddamn you, George.

You let him open old wounds and make you cry like a weak sister. So let me handle things for you, Charlie. He's asking for it anyway, so, yeah. Let me have him.

In all my travels with George he had never before spoken to me in such a way: cold and distant and eager, not just for blood but to end life. True, he had never spoken to me like that before because previously I had inhabited a sane estate just on the inner border of lunacy and he did not talk to me at all. I had moved from that place. But even in the early stages of my decay, when George first took a voice, he spoke only in a language of defense and protection. He spoke only when my ass was imperiled to a point beyond my brain's ability to salvage.

But now, with distinct clarity, George was asking me to . . . was asking me to allow *him* to . . . George wanted to bring Death.

"Please, Charlie . . ." And there was Stupid Dumbass begging to get some.

And there was George in my grip.

How much would it take to make both of them giddy with mortality? Amputating Dumbass's hand required all the effort of whacking a weed, turning a spadeful of dirt in a garden. It had been a simple chore. So what class of chore was murder? How much effort was required to send George skating over Dumbass's throat, to let his trick slide deep into Dumbass's ticker?

Very little.

Very little.

"Please, Charlie."

Charlie, please.

I moved in Dumbass's direction.

George fairly crackled with energy: Thank you.

I moved in Dumbass's direction. I moved, I stooped, I picked up George's hollowed end from the ground where Dumbass had been standing on it. I sheathed George's trick and quieted his voice.

Stupid Dumbass, he kept up his begging. "Charlie . . ."

"I'm going to get to a phone, call nine-one-one."

". . . Not going to make it . . ."

"Ambulance'll be here in ten minutes."

"All the while I'll just be dying. Christ, Charlie, I'm fucking dying!"

"Yeah, you're dying, Dumbass, but . . ." But what? What do you say to someone whose last moments are being played out before you in real time. There are no words of comfort or wisdom or sweet salutation. There is no glorious final scene brilliantly played in Peter O'Toole fashion. There's only the reality of things. "You're dying. Deal with it."

I got my pack. I walked. Stupid Dumbass's voice behind me getting smaller and smaller until it was nothing.

I called nine-one-one, told them there was a kid in a field across from a KFC that had his hand cut off. I told them they had maybe five minutes before he was gone for sure. They asked me my name, would I be around when the paramedics got to the scene?

I hung up.

I picked up the phone again, sank a quarter, dialed.

The other end picked up. "Yeah?" It was Kessler.

"You fucked up. Your little boy missed, and he's lucky not to be dead. Yet."

Nothing from Kessler.

"You won't get to Corina before me, and I'm sure as fuck not leading you to her. How's it feel, Kessler? You need a black man to help you, but your torpedoes aren't enough to sink him when the time comes. So how's it feel; how's it feel to be less than a nigger?"

Kessler started in on how I was dead, how I was worse than dead, how I'd better enjoy every tick of the clock 'cause it was just a matter of time before he made me dead.

I hung up.

I had a train to catch.

Pullman, WA.

I did two things when I got there. Three if you count keeping my head down, working not to get spotted by Haxton or SA Smikle, one of whom would only be slightly less pissed than the other to find me in town.

Thing one: I got a newspaper, read up on the killing. A train bum found dead, knifed in the back, balls hacked away. The story got more column inches than a dead train bum deserved, but the killing had been linked up—by the paper's speculation, but rightly so—to the killers who'd shanked and hacked the other vics, Insurance Kid in particular. The police were in high gear, the paper assured. The Feds, they reported, were coming to town. The Bulls were choking off the lines into and out of the yard. That I knew firsthand, having had to jump train half a mile down the line to avoid the hyped-up security. Barely any way into the city. No way out. If the killers were here, the paper asserted, here is where they would stay. Here is where they would be caught, or killed avoiding capture, and you, Dear Reader, would get every detail. I imagine a lot of papers were sold with that kind of attitude.

Thing two: I started marking territory. I did a little looking around, found an IHOP in a part of the city that was going through an extended depression. Plenty of Home Guard around. Some bottom-of-the-totem-pole civilians. I—we—would blend to the point of inconspicuousness there. There is where I would set the meet.

I went round a hardware store, bought a can of spray paint. Tried to buy a can. The first place I went, all I got was the third degree: what did a bum need a can of spray paint for?

Hey, I'm not a bum! I'm a hobo.

What did a hobo . . .

They didn't go for: "My yacht."

Second place I tried I got no trouble. They didn't care if I was going to spray paint the PRC flag on the president's forehead. Didn't matter I was a 'bo. Didn't matter I stank. Didn't matter I had no good reason for needing spray paint. I could pay for my purchase in cash. Cash mattered.

I went marking.

Railroad overpasses. Highway underpasses. Near the Sally and on walls next to missions. I nailed the back wall of a church, too. Didn't give a fuck. Was too close now. I had to get the word out, the same message over and over again.

C OF LOVE/BNC AT IHOP—NOON

Shorthand. Had to shorthand it. The cops, the Feds and Bulls, Haxton; they would be looking for signs, looking for clues. The less I gave, the better. I had to hope Corina got it, and put hope on hope she remembered all Walt had told her about me.

To my tag I added: + ◡̇ . Rail symbols for "it's safe," and "no police." I wasn't sure if Walt had ever taught her those, but I was running on faith as it was. A little more spent cost me nothing.

My spray can ran dry. I bought another and sprayed that one dry as well.

One wall, a mark: THE DEVIL IS NOTHING BUT A FALLEN ANGEL C OF LOVE

She was here.

And then I was done. Whatever proactivity I'd brought to the mix was spent. I made a jungle of one in an empty lot. I had no food. The two cans of spray paint had thinned my savings. Half a Snickers bar constituted my dinner. The other half was saved for a late nite snack. Then I got down to the business of waiting. That night would be down payment on an undetermined number of days to come that needed to be filled, and with no good way to fill them. I felt every minute that passed. I was not in the mood to masturbate. At best, anyway, that would have been only three to five minutes killed. There was my radio.

There was whatever AM talk was in the airwaves to listen to. In Pullman there was little. I could think of no way to entertain me. I was totally bored. There was nothing for me to do but sit and wait for the night to pass.

I was thankful for the first light of morning and the variety day gave to the continuing task of marking time. But real soon, the reality set in that the only real variation was that my waiting would be done in sunshine rather than darkness.

And then came noon. Noon brought with it the only thing I had to do each day: wait with purpose. I was at the IHOP by eleven-thirty, in a booth with a tea I did not particularly want. But the clientele was almost exclusively from somewhere below the bottom of the barrel; were at the IHOP as much because they had nowhere else to be as they were to eat. So the house imposed a table minimum. You gonna fill space, you gotta spend cash. My unwanted tea just about covered things.

The first afternoon I sat in the booth two-plus hours. Two fifteen altogether. The smell of eggs, bacon, and batter-fried foods was cruelty to my nose, some kind of nasty trick played on my stomach kin to taking a kid to a toy store, making him watch you buy gifts for someone else. My stomach made me aware of its displeasure with an internal eruption of bile.

Too bad. Sit there.

There would be no eggs or bacon for me. No pancakes or crepes or blintzes or French toast. A Rooty Tooty Fresh 'n' Fruity breakfast was beyond the realm of possibility. There would only be my cup of tea, the slow sweep of a second hand.

There'd be no Corina.

I had no disappointment in her nonappearance. I held no real hope she would show. Hope was an emotion I had quit long ago—a false idol I refused to worship.

I got up and left.

My tea remained.

The hours before noon and after became deserts traveled slowly and with great difficulty. There was no library to speak of in Pullman, and the town's small size made the presence of a black tramp all the more conspicuous; restricted my movements to a tight geography around my hidden jungle. There was little—there was nothing—to occupy my time other than the act of waiting itself. Waiting for the arrival of eleven-thirty, the time I'd go to the IHOP and elevate to a state of similar existence: waiting in a booth with my requisite cup of tea for the arrival of Corina that did not occur. Not the third day of waiting. Not the fifth.

I was becoming a regular at the IHOP.

I was not alone.

Regularly I saw a Home Guard who sat at the counter to take his meals. The second the plate was set down he went at his food as if he were eating for the first time in ten years of watching others enjoy the pleasure. He put both hands to work. His left clutched a fork as if it were platinum precious. His right gripped a roll, used it to sop up any and all liquids on his dish. He hunched low, shortening the distance the food had to travel from counter to mouth. He was like an efficiency expert on gorging. Only on occasion did he truly stop eating, and then only to reach into his mouth and pull out a mass of chewed food that was mortared by saliva. He would give it all a good inspection as if trying to find some fault. Fault found, he would reject the mass to the side of his plate and continue eating with minimal downtime.

Regularly I saw a couple—man and woman sitting together, across from one another, in a booth. The man over an open-face turkey sandwich, gravy, and cranberry mold that looked to be lacking cranberries as an ingredient. The woman ate a western omelet no matter it wasn't omelet time of day. The man—the gray in his hair, hair that was still thick and full, said he was . . . forty-six? Forty-five? The wrinkles around the woman's eyes, the small but growing layer of fat that circled her waist and only her waist, said forty-four. The tarnish on his wedding band, its dullness in the light, said they had years between them. Twelve maybe. Not too terribly many. Twelve years of marriage travels by like a cloud on a windy afternoon. Add a kid, a couple of them, let them gnaw away at your time, and twelve years seems like the day before yesterday. Years together, they sat a mere three feet apart, but each foot could be converted into ten-times-ten miles in the mathematics of a relationship in decay. They sat in the silence of the dead, their eyes looking down at their plates, only down, watching intently as their forks did the rote business of tearing into their food and shoveling it into their mouths. Their eyes looked at the food, the shitty fading wallpaper, at this or that . . .

The woman looked up at the man. The man looked at the woman. The woman smiled. The man reflected a distorted, funhouse-mirror version of it back. Then their eyes looked at the food, at the shitty fading wallpaper, at this or that . . . at anything but each other.

I was especially a regular at the IHOP with an old woman who sat in a booth by a window. She sat and looked out the window. That's all she did. She ordered food, but never ate it. She was always alone, never responded when anyone tried to engage her. It was like any other thing she did would distract her from looking out that window. She had a manner to her chore, she stared with expectation as if, like me, she was waiting for someone in particular. An old friend. A family member. Death. Didn't matter. Whoever it was, they didn't show. They left the old woman to wait.

And all of us were serviced by a waitress older than she should have been for her years, more haggard than she would've been if she didn't have to work double shifts to pay for her fatherless children or support her deadbeat boyfriend or whatever other rendering of white trashdom my prejudices cared to conjure, and she was, above all, happier, friendlier, more pleasant than a woman who assuredly lived a version of that life deserved to be.

I hated her. I added her to the list of people I hated for being more content than I.

Each afternoon at exactly one-fifteen I would get up and leave the IHOP. No extra time given Corina. If she wasn't coming in the one hundred five minutes given, she wasn't coming. And I laughed at myself. What was that: I wouldn't give the girl ten, fifteen extra minutes to show herself, I would not tease myself like that. But I would return the following day with a fresh belief that Corina would arrive. Was there sense in such nonsense? Probably not. But I was just so close to endgame there was nothing else for me to do but ride a runaway train to its termination.

Anyway, what better did I have to do?

Nothing, except to sit with the others who waited at an International House of Pancakes for whatever was going to happen next in our lives.

After each excursion I would ride the shadows back to my jungle and wait to wait again.

I missed Stupid Dumbass. I missed the Stupid Dumbass I knew. The one born different. The one who stared at strawberries floating in his cornflakes and wondered of things beyond the tiny little world he lived in. I did not miss the Stupid Dumbass who wanted to use fifteen dollars' worth of gun to end my life. I hated him for that; trying to kill me. Think that goes without saying. But even as I hated him, I missed having him around, the bit of human contact that came with having him jungle with me. I missed picking on him. I didn't miss it in a cruel sense, the way a sadist misses putting safety pins through a woman's nipples. I just missed having someone to kid, to joke with. I had joked with him, hadn't I? It hadn't all been abuse upon abuse.

Had it?

I missed, too, seeing him make the same mistakes I'd made in my early travels, each one reminding me that once I'd been a stupid dumbass as well.

Once. Still.

I let myself sleep.

I was so desperate to not be alone I tempted sleep. It came easy and took me quickly, and waiting just beyond waking was my deformed child, his crystal blue third eye staring me down.

I snapped to, cursing myself for thinking sleep, for me, could ever be anything but a kind of torture. I downed a couple of E tabs, my supply running short. I needed to score some soon, but my situation prevented me from actively looking for a source. That fact produced anxiety. I did not want to face sleep, The Drift, unarmed. I could not fight it without my ladies.

The night passed around me as I sat isolated in my manufactured bliss. The E kept me up, kept me happy, kept me in a state of perpetual love. I loved being alone. I loved being alone and awake in the dark. I loved being, at best, a hobo, at worst a train bum whose insignificance in the world was unmeasurable by any known means. I loved God who in His infinite wisdom had allowed me to get fucked up, fry every circuit I had, and arrive at such a station in life.

I loved, I loved, I loved.

And then the drugs wore off. I crashed. Got real depressed. Not quite depressed. I felt, as I sometimes felt, an ultimate calm. No worries.

As the first rays of a new day bled toward me from the horizon, I felt ready to give myself over to events. I would not fight them or try to coax them one way or the other. My fake tranquillity gave me the sense of being wrapped in a warm comforter on a cold night. I was where I was because where I was is where I was meant to be. What is going to happen, is going to happen. Why try to pretend otherwise? And the moment I acknowledged that, I knew that this would be the day Corina arrived at the IHOP. The placidity I felt was just about paralyzing.

No worries.

I sat some, let the rising sun, let its warmth spill over me. I found a bathroom at a filling station that didn't force me to beg the attendant for a key. I do not recall the bathroom's condition of dinge or level of smell. I remember only how good the water felt on my flesh, how much cleaner I smelled to my own self.

Different from previous days, eleven-thirty came quite quickly, but I made no panicked rush to the International House of Pancakes. Nothing would happen until after my arrival. I walked at an absolute stroll. Took a booth. Ordered tea. I tasted it. It tasted okay. I did not mind the clock. I did not eye the door. There was only one time I looked up from the top of the table before me. It was when she walked into the restaurant. C of Love. Corina Leslie. Slow, cautious, baseball cap on—team colors sweat-stained from blue to bluish brown—head low and eyes avoiding all others. A poor, dire attempt at being inconspicuous. That she felt the need to hide herself at all meant she knew how desperate her state was. She looked up enough to see me in my booth but remained at the door, hand clutching the handle; it was her eject leveler. I imagined the mental debate that raged in her: trust / don't trust. Stay / run like hell. Get help / kill yourself. They were the same choices I canvassed with myself when Corina's uncle, years ago, first extended me his hand.

I offered her nothing. I remained where I was. The choice was hers.

Eventually Corina ghosted over to me, stood at the edge of the booth and, for a sec, stayed quiet. She wore a long and filthy duster that hid her sex. I wondered how many attempted rapes before she learned that trick. How many after that before she learned most bums don't care—girl or boy—as long as there's a hole to fuck. From her side a hand came up and out. Not to me. Very gently she lay splayed fingers on the tabletop.

"Brain Nigger?"

I said: "Yes."

"Is it okay for me to be here? Is it . . . safe?"

I said: "Yes."

Her fingers made a synchronized S pattern over the table. She sat, her ass covering a spot on the seat where the vinyl had torn and the stuffing bulged through.

I asked: "You hungry? You want something to eat?"

"Hungry's a constant. Money's what I'm wanting for."

I flagged the perky waitress, who was real happy to be finally taking a food order from me. Corina wanted the low-rent ham and eggs. Eggs scrambled. From the waitress I got showered with "hons" and "sweeties," and even got a wink. My misery did not take to her happiness. As she quick-stepped away to place Corina's order, I wanted to hunt her across the restaurant and kick her teeth in.

Corina looked side to side, clearing the coasts. She took off her cap. She looked different than I'd thought. In my mind I had added age to her high school picture, sure that her time on the rails would have left their mark. Furrows running north-south near her mouth. Deep tracks bleeding outward from the corners of her eyes. I'd thought she would have looked old and worn and haggard and defeated. She looked none of those. Tired, yeah. Black half-moons sat beneath her eyes, her eyes themselves webbed with veins that were purple in their redness. But wash her, clean and comb her mangle of short hair, and she was as she had been in the picture I carried: young-looking. Sort of pretty. Maybe a little more so with the weight that had been starved from her frame.

"Walt sent you?" That was soft and low, and I had to have her repeat it.

"He asked me to try and find you."

"He cares about me. Only person who does. He talked a lot about you. When I saw your tag it took me a minute to work it all out, but then I remembered Walt talking about the Brain Nigger."

*The* Brain Nigger. Nearly made my name sound good.

Corina said: "You don't look like a brain nigger." Almost a smile: "Look like a nigger, but you don't look like how I figured."

"How'd you figure?"

"That you'd look smarter. Little guy with glasses."

"Little guys with glasses don't normally do very good on the rails."

She nodded. She put back on the cap, went back to hiding. "Am I what you expected?"

"I don't know I expected anything."

"You came a long way, and you must've looked hard. You had to expect something."

"A scared little girl? I guess I expected that."

Corina moved uncomfortably against her seat. "I'm not a scared little girl."

"Seventeen? What's that make you? And you go around with your cap pulled low, you creep like a mouse too goosey to come out of its hole. You are a little girl. Nothing you can do about that. And being scared, that's nothing to be ashamed of."

Again Corina looked toward the door. I looked too. No one there.

Corina's hand had never left the table. Her fingers maintained their light touch in the manner of someone reading the fine convextions of Braille. As I stared at Corina I thought, with hollow eyes unfocused, if I were across the restaurant I might just guess the girl for blind. I wondered how we looked together; a black man and a young, sightless woman. I glanced around the room. The Home Guard eating at the counter. The old woman looking out the window, the couple who sat alone together. None paid us any attention.

"Brain Nigger."

I looked back to Corina.

"I wish that I'd never come out here. I don't mean wish it a little; wish it casualistically."

That little malapropism. I felt queer. Her misspoken word made virtual a girl I'd known only through an old picture and handwritten letters. I wanted to reach out and touch her, feel her flesh and warmth, make her real to myself. I wanted to take her, take her by the hand, take her away from this place, this city. This life.

"It's all messed up, Brain Nigger. It's undone so far and so bad I don't know how to make things right."

"I know."

"You don't know."

"Not all of it. There are a couple of things I can't figure. But I know how most of it lays. You wanted to ride the rails. Why is your own reason. Stupid as it might be."

"It is stupid."

"Doesn't matter. Anyway, you caught out, you rode, and it was . . ." I caught a glimpse of myself hopping a train for the first time, riding out of LA, thinking all I was was now behind me. "It wasn't fun, but, for a while anyway, it was good."

"It was, Brain Nigger." Little hints of life crept into Corina; soft light in her eyes. Her hands, both of them now, clutched at the tabletop as if, by sheer force of will, she were trying to reach through the Formica into the past and set all things wrong right again. "I was free, Brain Nigger."

"Shit. I hear one more—"

The waitress, teeth set to high beam, brought over some chipped porcelain and silverware made of tin. On the plate was ham and a couple of scrambled eggs that appeared to come from a helluva stingy chicken. Corina had at it. Her fork did double duty as a knife in a time-saving effort. The food looked good, smelled good. I wanted some. I could only afford what was before us. I let the girl eat.

Finishing my thought: "I hear one more goddamn person talk about freedom on the rails . . ."

"But I was. I was . . . I was free."

"Free how? What from? Free from fear of getting raped morning, noon, and night? Free from being warm and dry? Free from food? I know you were free from that."

Corina stopped eating, scrambled egg perched on her lip that she refused to lick away as if to prove me wrong. I kept up my stare. She couldn't fight me and hunger. Her head sunk a little, hid her face, hid the shame living there. Corina sucked away the egg on her lip. Her fork went back to butchering the ham.

"So things went south: no money, cold, tired. But you stayed out on the rails."

"I couldn't go back home. Wasn't just about pride. I couldn't . . . I didn't want any of how my life used to be. You understand?"

"I do."

"So, I couldn't go back. I had to find a way to live."

"Kessler."

Corina looked up at me. No shock. No surprise. She looked, she said matter-of-fact, in pure assessment: "Brain Nigger."

"You moved dope for him."

"I was so hungry. I was so hungry, Brain Nigger. I was afraid to steal. I didn't want to go to jail, and I wasn't gonna sell myself; let some man have me for the price of a Happy Meal. Drugs, I mean, fuck it; people are going to do drugs anyway, right?" Once more, really desperate to know: "Right?"

Yeah. Most likely. There wasn't a force on earth that could keep me from my necessary bumps.

"Do you . . . do you think less of me for it?"

I didn't think anything at all. "So, you muled for Kessler."

"He would get people like me: girls, kids, people who didn't look like they were mules. All of us young and hungry. And stupid. Told us if we wanted to make money, all we had to do is move his meth for him. First he tried to fuck me, then he told me I could be his mule."

"You'd catch out, ride the line, get them to his NLR dealers."

"Yes."

"They give you the money to take back?"

"Yes."

"And Kessler trusted you like that; with his drugs, his money?"

"Got nothing to do with trust. He's got eyes everywhere. Where you wouldn't even expect them."

I thought of Stupid Dumbass.

"You learned that quick, and you learned to do like told."

"But you got greedy."

She said nothing. Corina said nothing, but suddenly her eyes went from tired and dull to sharp and narrow. They reprimanded. They demanded to know: how dare you?

I said: "You were supposed to make a drop, the drugs or the cash, but you didn't. You kept it for yourself and ran."

"Is that how you got it figured?"

I nodded.

"Bastard! A bastard is what you are!" That came from her full scream. "You say you're gonna help me, you say you come out here to help me, but you think I'm nothing but a . . ."

No one else in the restaurant looked. No one cared. Even so the manager, previously unseen, paraded his brown vest across the floor, jangled the fistful of keys in his pocket . . . made his presence felt. He let everyone know that he had every little thing in his IHOP universe under control.

"Why you did what you did, it doesn't matter. What matters is you got yourself in a tight place."

"I didn't do anything!"

"Kessler wants you dead for nothing?"

The waitress came around, bussed Corina's plate, asked if there was anything else we needed.

Yeah, I needed her to lean closer so I could bust her one right in the choppers.

I said: "No."

The waitress smiled, said she'd leave the check right *there* for us on the edge of the table. Whenever we're ready. No hurry. You-all have a nice day. No hurry at all.

She went away.

I said: "I know you took something. Kessler told me."

"You talked to Kessler?" Her tone ran between abject fear and utter admiration. She was impressed, probably, because I'd had a sit-down with Kessler and lived to tell. What she was afraid of: That I'd bought my life by selling her out.

Reassuring: "It's okay. He tried to use me to track you. Didn't work."

"Who'd he put against you? Felix?"

"Tall thin guy?"

Corina nodded. "Him and Hester. Them are two you gotta be causistic about."

"Her, the girl; what's her deal? She doesn't talk?"

"She talks." Corina raised up her balled fists. "With these."

"Anyway, we got clean of 'em."

"We?"

Later, I'd introduce her to George Plimpton. "But Kessler said you took what was his."

"A dope dealer Nazi fuck said I stole from him, and you believe it?" Corina gave me a hard look, waited for me to back down or apologize or modify myself. When she got none of that from me: "Know what a flesh suitcase is?"

"No."

"A particular kind of mule. Know how a flesh suitcase carries drugs? Kessler would sit me down at a table. He'd take a bunch of balloons, condoms, filled with meth and put them on a plate. His idea of a joke. Guess what I'd do with them meth-filled condoms and balloons?"

I could guess.

"You ever try swallowing rubber or that laytaxical shit or whatever? Give a try at downing twenty or thirty of them. No matter they slather them up with, like, cooking oil, you choke and gag, cry so hard you can't even see. First time I got three down before I puked 'em all back up. All that just scrapes up the inside of your throat. Pretty soon, you're tasting blood with every swallow. Twenty, thirty, or more swallows of blood, oil, and rubber. And all the while Kessler was just sitting across the table smiling, laughing like he's watching his favorite comedy program over a TV dinner. And then you get 'em down. And then they're sitting in your stomach, and the whole time it all feels . . . it feels wrong. Your body feels wrong to you."

I looked down. Didn't even know it. My hand was gripping my gut.

"That's how it all starts. How it ends is with you digging the drugs out of your own shit when it's time to do the deal. You in some nasty little shack out in Nowheresville picking through your crap while Kessler's connection is watching. Watching and drinking a beer and laughing. Ha fuckin' ha."

Deflecting: "I don't care that you stole the drugs, so I don't care why."

"Few weeks back I was making a run. Came time for me to shit the drugs out, they wouldn't come. They're in me, Brain Nigger. They're stuck up in me somehow."

The waitress came back around. Check still sitting at table's edge, she wanted to know if there was anything else she coul—

Me: "Leave us the fuck alone!"

She stumbled back, hand clutching her uniform at center-chest, got clear of us quick as she could. The waitress left us the fuck alone.

To Corina: "How is that possible?"

"I know? How am I gonna know? You're the one with a brain."

Yeah. But my knowledge of the gastrointestinal system ended with its correct pronunciation.

"I just know I got a problem with my shitter, that's all. A couple of 'em have come out. Still got, I dunno, maybe fifteen, twenty of them up in there."

"Why didn't you tell Kessler—"

"Tell him what? You don't believe me, and you're supposed to be out here helping me."

"You go to a doctor?"

"Doctors cost money and ask questions, and the ones that don't would just cut me open for what's inside. So I did the only other best thing I could. I ran."

"But you only got as far as Harve."

Corina kinda tilted her head some, took measure of me. "You have got this figured."

"When you don't sleep, when you use all twenty-four hours in a day, it gives you nothing but time to think."

"I made it to Harve. Like I said, Kessler's got eyes everywhere. One of his Nazi boys found me hiding out in the yard. He was gonna earn some points, get his boss's drugs back. He was gonna stab them out of me, or beat them out of me, or fuck them out of me, or all that depending on his mood." Corina's palms came together like praying hands and dropped down between her legs. The whole of her tightened and narrowed. She was collapsing in on herself. "He stood over me with a big stupid grin, spit dripping from his mouth like a wild dog. And I thought: that face, the dirty ground I felt through my torn-up shirt, the stink of the yard; oil and diesel soot: they were going to be the last things I ever saw and felt and smelled in all my life. And then I let myself go. I let go like . . . like I was letting go of a rolling train just as it was passing into a tunnel; I'd just let go and fall back and smack up against the ground and let my neck snap and then I'd be free. Really free. That's what I was riding the rails for anyway, right? . . . So, I just let go . . .

"But before I could let go all the way, I came out of the dark and there was this horrible, awful screaming, and he was there."

"He who?"

"Guillermo. He was just all a sudden there kneeling over that Nazi, blade of his knife shining like a vengeful shaft of moonlight, carving that redneck's pecker off, blood all misting up in the air and glowing scarlet in the yard lights."

Even with her weakness with language Corina had a sickening way of making the ugly act of castration sound like a gorgeous art.

"Who's Guillermo?"

"Just some train bum. He was. Now he's . . . Brain Nigger, he's like my own angel of death. I didn't think that right off. First I thought he was just a filthy Mexican that was whacking off that Nazi's dick as warm-up for raping me."

"He's Mexican?"

"Yeah."

I was right. Righter than Haxton.

"But he didn't rape me. He reached down a hand for me, lifted me from the ground. He told me that everything was gonna be all right, that nobody was gonna hurt me. He was gonna protect me now, and anybody that crossed him was as good as shanked. That's when I thought he was my angel of death."

"So you ran together."

"We ran together."

"Shelby, Spokane."

"Kessler's Low Riders looking for me. Guillermo took them out. He protected me, just like he promised. I don't even want to consecrate how many times I'd be killed if it wasn't for him."

"What about Insurance Kid?"

Corina looked at me for a second. I was about to elaborate when her face told me she got my meaning. "That insurance kid. Yeah. I read the papers. Good little college boy out looking for some fun. His kind of fun was finding an ass he can hold down and ram 'cause he's not man enough to get a girl to suck him without his rich-fuck daddy paying for the whore. He tried to ram me. His lily white got some of Guillermo instead."

Pure venom.

"You got a lot of anger in you."

"Four months on the rails swallowing drugs and dodging dicks. Yeah. I've got a whole lot of anger up inside me."

Corina looked around the restaurant. Not at anything in particular. Just around, hopeful that something would catch her eye, give her some other thing to think about besides men—young and wealthy, dirty and crazy—who wanted a piece of what she had and would take it however they could.

Nothing.

She looked back to me.

"So, anyway, maybe Guillermo went a little overboard with that insurance kid, but the thing is: he saved me."

I stared at Corina. I stared at her. I said: "He's insane."

"I know."

"He's a goddamn psycho nutcase. He stabs men in the back and cuts off their balls."

"I know. I seen him do it."

"And you run around with this freak?"

"I don't have a choice."

"You get away from him. You go to the police if you have to. Tell them that— "

"I—DON'T—HAVE—A—CHOICE!" Each word thrown like a jab to slow me down, straighten me up. Make me listen. "I'm his woman now. He . . . he loves me. A guy like that loves you, he loves you all the way. There's no getting free of him."

"Where is he?"

"Somewheres."

"Cut the coy!"

"I'm serious. He's somewheres, always close. I told him I wanted to eat alone, but he never lets me get far off. He worries about me."

"He's controlling you."

"He protects me."

"He's obsessed with you."

Corina shook her head a bit, pitied me for not getting things. "Obsessed . . . Labels like that are misleading. Like how they call Rocky Road 'Rocky Road' when there's only some almonds and a couple of chunks of chocolate in it. That ain't real rocky."

I stared at Corina. I stared at her. I said: "Are you fucking stupid!"

"So he's obsessical; so what? After a whole lot of nothing in life, it's good to have someone want to give me everything they got. Brain

Nigger, I've given up on trying to figure if people are good or evil. All I care about now is: do they serve my purpose. My purpose is staying alive. Guillermo serves the hell out of that."

It was like talking to a child. Except, how would I know? "He's dragging you down a bad road. This is way beyond Kessler now. The police, the Feds, Bulls; they're all looking for you." I paused. "Sort of. Your skin, your hair; they think you're a white boy."

In shock, equaling the most emotion she'd given me all afternoon: "I look that bad?"

My mouth stalled in disbelief. "This isn't a looks issue. This is about whether you end up alive, dead, or in jail. If alive is what you want, then you leave here with me. Now!"

"Leave and go where? Where am I gonna go Kessler's eyes can't see me? Where am I gonna go he's not gonna find me? And as long as I got his shit in my stomach he's never gonna stop coming."

"I dodged him once."

"You got lucky once."

"Don't fight me."

"Don't push me! I'm already getting pressed two ways; the Low Riders and the law."

"So you get yourself a killer and throw in with the Devil?"

And she said, as I'd seen her tag, with the dispassionate conviction of someone speaking the gospel truth: "The Devil's nothing but a fallen angel. He'll take care of me. I'm doing you a favor letting you walk. Stay with me, all you're going to end up is limp in a ditch."

"I'll take the chance."

Lacking any understanding of me: "Why are you doing this?"

"Your uncle sent me to—"

"Nobody puts their neck out for nothing." My words to Haxton. Corina's words to me. "Nobody I ever known. So why you?" She spoke with a desperate, desperate need to understand. "Why . . . what do you get out of this?"

Like talking to a child.

Except

How would I know?

"It don't matter anyhow," she said, voice soft again as it was when she first sat down. "I got, like, fifteen packets of meth I'm carrying around inside me. Sooner or later my stomach juice is gonna eat through them balloons. Guess what that means."

I could guess.

". . . Never even tried meth before." Wistful. "Wonder if I'll get high first, or just die. There ain't no way out of this, so just leave it. There ain't nothing you can do. You're just a nigger. Even if you are a smart one."

I fell back in the booth, was pushed back by defeat. Corina. To be so young, and your only options are the manner in which your life ends.

I did not know what to do.

You got lucky, she'd slapped me with in regard to getting out from under Kessler. And I knew I had. Could I get lucky twice? Did it matter? Did it matter if, at the end of the line, it was Kessler or the cops or her psycho savior or her own body that took Corina out?

I did not know what to do.

Do I say "Fuck it. I tried," save my own black skin, and let the girl go her own way? I wasn't saving Corina for Corina's sake anyway. Wasn't doing it for Walt or a higher calling. I was doing it for me. I was in it for what I could get out of it.

I did not know what to do.

But I did know I could not let myself be nothing but a nigger.

I took Corina by the wrist, pulled her behind me for the door. As an afterthought: "C'mon."

"Brain Nigger . . ."

"We make the yard, catch out . . ."

"Kessler's not gonna—"

I hit the door, kept going. Eased around the side of the building. The back way was the best way.

"My pack! Guillermo's got—"

"Forget your pack. Don't need it. I'll get you home, get you to a hospital . . ."

"Kessler's never gonna give me up. Long as he's alive—"

"Fuck him!" I yelled back at her. "Fuck him, Corina!"

I moved us at a fast walk. No running. No calling attention to us.

As I led Corina I did some calculating: I had my pack, so no need to go back to my jungle. George was always at my side. Maybe we should catch out south instead of directly east; get off the High Line quick as possible. Going south would add time to getting Corina home, but better to take the time. No Nazis to the south. Fewer Nazis anyway. Probably. And there was that FTRA guy I had bad blood with. How ironic would that be: so close to making it only to get cut down by him and his crew. So take a little time, swing wide, then get to Walt. It could be done. This was all doable. I felt good. It felt good to be smart. I felt warm and I felt light. My brain had been thinking at the speed of light, and suddenly I felt the need to slow down. My whole body wanted to slow down. It did that. Then I felt like I wanted to float. Not float. Melt. Melt like I'd just been kissed by Lady K. But Lady K hadn't kissed me. Lady K hadn't kissed me, so why did it feel like she had?

I turned. Slowly. The world sloshed around me; liquid in a pool I was swimming through. There was Corina. Corina was yelling something to me, but I couldn't hear her—my ears too tired to function.

I turned a little more, the world sloshed a little more. Just off to the side of Corina was a guy. Sweet-faced guy. Mexican-looking guy.

Guillermo?

My hand seeped to my back, where something flowed warm and wet, and I didn't need to see what I touched to know what it was.

Guillermo.

Catch out south. Take the long way, dodge Nazis and Feds and killers. Get your child . . . get a child back to her family. I'm such a smart nigger. Such a smart nigger. Some smart nigger. I couldn't even make it out of the parking lot of a pancake house.

I was going down. Down to the pavement and down beyond that. I felt like I was dropping into the heart of the K-hole. And I felt good. If this was what being stabbed was like, being stabbed was like nothing. It was just like being on K.

And then I remembered.

I remembered the thing about K—what it felt like when you were on K—it felt like you were dying.

I did not expect to wake up. When I did, I did not expect to wake up in a hospital. Even a county one. County hospitals are where poor people are sent for medical treatment. Poor, but still rich enough to occasionally pay taxes or own a home even if it was a mobile one. People like me, so far below the poverty line we'd snap our necks trying to look up at it, who'd been anonymously stabbed and left to bleed in parking lots, ended up in shitty little volunteer clinics. If anybody bothered trying to keep us alive at all.

So imagine my surprise waking up in a hospital. Even a county one.

There was a dull throb in my back that my higher brain functions told me was pain, but which my lower brain functions couldn't feel thanks to some mean pain blockers.

I heard a noise. A low mumble. I looked to my left. There was a curtain. On the other side of the curtain was another patient. Couldn't see him. Could only hear him. Sort of. I listened some, but wasn't able to make out anything he was saying so I quit listening and let the mumbling go on as vocal Muzak. I looked to my right. Sitting in a chair diagonally across from me was Haxton. I hadn't expected to see him. I also hadn't expected to wake up, or wake up in a hospital, so the day was full of surprises.

I tried to talk. My throat was coated with pure desert; dry and harsh.

Haxton leaned, reached for a cup with a flexi-straw on a tray next to the bed, held the cup while I sucked water.

I tried talking again. "What are you doing here?"

"Asked me that yesterday." Haxton sounded bored.

"Yesterday?"

"Day before today. Yesterday. Just like the song." Haxton sounded annoyed.

"You were here?"

He nodded. "And we talked."

"Don't remember any of it."

"They stitched you up, fed you a lot of drugs."

They had the best drugs in hospitals. It was a crime against humanity that you had to be seriously jacked up and/or dying to get them.

"How'd I get here?"

"Waitress found you outside the restaurant. She ran out there after you 'cause you didn't pay your bill."

Irony. I felt very poor about having wanted to kick her in the face.

"You're not too bad. Nothing real important hit. Paramedics got to you before you bled too much. You'll just have some pain from the wound."

Would have, except for the meds.

The guy next door, behind the curtain, started crying. He said he was dying, begged someone to come hold him 'cause he was dying. I didn't think he was dying. When you died in hospitals all kinds of alarms went off and people rushed in to save you. On TV they did.

Haxton: "I heard a bum got stabbed. Thought it might be our guy at work. Hell of amazed to see you. They were gonna move you out to some clinic. I asked them to keep you here."

Thankful for a second, a second later I was scared with worry. "Am I in trouble?"

"No law against being a victim."

There was edge to that. I knew I was in trouble. Maybe not officially, legally, but I was top o' Haxton's shit list with my name highlighted and underscored. I figured, right about then, the best thing, the only thing, was for me to come clean.

"I want to come clean. There's more to things than you know."

"I know."

"I want to tell you everything."

"Brain Nigger, I know. You told me. Told me yesterday."

"Yesterday?"

"Let's not go through this Shinola again, if that's okay."

And Haxton told me what I told him. Everything. All of it, from Chocolate Walt calling me to Britt, me catching out along the High Line, Kessler, Stupid Bitch Dumbass, George doing a job on Dumbass's hand—I asked if he knew anything about a one-handed kid turning up somewhere. He said he didn't—Corina, and how I'd used him to find her; let him think I was going to dig up info for him when really I was just waiting for Haxton to tip me to the next body so I could race him and the cops and the Feds to the scene. When he got to that part his expression didn't change; he didn't spit fire at me with his words. He didn't out-and-out hate me for my deception. Worse. I could tell he was hurt. He'd trusted me, and I'd busted his trust. Haxton finished telling me what I'd told him about Corina's angel of death.

"If you'd let on from the start I coulda helped you get her away from him."

"I didn't know. Not for sure. At some point I figured she and the murders were connected, but I didn't know how. If she'd been the one doing the killing—"

"You would've tried to get her out of here just the same."

"Yes."

"Never mind she would've been a murderer."

"Of some Nazi train gangers that were gunning for her."

"And that young kid?"

"Insurance Kid tried to rape her."

"Rape's wrong. No two ways about it. But they don't execute people for it."

I realized, just then, the guy next door, behind the curtain, wasn't making noise anymore.

Haxton said: "They're going to release you tomorrow."

"Am I doing that good?"

"No, but I'm paying for this, and another night is all I can afford."

I started to say something, but—

"Don't even bother with thank-yous. I don't want to hear it."

"What happens after I get let out?"

"What happens about what?"

"With me; what happens next?"

"Told you: no crime in being a victim. Do what you want. I gotta do what I can to track a killer."

"They still here, Corina and her man?"

"All the law in town, I don't know how they'd be anywhere else."

Then we were quiet some.

Then: "Haxton, if you catch up with them before the Feds, do what you can for her; for Corina. She's a victim, too. Like you said: no law against that."

"Yeah."

Then we were quiet some.

Then: "Haxton, I'm sorry I lied to you, but I came out here to bring Corina back home for a friend. That was my job. My only job."

Honed to a point that could kill: "Well, you sure fucked it up."

Haxton got up, left.

I did not want to be in the hospital any longer. I did not want Haxton's charity. The weight of it hung on my guilt and choked me. But I also did not want to leave the hospital. I was clean, having been scrubbed that way by a nurse. I smelled good. Anyway, I lacked a smell. What food I had was edible, the bed was soft and was good for lying in. I had no fear of falling asleep. I was not tired, having spent the better part of two days passed out or semiconscious, but undisturbed by visions of a horrid child. Hospitals indeed had the best drugs. I lay comfortably awake all night trying to figure what there was for me to do next.

In the morning a nurse came around to discharge me. Like a hotel, they wanted me out by noon. I asked the nurse if it was okay for me to be walking around with a fairly fresh wound to the back. She said yes. She didn't look me in the eye when she said it. My clothes had been bled up and cut from me by the paramedics. Haxton had bought me new clothes. Nothing fancy. Goodwill chic. A T-shirt, Levi's—okay, for me, those were fancy—socks, some cheap shoes, and an equally cheap jacket. Members Only. The whole of my wardrobe topped maybe seventy dollars when new. But once on me, as I stared in the mirror, the clothes and clean flesh made me look vaguely like a human being. I reminded myself of someone. I reminded myself of Charles Harmon.

I collected George and my pack where my ladies remained safely hidden. In the pocket of my coat I found one hundred fifty dollars. The noose of obligation around my neck tightened one notch.

I left the hospital.

I stood around outside for a while.

Then I decided it was time to go home.

The yard in Pullman was like an anthill on fire. Bulls everywhere. Looking for a Mex killer and the "boy" he was traveling with. Good luck finding them. Not my problem. Not anymore. Mine was getting out of Pullman. There would be no catching out from inside the yard. Catching a moving train was never easy and only made harder with a healing wound. That hundred fifty dollars Haxton put in the pocket of the coat he bought me would pay for a bus ticket home with some left over. Greyhound: Pullman to LA—$125.00 on the nose. One day, fourteen hours, five minutes of riding. As scheduled. But I would not have to huddle up on the floor of a boxcar or flatcar. My new clothes would stay clean. That was suddenly important to me: wanting to be warm and dry and presentable, and not live like some stray dog. I felt myself changing. Seeing my washed skin in the mirror, seeing what new and halfway decent attire looked like on me, made me feel like *not* Brain Nigger Charlie. I didn't want to feel like a nigger anymore, and I didn't feel like a brain anymore. It wasn't that I'd been sent to do a job and had failed. Wasn't just that. Failure was as comfortable to me as old shoes. I didn't feel like a brain anymore because I was sent to do a job and had been outsmarted at every turn. In a world of bums and lowlifes, in a barren place where essentials—food, shelter—were never easy to come by, I always had my wits to elevate me. Now, time and again, I had been outwitted. So if I wasn't a brain and didn't want to be a nigger, what did that make me?

I remembered looking in that hospital mirror and seeing Charles Harmon. Is that who I was again?

I thought about that as I rubber-tramped south feeling odd and uncomfortable over every mile—riding upright with the other fifteen paying customers affected me like a bad graft my body was deciding whether to accept or reject. We rolled through Cheney and Ritzville and Ellensburg to Seattle.

What had I been doing out on the rails? Did I actually ever eat out of garbage cans? Did I eat garbage? Just thinking of it made me want to retch.

Tacoma, Fort Lewis, an hour's layover in Portland, OR.

God, was I insane. Did I survive off food stamps? Did I jungle in the open, in junkyards and nasty shit-covered fields? Did I go days on end without cleaning myself, and when I did only as little as required?

Salem, Cottage Grove, Grant's Pass.

Every mile away from how I used to live was like a shovelful of dirt tossed onto a well-dug grave.

A mile further Corina was left behind.

A new ornament hung on my collar of guilt and pulled it tighter. I had been sent for Corina. I had left without Corina. But what had Walt expected? That I had found her at all qualified as a miracle. To bring her back safely along the High Line where she was wanted dead would have amounted to the Red Sea parting. Me still being alive was luck, nothing more. C'mon, Walt, really, what did you expect? Anyway, she had the crazy Mexican to protect her.

Unless he killed her.

Not my problem.

Yreka, California, and Dunsmuir and down through Redding. A forty-minute stop turning into an hour and a half.

I rode south thankful for the time to think and the feeling of safety that came with using accepted means of transportation. I felt conspicuous in my new/old skin. The bus was not a train, but I had a self-sense of being Yuppie Scum slumming that advertised, by my nature, easy pickings. I was probably safe. George was still my companion. But even George was altered. Silent, as if on my journey back to normalcy he had lost the ability to speak. Or maybe he didn't have the desire to talk to Charles Harmon. He was a friend to, a construct of, Brain Nigger Charlie. What would he want with a sellout, middle-class brother? My ladies remained faithful. They did not comment on my life change. They did not care. Happily they serviced me, kept me from sleep, gave me extra hours to think and plot. But by the time I'd reached my destination I'd thought of nothing. Had no plans.

A two-hour, forty-minute ride from Coalinga JCT RS, then Los Angeles.

Los Angeles. Downtown. 1716 E 7th. The Greyhound station. I got off the bus and stepped into sunshine and warmth that seemed to take me on and welcome me home. Sort of. Eleven years I had lived in the city. Now it was foreign to me. There was little of it I did not recall, but there was none of it I recalled living among. More like, it was the canvas of a dream I'd once had. A point on a map I'd studied and studied and studied about but never traveled to. But a city where I'd lived and worked? Was that the coffee shop you used to stop by in the morning, especially on cold winter mornings—fifty degrees. LA cold—where they made this terrific hot cider with caramel in it? Did you used to sit and talk some with the owner because he was the only other person you knew, personally, who'd actually read all of *Atlas Shrugged* and you talked about it and talked about it and talked about it until you were sick of talking about it, but you got free bagels when you talked to the owner about it so you kept talking about the book long after every piece of it was picked dry? Was that the chophouse you used to go to for lunch at least two days out of five, order some kind of steak with onion rings, and say when it arrived—every time it arrived—they out to serve a body bag with this? And that little corner store; was that the corner store where you'd go when Beverly called you at work asking you to pick up this or that? Was it the store where you went to get this or that not because this or that was cheaper there, but because the store was where a checkout girl worked who was fairly pretty but had a tremendous rack and factory-installed matching ass, and who was fun to flirt with—every man believing the flirt muscle had to be constantly, continually flexed for fear the whole of him would atrophy into middle-aged undesirability. The checkout girl was good for a workout, wasn't she, until the day she mentioned she had a boyfriend, and, no matter you had a wife, you thought of her as a teasing little whore and wanted nothing to do with her anymore.

Yeah. Those were the places.

Maybe.

Was this how amnesia vics felt when shown old pictures and were then told incessantly "You remember this!"

I hopped a cab, told the cabbie I wanted to go to Woodland Hills. I only had enough dough to pay for a ride up the one-oh-one to Barham in Studio City: a piece of LA County that got its name because one of the big film studios was located there. I guess Studio City is a better name than We Make Shitty Movies City. I paid the driver with enough to spare for a tip that was not a good one. I felt bad about that. Brain Nigger Charlie would never have felt bad about it. Studio City to Woodland Hills was a hard but makable walk. When I had my BMW, my office to home was a twenty-five-minute drive when traffic cooperated. When I had my BMW. Now I had my legs. And my thumb. But my thumb was attached to the rest of my black body, so there would be no hitching a ride.

Maybe I should call my old office, see if any of the boys are around: Scott and David and Jay. White guys all who accepted me—read that as tolerated me—because my paycheck rivaled theirs.

Now?

Would they still invite me Sundays for barbecue and to watch the game?

No.

But I wouldn't invite myself.

Not now.

But soon. At the end of the road when I rejoined all that I was, there would be football Sundays and golf outings and weekends away from the wives in Vegas. And to get those all I had to do was make it to Woodland Hills.

I started walking.

Was I making three miles an hour? Less. Was it a rule of nature that the closer you got to your destination the more slowly you traveled? As I suspected, my raised thumb was ignored. At least, it got nothing more than nasty stares and cold glances from the cars that kicked gravel at me and spat toxic exhaust. Some Mexicans, gardeners, let me ride in the bed of their two-decades-old Ford.

Mexicans.

Guilt was again hard-charging my ass.

I sat among a couple of mowers, a leaf blower, a can of gas that slid around dangerously. Well, that would be just perfect. That's all I'd need. After everything else I'd been through, so close to closure, for that gas can to ignite and consume me. Would that be ironic or poetic? I gave myself the assignment of trying to figure which and spent the ride comparing and contrasting the two, drawing no conclusion by the time I reached the outskirts of my old home.

I traveled the remaining distance, Fallbrook to San Luis to Dunman, on foot. Each step taken, the more vivid my past became. The neighborhood; the dog park where people like me drove our hounds in our SUVs to commune with others like us. The street: nice, inviting houses to which neighbors rarely invited each other. Good neighbors are quiet neighbors who mind their own. And, finally, the house: our house. The house where, when Beverly and I went to view it, the realtor subtly turned the radio that filled it with ambient sound from classical music to rap, then asked in a greasy, implying manner if I had been preapproved for a loan. He was asking: was I wasting his time? He was asking: could someone like me afford a place like that? I practically, in spite, bought the house on the spot. Really showed him, huh? But the bitterness faded. The house became the place where I was to be a husband and father and raise a family.

I'd done none of those things.

I'd done nothing more than conjure a disfigured offspring, completely lose my mind. But I was better. So much better. And five years late I was going to live up to all my expectations: be a loving husband to my wife. Be a good father to my child. Raise a healthy family.

Now.

I started for the door of the house. My house. I stopped. What was I thinking? I wasn't. I wasn't thinking. Cleaner than I'd been, but still dirty and older and years different, I could not merely ring the bell and wait for my wife to answer, smile, say "Hey, honey, I'm home" as if I was just a little late from running errands. I laughed. The first genuine laugh I could remember. Ring the bell? Maybe I was still slightly touched. Ring the bell? I couldn't do that. Instead I would . . . stand where I was. That's what I would do. I would stand where I was across from my house. Stand there and eventually Beverly and my child would come out and we would reunite.

So I stood. I waited.

As I stood, as I waited, a few cars passed, slowed, gave me curious, suspicious looks. Didn't blame them. A black man in this neighborhood? In my time in suburbia I had been similarly indoctrinated. More than once, seeing an unfamiliar black face, I asked myself what the hell were *they* doing *here*? I called the private security company that circled the blocks for just such occasions. Free of the yoke of citizen review boards, they escorted *them* to some other street. Some other neighborhood.

Now I was *them*.

In the garbage of a house nearby was a rake that was missing just enough teeth to be useless. I took it, raked the street in front of my home. No more cars slowed. A dark-skinned man doing menial, subservient labor? What was unusual about that?

So I raked. I raked. The hour was getting late, but at that time of year there was ample light remaining in the day. Good light. The sun, just then descending, was made soft by low-lying haze and lit the sky with a golden glow which made all the valley beautiful in a way usually only seen when the big Hollywood star kissed the big Hollywood starlet at the end of act three. In other words, the world seemed magnificently, artificially unreal.

And then the door to my house opened. Beverly stepped out. And then my son. Yes. I had a son. I had a boy. Almost five now. Caramel-colored skin. Dimples. Those were his mother's. So was his good hair. And I could do nothing except stand where I was and . . . and marvel at him; at this wonderful little life that I had helped create. And as I stood and stared he stared back. My boy recognized me, before even Beverly. No matter he had never known me, he saw me, now, with more than his eyes. He looked at me and knew me with his heart. And no matter my dated clothes, my dry scaly flesh, he ran to me and hugged me and held me, held me tight with his little hands. I dropped down in the middle of the street, leveled by my child. I cried. And while I cried, my son's little hands gripped me tight given strength by devotion. And his little voice said: "It's all right. It's over now. From now on everything will be all right." My crying began again in earnest. I ran my hands through my son's bushy hair, down his head, over his cheeks where my fingers felt his third eye.

I sprang awake.

And then the door to my house opened. She stepped out. She walked along some moss rock the landscapers had talked me into laying in the front yard, down to the mailbox. She got the mail from the box. She stood a minute in the dimming sunlight sorting bills, junk mail, magazines. A catalogue. She was an older woman. At a distance I would say she was gently into her fifties. She was Asian. She went back up the moss rock. She went back into my house. Within eight minutes the garage door opened. A late-model Mercedes-Benz pulled out. She was driving. As it turned past me I saw no child seat in its back. And then the old Asian woman was up the street. And then she was around a corner. And she was gone.

She was not my wife. This was not my house. It was, but no longer. Five years. More than enough time for an abandoned pregnant woman to put the property on the market, sell it, move somewhere that wasn't here, and start all over again with her son. Maybe she had a son. What the fuck did I know?

And I started walking back toward downtown. I made about a mile before I realized I was still carrying that rake. I dropped it and kept walking. It was well into night before I got to the rail yard. It was midmorning before I got on a train that was heading north. I rode on a flatcar. I got dirty. I tore one leg of my pants. I didn't care. Somewhere along the way my ring started hurting me. I worked it from my finger and tossed it.

As I rode toward where I'd come from, as I rode toward where I'd been, George said to me: Welcome back, Brain Nigger.

Little more than a day's travel and I was back in Spokane. I jumped train short of the yard. I walked some, found a pay phone. Finding a phone was the only question mark. Everything else, everything that was about to happen—it's what I'd spent the last little more than a day thinking on.

I dropped a quarter and dialed.

"Haxton."

"It's Brain Nigger Charlie."

"Yeah." He was curt with that. Yeah, as in: Yeah, what about it? Yeah, so what? Yeah, c'mon, you're holding me up from whatever else I have to do even if whatever else I have to do is nothing at all.

"I wanted to thank you for what you did; taking care of me in the hospital. For the clothes and everything. The money. Would've called you sooner, but I went away for a while."

To all that Haxton had nothing to say.

I asked: "Anything new with the Mexican?"

"Not really." I waited for elaboration. None came.

"This whole thing with Corina . . . she's so caught up. You've got to know that. You have kids, Haxton. Can you imagi—"

"Something you wanted?"

A month ago I didn't know Haxton. Four weeks. Before, if I'd read in a newspaper he'd been hit by a bus I wouldn't have recognized the name or lingered over the story.

Now

I felt bad about having lied to him. I felt bad I couldn't bridge our divide.

Okay. All right. Great. He hated me, hated my guts, hated everything I stood for, which was nothing. Fine. What did it matter? It didn't.

So, let's get to it. "I'm in Spokane. Something's going to happen up here. When it does, if there's any way you can make sure it gets some play down there in the paper, I'd appreciate it."

"What's going to happen?" Haxton got curious. "Brain Nigger—"

"If you can. Please."

"What's going to—"

"You'll know. Good-bye, Haxton. I mean that, too. Good-bye."

I could hear Haxton calling at me, "Wait, Brain Nigger, what's going to happen?" as I hung up the phone.

What was going to happen? Nothing of consequence. I was going to die.

Track. Talk about trains, say track, and rails are all most people think of. But there's more to it. Railroad track is the rails, crossties, tie plates, spikes, fastenings, and ballast. It is all of that. Two hundred thousand miles of commercial track in America, and it is in constant need of renewal, repair, and replacement. Tools of the trade: tie tongs, spike maul, spike remover, lining bar. And men. That was the other tool. And they were tools as much as humans. Big, brawny men working in gangs of a dozen-plus, tearing track, lifting track, laying track, lining track. Long work. Hard work. Hard and dangerous when you added they were working hot sections of the line; traffic rolling, trains ripping by, making schedule. The rails were the veins of a system that had to be fed. You didn't cut a vein. You didn't shut down a line. So you worked a track, your best friends were the dispatcher back at the CTC who you prayed to like God in heaven that he was letting the engineers know where you were and what you were doing, and the flare just up the track that burned its red warning: I'm working here. It was not much of a lifeline. But then, it was not much of a life lifting rails and dancing around Units to earn your pay. But those were men doing work, not frightened little girls. Men. I sat in the dark on a hill off the line watching the trackmen work the rails, dodge the trains. Mostly watching the trackmen, also watching my back; keeping an eye out for any stray NLRs or FTRAs that I'd begun to feel were continually creeping for me.

The trackmen worked till the early hours of morning. Close to clocking out, they packed their tools, locked them in a shed. Beers got popped. They drank away some time waiting for a BNSF van to come around, pick them up, take them to wherever it is those kinds of people go when done with their labor. Small homes. Trailer homes. Little lives filled with Trans Ams and passable women at cheap bars and anything that distracted from thinking and remembering that come nightfall it was back to lifting rail and dodging trains.

I sat where I was for a while. Waited. Before the sun took over too much of the sky I went down to the work site. George and I broke into the shed, and I helped myself to what I needed.

"Yeah?"

For a near-friendless tramp, I was quite suddenly making a lot of phone calls.

"Kessler."

He knew my voice right off. "You still alive?" Excitement more than disappointment: happy the opportunity remained for him to be the one to take me from living to dead.

"Still alive."

"Do yourself a favor, dude: slit your throat before I do it for you."

"You want to talk like a hard guy, or you want to talk a deal?"

For a couple of ticks Kessler was quiet. That was the sound of curiosity at play. "What are you talking, man? You gonna deal with me? Now what the fuck is a thing like you got to—"

"What do you want worst in the whole world?"

More quiet. It wasn't the answer to the question Kessler was thinking of. That he knew. He was thinking of angles, and which one I was playing. "You gonna give me Corina?"

"I'm going to tell you where you can find her."

Kessler gave the maniacal cackle of a cartoon villain ready to fire up the death ray and wipe out half of Metropolis. "All a sudden you gonna sell your girl out?"

"I'm alive. I'm lucky to be this way. After I talked to Corina—"

"You talked to her? You really know where she's at?"

"After she gave me her version of things, I know my luck's not likely to stay good where you're concerned. I got into some nasty business. So, yeah, now I'm looking to sell out. Her to you."

"Maybe you are a brain nigger, huh?"

"Maybe."

"So, where's my little bitch?"

"We've got to do a deal first."

"Deal is you get to live, dude."

"There's living and there's living right. I'm tired of getting by like tumbleweed. I want to live like I amounted to something."

More cackling from Kessler. "I don't know how to turn a nigger into somebody. My magic's not that good."

"But your drugs are. I had some of that, I started dealing—"

"Don't need the competition, coon."

"You think I'm going to stay out here so I can get squeezed between you and the FTRA? I never want to visit this part of hell again. I get the drugs, you get Corina, I'm gone."

Quiet.

I said: "Look, way things are I'm good as dead anyway. You don't want to write me a pass, I'll hang up the phone and take my chances."

"So do it."

"You know that's not what you want. How many of your boys've been taken out going after this girl? How long can you stand not looking her in the eye while you let her bleed?"

Quiet.

"Hey, here's something, Kessler, just between us. Know how you call her bitch all the time? She says the same thing about you."

"Maaan, you're fuckin' strokin' me. I don't like that."

"That gas station where you and I had our talk. I'll be there. Bring the drugs."

"Fuck that. I don't carry my own weight. That's a good way to land my ass—"

"Then send your boys to get me. I'm waiting." And I hung up the phone before Kessler had a chance to add to things, change things. I needed his high minions to come retrieve me. Anything else would not work.

I walked from the phone for the gas station at a meander. I was looking for something. Wasn't sure what. Just a meaningful place. Found a big empty field of overgrown weeds. It was circumferenced by a chain-link fence; the fence an odd sign that read: We own all this nothing, so stay off it. I stood where I was feeling like Galahad at water's edge ready to return Excalibur to the Lady of the Lake. I looked down to George in my hand. I wanted to say something to him, but I was already borderline insane and engaging my goonie stick in good-byes would only make me decidedly so. I rotated back, heaved forward. George went flipping through the air, hit the ground far beyond the fence, bounced up . . . for a moment, balanced on end, perpendicular to earth, he looked like he was standing—independent and free of me at last. Then he tipped and fell and disappeared beneath the waves of grass. Better he should be out there. Where I was going, he'd only want to try and help me. There was no helping me. Better he was returned to nature to be found one day by someone more deserving than I.

I started away from the fence. Stopped. Walked back. I stared to where I thought my friend had fallen. I was crazy. Why deny my craziness?

I said: "Thank you, George Plimpton. Good-bye."

I walked on for the gas station.

They were already there. When I got to the gas station I saw the Imperial, swore to myself. If Kessler was in the car I was dead. Was dead anyway. But I would be dead in a Mobil parking lot and that did nothing. As I approached, Buzz Cut Girl—Hester—got out of the car. Then Liquid Evil—Felix—with half an X spliting his face. George's work. No Kessler. I felt better, if having to face down only a couple of psychos and not the head Nazi was anything to feel good about. Felix, Hester; their hate for me was plain, though not overt. They just seemed so very tired of my being. In a perfect world—in their perfect world—they would end my life one of ten thousand ways and be done with me. But like the rest of America, they had a boss who didn't care what the employees wanted. Boss says fetch, they fetched. Was the same for hired guns as it was for assembly-line workers.

Felix started to say something, but I went right past him, opened the back door of the Imperial, and slid in. "Let's go." I slammed the door.

A couple of seconds passed with Felix and Hester standing wordless, or Hester wordless as usual and Felix equally so. It was, I imagined, a couple of seconds where they deliberated the consequences of offing me right then and there. I considered, for no other reason than to be an ass and enjoy the moment of being an ass, tapping on the glass of the window and indicating to my Armitron in time's-a-wastin' style that I had to see a man about a horse. But just because you can do something doesn't mean you should. Pissing on a pit bull. Telling the heavyweight champ you fucked his wife. Twice. And, later, queer as it sounds, I did not want Felix and Hester extra furious at me. It was enough that they hated me. If they hated me, merely, I held out hope that what was to come would come with merciful rapidity. And just then I got with the reality that I had started to climb the thirteen steps for that quick drop from the end of a short rope.

Hester got in on the passenger side of the car. Felix took the wheel.

"If I had things my way . . . You are fuckin' lucky."

Yeah. Lucky me. I settled in for a ride, rested my head against the window, looked at nothing in particular as Spokane passed outside. I let my head roll a little over the glass. I looked at Felix, at Hester. She really wasn't unattractive for an Eva Braun kinda girl. I wondered, could you kiss a girl like that? Would she kiss you back? Did Felix kiss her? Do Nazis kiss, or is it just rough love among them? Any love? Did they ever hold hands and talk about the future?

"You two hold hands?"

From them nothing.

"Just curious."

Nothing from them.

I rolled my head and went back to watching the world go by.

There wasn't much watching to be done. I'd expected to be driven somewhere remote, secluded. Where I was taken was neither. It was a neighborhood house, a row house on a hill in a blue-collar section of Spokane not even far from the yard; the geography of the land gave you a fair view of it. Felix parked. Felix and Hester got out of the Imperial. Felix opened my door. Squatted down to my level. His eyes came at me like they were clutching butcher's knives. Ticking his head toward the house: "That guy in there is the only reason you're still aboveground. Whatever you've got to say better make him happy." A beat, then: "Know what? Fuck that. Get him hot. Do me that favor."

And then I was in the dirt and gravel, scrambling forward, trying to stay even with Felix who had my left ear in his grip and was leashing me by it for the house. I stumbled, slid, got dragged, tried to keep myself on my feet, then tripped up the porch like a spastic salmon. I was through the door of the house, pulled into a room, dumped on the floor. On the floor is where I stayed, huddled, clutching at the flesh of my ear. It was all numb. Couldn't feel it. Couldn't feel blood either, the only indication it hadn't been ripped from my skull.

"Hey, dude, you pissin' people off?"

I looked up. Kessler. I opened my mouth to say something smart and I started to choke.

Kessler started to laugh. "You a fuckin' virgin, man? First time you been in a lab? Yeah, that ammonia, man; that shit takes some getting used to. I'd open a window, but, you know. Cops."

"Cops . . ." talking was a strain, "and FTRA." My throat and nose burned. I'd come into—I'd been dragged into—the house breathing hard and the ammonia I'd sucked in scoured my passages nearly raw. I couldn't see the lab, but if the cooking supplies were hurting me it had to be close.

"Fuck the FTRA. They wish they had a slice of my shit." Kessler jerked a thumb at a door across the room. Across the room, past Felix and Hester and a couple of other guys—big, not husky, just plenty nasty—who looked like their sole function was to keep people the fuck away from the door and what was on the other side of it.

I rolled myself off my back and onto my ass, sat, kept rubbing at my ear. "Your shit good?"

"Wanna try?"

"Don't do meth."

"But you do drugs."

"Helps keep me from sleeping. Don't like what I see when I close my eyes."

" 'Fraid of the dark? That's little-boy shit."

"You're the one hiding out."

"Fuck that, man. Hidin' in plain sight, and those FTRA bums are too stupid to see. They got labs blowin' up every other week. Bunch of dumbasses trying to cook their shit." Kessler started talking to Felix and Hester, the two goons; preaching to the choir, as if he couldn't care less if I got his meaning or not. "We been here six months. Cookin', sellin'. Before that we really were just about down on their asses. Meanwhile they're lookin' two, five miles from here 'cause they figure I'm runnin' scared. I'm not scared of shit, man." He brushed back his golden hair. "That's why I'm makin' ends and they're nothin' but bums. Fuckin' bums." He turned his attention back my way. "Corina."

I wanted to puke. I was frightened so bad I wanted to empty my guts. My ear hurt like hell, and that was nothing when put next to what

I knew was coming. I was approaching the end. My end. I did not want my end to be this way. I wanted it to be as if I was on K—soft and gentle; a floating feeling while I sailed to nothingness. But not like . . . not . . .

If I could take it all back, if I could take back every part of my life that had brought me here—this floor, this Nazi drug lab . . . Christ, if you could see from your beginning where and how you would end, if you could dodge every mistake you made that would travel you to a bitter finish . . .

But you can't. Here—this floor, this Nazi drug lab—is where I had to be. Here is where I would die.

Okay. Fine. Not fine, but . . . if I'm going to die, just let me not die for no good reason. Let me not bitch out. And let me, for one time, for the only time in my life, do as I'm obligated.

Kessler said again: "Corina."

I sat where I was. Scared. Scared to my core, too scared to move or say or do anything.

So much for not bitching out.

I don't know what transpired between Kessler and Felix. Just a look, I guess. I heard no orders given. Maybe none were needed. Maybe their routine was so commonplace Felix acted by habit. Real quick he was over to me, pulling my hand from my head. Then, and I don't know how many times, he beat me in the head, beat the side of my face. He beat me long after I'd slumped down and beat me some more as I lay on the floor. Every punch dead to the ear as if it were the eye of the bull. Already tenderized, that was where pain would be at its maximum. My cheekbone cracked, swelled. Felix kept on beating me.

He stopped beating me.

I felt the warm wash of blood over my skin. My outer ear torn? My inner ear shattered?

Kessler said, and I heard in mono: "Corina?"

I did not try to lift my head, my head felt lopsided from the battering. I did not try to look at Kessler. I did not own the willpower.

I said into the floor: "You know . . . y-you know Corina's black?"

A lot of quiet.

I said again: "Do you know—"

"Do I give a fuck?"

"You did. You wuh . . . wanted to fuck her. Na-Nazi, and you got a hard-on for a black chick. Then she stole your crank. Then you suh . . . sent your boys for her." I was building a fire. "Know she's got a Mexican looking after her? He's the one who cut your boys. A blahh . . . black chick and a Julio, and they're taking you out one by one."

"Man, you better just tell me where she is."

I lolled my head to one side. I looked past Kessler and Hester and Felix, past the Nazi goons—the goons. I could feel their mirth. Most times, I figured, they just stood around playing tough, doing nothing. Tonight they got a dinner show. I looked past all them to the door that gated the lab.

Kessler: "You wanted a deal. Gave you one. Better than you deserve. So let's get to things, man. Where's Corina?"

I wondered. I wondered if Kessler really would've given me the drugs. Doubted it. Too bad. Could've moved that stuff. Could've made some dough, bought some things, dressed nice. I could've built myself up and . . . Ahhhh. I probably would've just taken the stuff and gotten high. Didn't matter. He wasn't going to give me the meth. And I wasn't going to tell him shit.

I lit the fire: "Know something, Kessler? Corina, when she told me how she took your drugs, got your boys killed . . . she was laughing at you."

Nothing from Kessler.

And onto the fire I threw some gas: "I'm laughing at you, you goddamn white trash peckerwood stupidass cracker fuck."

Burn, baby, burn.

I didn't know who was doing the punching and kicking and hitting. I just knew I was being punched and kicked and beat to hell. There was a fist or foot or some of both at every turn. Like dodging water in the rain. No escaping it. I was caught in a downpour of anguish. My head snapped from one blow, snapped back from another. I could hear, could feel the crackle of bones as they splintered inside me. Tried to protect my skull, but my ribs took abuse. Protect my ribs, and my back got it. It was my own little Sophie's Choice: which part of me gets saved, which gets sacrificed. None, actually, in particular. The Nazis were going to have all of me.

And then it stopped. The beating stopped and I thought—instinct told me—fuck whatever else you had planned because your plan has gone to shit. Time for self-preservation. Get out. Get out before the beating begins again, harder and harsher after the warm-up.

I agreed with instinct.

But I could not move.

My concussed brain sussed things. I was on my back, wrist held by Felix. Hester was straddling me. Okay. I had to fight. I hurt too much, was too weak to do much damage, but I had to try. I could not die. Not just yet. So I had to fight. I struggled some. Took a couple more shots to the head from Felix. My fighting was over. Blood left my head and I floated. Not nearly far enough away.

Kessler talked: "You don't fuckin' get it, man. You think you can come in here and play me? Don't know what you think your game is, but you lost."

"Fuck him up," came the word from Kessler.

I knew nothing of torture. I always figured—not really figured, but as I was so informed by movies and TV—that torture was handed out by snarling psycho-villains at a metered pace maximizing the agony for those who received, pleasure for those who gave.

That was movies. TV.

Torture's just another kind of violence. Like every other kind of violence it came quick. Hester pincered me by the jaw, flicked open a knife. She cut off the lid of my right eye. She slashed it away—fast, brutal—and the only way I knew the deed was done was by the pain that followed: a white-hot coal strapped to my face. For a second I saw two worlds; one normal, one hidden behind a flowing red curtain. Energized by agony, I tore free of Felix, bounced Hester the fuck off me. They didn't care. They wanted to see me stumbling around screaming. They laughed. Kessler laughed. The Nazi goons whooped it up. I grabbed at that coal scorching my skin. It was there to stay, and the hurt with it. The hurt underscored by the inconceivable: she took my eyelid! The bitch cut off the lid of my eye! Who the fuck cuts off an eyelid? Who the fuck . . . ? Those thoughts reinforced the reality of the event and turned up the volume on the agony. I screamed more, screamed all I could. I screamed to let out the pain, drive off the pain. I screamed because, someone takes your eyelid, what else is there to do? The pain and the screaming fueled more laughing and brought on humiliation. It didn't matter much, but the humiliation was there as I flopped around dripping blood from my eye and shitting my pants and cleaning out my stomach by way of my mouth and did other glamorous things and

And there was a voice. Whose, I wasn't sure. Corina's, maybe. Maybe it was Chocolate Walt's. I just know that there was a voice saying to me over and over something about a door. A door and how me getting close to Kessler and even getting beat near to death was all something that was supposed to be happening.

Supposed to be happening?

Why would I want this? Their laughing, my screaming and the shitting, the puking . . . Why would I—

A door.

The door.

Okay.

The door. Let's go, Brain Nigger. Enough with being psuedo-intellectual. Time to be purely physical.

Being physical, at that point, for me, was reduced to stumbling, tripping over my new lack of depth perception and acquired demi-blindness. And good for it. Good for it because my gimpy, seal-boy movements, my blundering all over the room, masked my actions as I tried to orient myself for *the* door. I saw it for a split second, lost it as something caught my legs and sent me to the floor. I scrambled on three points, one hand still occupied with holding my now forever-open eye. I prayed, prayed hard I'd somehow get where I was going before I got boring and a new round of torture was needed to make me fun again.

The door.

I saw it spinning ahead of me. I lurched and I lurched and I threw myself against it, praying, praying hard, that it wasn't locked.

Prayer answered.

I fell into the adjoining room. Kessler's meth lab. Couple of people in there, maybe, wasn't sure, cooking up some shit. Wasn't sure. Too dark, the one window blacked out. Didn't matter. All that mattered was me crawling as deep as I could into the room and praying, praying hard, one more time that Kessler followed.

Kessler: "Thought you didn't like meth?" His laughing slowed, but me flopping into his lab was still good for a chuckle.

I rolled, tried to spot him. He was beyond the door, still in the other room.

"Better not fuck up my shit, dude."

Felix came strolling in. Hester came with him. The goons were at the door.

Kessler stayed in the other room. "I don't get you, man. Why you come here, just to get yourself killed?"

I tried to call to him, tried to bait him. My screaming, the ammonia stronger than ever; all that constricted my throat, made it useless for anything beyond whimpering.

"You want to die, black, that's cool with me. Corina's gonna get her little nigger ass killed, too." Kessler stepped to the door, leaned against the sill. "She's gonna get her ass fucked, then killed. I promise you on your own fuckin' grave it's as good as done."

I tried to will him closer to me. Closer. Please, God, my dying wish: bring him closer to me. My hand fumbled in the pocket of my coat.

"Shit. You just a fuckin' waste. I'm doing you a favor takin' you out."

In the manner of their well-practiced silent communication, Kessler sent Felix and Hester forward to end my life.

And then Kessler stepped into the room.

One step.

Good enough.

A meth lab, besides a place to make drugs, is nothing but a big fat collection of unstable chemicals. Mixing them is about as safe as storing gas and nitro in a toaster oven. It doesn't take much to set it all off. Overheat the ethyl ether or the sodium hydroxide, mishandle the sulfuric acid . . . drop so much as a match and say "hey" to your ancestors.

From my pocket I pulled a railroad flare.

Why did I come here, Kessler? I came to kill you.

I ripped the flare lit.

Hester, Felix stopped. That I could see. I could not see the "oh shit. I'm gonna die" looks on their faces. Too bad. Woulda liked that.

Bye, Nazi motherfuckers.

I tossed the flare at the tables of chemicals.

It felt as if I had a moment of clarity. It was impossible. The actual flow of time would not allow for such an event. But it felt as if—as I watched the flare rotate, rotate, twisting its luminescent red tail through the air—it felt like I had the cold metal of both barrels in my mouth. And as my big toe pulled the trigger that would trip the hammer that would fire the shells that would vaporize my skull, I came to a too-late conclusion: shitty as it was, useless as it was, as little as it ever amounted to, I liked my life. I liked *being* alive.

In reality, it was not clarity or vision or an epiphany that converted me to the belief that even a sucky life was better than no life at all. It was nothing more ersatz than cowardice. The burst of energy that got my broken body off the floor nothing more heroic than self-preservation driven by abject fear: Death would hurt. I moved for the blackened window, jumped for it. That was all I managed on my own; making the leap. In the next moment I was punched in the back by a fist of heat and greeted with a screaming boom that, together, threw me through the glass. I traveled just ahead of a firestorm that expanded in an instant and swallowed all that stood before it: wood and fabric and flesh. It fed and it grew and it fed more in a locked cycle of destruction. It chased me from the house, tried to add my blackness to its menu, its tongue and tendrils reaching for me. I hit the ground, rolled, rolled myself douse. The fire took most of my jacket, the skin of my back.

I lay where I was some—one hand still clutching my eye, the other clutching the ground.

I turned over some. My functioning eye looked at the house. Flames showed through the windows, clawed for the second floor. From inside the house came a noise that sounded like the fire inhaling oxygen. Or a scream. The fire took the house with a certain violence; raped away its paint, its fixtures, tore at its supports, made it weak and turned its weight against itself. I could only imagine what it would do to a person. I could only hope Kessler wasn't killed immediately and was left to suffer.

I enjoyed the moment.

Sirens in the distance. Faint, far off, but they were coming. I could see, barely, lookie-lous watching the exploded, burning structure—people dead or in the process of dying inside—with all the detachment of an audience watching a bad movie that they'd paid to see and refused to walk out on.

I did not stay. Police would arrive soon. Beat up, cut up, burned, outside a blown-up meth lab was not a good place to be found by the guys who enforce the law.

I got up off the ground. That was the first miracle. The second. I guess being alive was miracle number one. Anyway, my legs worked and I was functional enough to operate them. I let what remained of my jacket fall from me, my arms too weak to take it off. I tore a sleeve free, wrapped it around my head, covered my delidded eye. It would do for a bandage. I started limping down the hill, headed for the rail yards. It was the only direction I could think to travel. Not far. I could make it. I'd figure out what to do next—what to do next being how to get myself some no-questions-asked medical attention—after I got there and gave myself an hour or eight to pass out.

One last look back at the house as I walked. A window in the upstairs blew out.

Corina.

That fire was her freedom. Sort of. She had told me she had to stay with the Mexican, that he was her only protection against Kessler. That Kessler would never stop coming at her.

But now

Flames were punching through the roof. The fire owned all of the house.

With luck—with a little more luck—Haxton would make sure news of the lab explosion, the hideous death of a particular train gang leader, got reported in the paper down in Pullman. And if Corina was at all a smart girl, safe now, she'd call the police, turn the Mexican in like I'd told her, save her hide while she had some to save. And maybe I—

Sirens getting closer. Time to walk on. I kept on down the hill. Moving was slow and unsteady.

So, anyway, maybe I could still get Corina out of here, out of Washington State, get her home, get her to a doctor, and get Kessler's time bomb out of her body. Then I'd get her back to Walt: here you are, Your Highness. Charge fulfilled. In old England you got knighted for shit like that. I got sixty-seven dollars in food stamps, minus costs, a trip to the free clinic, and an eye that would never work right again. Maybe the same with an ear, too. And I got that other thing that I may or may not have even known I was trying for when first I'd said yes to Chocolate Walt. I had purpose.

And there came a noise that to my mind sounded like the Devil trying to bust his way out of hell. I turned, looked. Sitting up the road at the top of the hill was Kessler's Imperial LeBaron sedan, the massive V-8 growling at me. A beast at feeding time.

Forget every single other thing he'd done to me. Just then I got why Corina was frightened to the soul of this cat. Apparently, he would not die.

Kessler revved the Imperial's engine. Foreplay. Getting himself hot and wet before the kill. And when he was ready he put the car in drive, sent it down the hill and missiling for me. I started to move away. My weak and gimp legs propelled me at little more than a walk. Not hardly fast enough to get clear of the car, its wide chrome grille a fat toothy grin sneering: Let's get it on. I could hear the engine racing nearer as I limped for cover. Didn't make any. Wasn't even close. I turned. The car was there. I think I jumped up as the bumper took out my thighs—some kind of fear reaction. Useless, except that it flipped me up onto the vehicle instead of launching me backward through the air on impact. Better that way. Maybe. I wasn't thrown forty or sixty feet up the road and splattered against the ground. Instead I ended up riding the hood of the car with all the skill of an untrained bronc-buster. I gripped hard at the metal seams. Kessler fishtailing wildly, trying to shake me loose.

I wouldn't let go.

Wouldn't let go when he jumped a curb, took out a fence, me getting hailed, getting shredded by snapped, jagged wood. The car bounced for some grass, an open field. It took air, rose, fell, hit ground. Hit ground hard. I thrashed on the hood. My face slapped the metal, took a pounding. My bad eye reminded me it was fucked up with a fresh jolt of hurt.

I wouldn't let go.

Kessler drove on, cranked the wheel, sharp turns, whipped me side to side. Cranked it, cranked it. Whipped me. Wouldn't let go. Fingers cut, bleeding. Wouldn't let go. Wouldn't do it.

Then he braked hard.

That's when I let go. Was forced to let go. Momentum tore me from my grip, tore away layers from my hands, sent me sailing up, out, then to the ground where I bounced and skipped tossed-stone-style and gave my burned back some other kind of misery to think on. I could barely see, had to slosh my head around to catch Kessler getting out of the Imperial. What was left of him was a horrible thing. Baked flesh, roasted flesh, missing flesh. Clothes melted and melded with what flesh remained. His beautiful Frampton mane fire-shaved, revealing a charred scalp. He looked the result of a science experiment gone frighteningly wrong: what happens when you splice man with fire. He had taken one step into the room when I lit the flare. The blast had probably, as it had with me, blown him clear of the inferno. Burned him, yeah. Mostly killed him. But hate was the apparatus that kept him alive. His was roasted to perfection. And with his skin gone, his pain receptors melted, Kessler was feeling fine because he wasn't feeling anything at all. His lab was exploded, his goons were dead, he was a wreck, but it was a lovely day to kill the nigger who caused it. He came at me screaming a language I'd never heard before. I wasn't going to stick around to learn it. I turned, clambered, clawed my way forward. I tripped, fell over something. Some*one.* I got shoved, and I fell into someone else.

Angry voices yelling at me: "What the fuck ya doin'? Get the fuck off!"

With their voices was the sick sweet stink of dirty bodies. Bums. Tramps. 'Boes. I was in the jungle. The jungle was full of people. People who could help me.

"Help me!" I screamed loud as I could to anyone who would hear. "Somebody help me!"

"Get off me!"

"Get out of here!"

"Get the hell away!"

I was pushed around, pinballed from body to body. But I got no help. Bottom feeders, just trying to keep themselves alive. Bottom feeders don't raise up their heads for anybody.

"He's gonna kill me!" I fell into someone, clung tight with all the desperation I owned. "Please, Christ, help me!" And then my head jerked from an explosion that blossomed across my skull. As the whole of me lolled around, tried to recover, realized I'd just been hit, another blast worked its way left to right through my brain. And there was that unknown language screaming at me. It was Kessler I was clutching.

"No! Kessler, don't kill me!" I was pathetic with my begging. Didn't care. Wanted to live.

And I took another hit. My head jerked up, probably a knee to the face. I let Kessler go, tried to roll away. I didn't go anywhere. He was grabbing onto me now. I opened my mouth to plead for my life—please, God, let me be pitiful enough to sway him—and something hit me in that region. Harder than a fist. A board? A brick? It stuffed whatever I had to say back inside me. I just let my jaw hang open and the blood flow.

And there was that screaming, on and on, barely decipherable. Die, nigger. Good as dead, nigger. Gonna fucking kill you, nigger. It was punctuated by my body jerking from well-placed blows. My head, of course. My ribs. My gut. He didn't hit me in the back. Good. Don't think my back could take it. Maybe it could. Honest, I didn't really feel much. I was somewhere beyond hurt now. I could accept the abuse and was glad to because as long as I did it meant I was alive. So I let my head snap and my body wrap itself around kicks to the midsection. Beat me all day if you want. I'll take it. Sure, I kept up with my begging and pleading: No, Kessler! Stop, Kessler! Please, Kessler, don't kill me, Kessler! But that was more an automatic response; the kind of thing you do naturally when you're being pummeled to death. But one day, when I recovered from being pummeled to death, I would go find George Plimpton and we'd come looking for Kessler. And then . . . watch out! One day.

One day.

Kessler kept on with his animal screams. Kept on. Kept on. I could hear them clearly. I could hear them real good because my head wasn't jerking around anymore. Took me a minute to realize that. I was just lying on the ground no longer taking abuse. Still the screams kept coming, but they weren't angry and chock-full of hate. Now his screams were like mine; weak, full of fear: "No! Don't! Christ! Please! Jesus!" It was as if Kessler liked my sissified wailing so much he'd co-opted it. But screaming like a bitch isn't something you do without cause. I worked open my eye that wasn't permanently so. Kessler had cause. Four, five train gangers holding him, grabbing what was left of his cooked skin. One of them was beating Kessler. Kept beating Kessler. Was sweating from beating Kessler; his midsection, his head. One time he snuck a shot to his balls. When the ganger got tired, he tagged off and another took to beating Kessler; his midsection, his head . . . really wherever he felt like laying in a free, unimpeded punch. And the gangers, each of them, they had black bandannas around their necks. FTRA.

Out of the frying meth lab

Into the fire.

One of the gangers, the one who had been smacking Kessler but who was now taking a breather, to someone near me: "What 'bout the nigger?"

I rolled my head, really I had to roll my whole body as my extremities weren't working too well on their own. Standing near me, towering over me, was Rat Dog Grady.

I mouthed his name. And for that, I took a kick right in the face.

I saw nothing after that. Nothing in particular. Just a glowing psychedelic tapestry that pulsated inside my skull in rhythm to a throb in my ear. I heard Rat Dog say: "Nigger ain't worth my time. Good as dead, anyway."

And then Kessler's screams slowly moved further and further away as he was dragged deeper and deeper into the jungle. And then his screams turned into some kind of hideous gurgle. And then there was nothing. Just the low rumble of a Unit pulling from the yard.

I lay where I had been left, and for a time watched the pretty colors swirling inside my head. I didn't know if Rat Dog was returning the favor of saving his life, or if he really believed I was just a nigger and not worth the energy it would take to kill. I do know that I'd never been kicked in the head as hard in my entire life. My brain shut down. I hoped that I was only losing consciousness and not, as Rat Dog had said, good as dead. I guess the proof would be in my ever waking up again. Or not.

I remember the guy, the paramedic, working on me. I don't know what he was doing. Shouting medical stuff to his partner, sticking needles in my arm. I didn't feel the needles. A cut-up eye. Cracked bones. Welts, bruises, lacerations, and burns. Needles were nothing. I remember riding in the ambulance. I remember the sirens, the feel of the vehicle slaloming through traffic. I remember the guy squeezing my hand and telling me: "It's going to be okay. You're going to be fine."

I remember thinking: All this trouble. I'm not worth it. I wanted to tell him that. Instead I passed out.

A few days later they let me out of—they told me to get out of—the hospital. I asked the nurse if it was okay for me to be walking around with a fractured rib, a couple of those, probably a concussion, and definitely a missing eyelid. She said yes. She didn't look at me when she said it.

I tried to reach Haxton on his cell phone. The first time I called he didn't answer and I got sent to voice mail, but I didn't leave a message. Nowhere for him to call me back.

Ladies E and K threw me a "get well soon" party.

Later, I called Haxton again.

He answered.

"Haxton?"

"Brain Nigger!" More enthusiasm than the last time we'd talked. "Lord Almighty, you good?"

"Heard about things?"

"What I read in the paper down here. I didn't have to do much to get play. They ran the story on their own. Saw about Kessler, figured you were in on that somehow. And when you didn't call any after that . . . What happened?"

I was wearing an eye patch now. If I was really rich—actually, not really, rich. If I was just Charles Harmon rich again, which, to most of America, is really rich—I could get some kind of surgery and have my lid fixed and kiss the patch adios.

If.

But I was Brain Nigger Charlie, and I'd be wearing the thing for the rest of my life.

I said to Haxton: "Long story."

"Now what?"

"I think . . . I hope something's going to happen."

"Something . . ."

"You know any cops down there?"

"A few."

"Stay close to them. They might get the word first."

"Word on what? What's supposed to be—"

"I'm going to try and find Corina again."

"You're coming down here? How you coming?"

"Train," I said. "I'm back to trains."

"Well . . . be careful."

A useless warning. After all I'd been hit with, what more was there to be careful of?

"Yeah," I said.

"Call me when you get here. I'll come get you."

"Haxton?"

"Yeah?"

"Something else."

"Yeah?"

"When you see me, I'm not going to be pretty."

I knew some things about the Berlin Wall. Back when there was one. I knew them from the library, of course. The Berlin Wall was not one wall, it was four generations of walls. The first one went up over the night of August 13, 1961, and it wasn't a wall so much as it was a whole lot of barbed wire and roadblocks keeping the East Germans in the east. In 1975 the fourth generation of the wall was erected. It was about twelve feet high, made of concrete slabs run between steel girders. It was 18 inches thick, ran a total of 96 miles, was ringed by 302 watch-towers, 65 miles of antivehicle fences, 79 miles of electric fence . . . Basically it was hard as hell to get around, over, or through. The Berlin Wall was gone. I would never have to get around, over, or through it. But with my cracked ribs, my fractured skull, my burned back, it was like facing the Berlin Wall trying to figure how to get around, over, or through the simple little chain-link fence that separated me from the field where I had thrown George Plimpton. I tried climbing the fence. Four times I tried. Never got so high one foot didn't always remain on the ground. I tried pulling a section apart.

Yeah. Right.

I tried digging under the fence with a soup can I found. That would work. Given enough years.

So I gave up. I was about to. Then I thought about trying the gate way on the other side of the fence. What the hell, right? I walked for it. I got close and I saw a heavy metal chain that looped the gate and the fence a couple of times, and I swore at myself for both having hope and expending the energy it took to walk way around the fence. Then I got close enough to see that the gate was chained but the chain wasn't locked. Someone had previously busted in, or someone had forgotten to put on a lock, or someone had just been too cheap to buy one to protect property that was empty anyway. I opened the gate and wandered the field sweeping through the wild grass. I think I spent about twelve minutes doing that. Eventually I found George. I picked him up. He didn't say anything to me. No greeting. No welcome back. I wasn't bothered by his silence. I knew, after I ingested enough drugs, he and I would chat plenty.

Should've taken the bus. The Spokane yard was still hot with Bulls. Hotter now after Kessler's lab got blown up and his carcass got found down on the rails severed several times over by an eastbound BNSF. Catching out inside the yard was impossible. I had to catch out on the move. Hard enough healthy. A magic trick with one useful eye and a fractured body. The first train I went for almost killed me. Took me a day to get up nerve enough to try again. The second didn't kill me, just hurt me bad. It yanked me along, stretched my body, made my ribs feel like twisted metal tearing me apart from the inside out. But I held on. I pulled myself onto a flatcar. I made the ride, Spokane to Pullman, on my back, breathing hard, in pure pain and with a single thought whipping around in my head: jumping off outside of Pullman was going to be pleasurable as a sip of hot grease.

About that I was a hundred percent correct. After I made the jump I lay in the tall weeds beside the rails. When the ache of detraining dulled enough to let me function, I limped with George's help for a pay phone. I called Haxton.

"Yeah?"

"Haxton? Brain Nigger. I made it."

. . .

"Haxton?"

"You're, uh . . . you're a little late. It's already gone down."

Gone down? My heart found another gear. "What happened? Is Corina all right?"

"Where are you? I'll come get you."

"Is Corina okay!"

"Honest, I don't know."

. . .

In the morgue, on a table, there was a body. There were a few bodies on a few tables. More than I figured I'd see in a small town like Pullman. There was one body on one particular table. Dead, of course. That it was in a morgue said so plainly. Blood staining the white sheet that covered it said so, too.

Haxton pulled the sheet back enough for me to see the body's face. It was the Mexican. It was Guillermo.

When Guillermo knifed me, no matter he was trying to kill me, I remember him as having such sweet features. I'd thought, later, his seraphimism was nothing more than the manifestation of a last-moment-of-life vision. I was dying, yeah, but I was being put out of misery by—as Corina had called him so many times—an angel of death. So why shouldn't the guy doing the mercy killing look sweet? And sweetness is what I saw. Yet now, alive and lucid, I figured Guillermo would look like the nutso serial killer he was. Emotionally bankrupt, unable to comprehend right from wrong. Other than young and fresh-faced, only thing Guillermo looked was very violently dead; his body seasoned with entry and exit wounds from the bullets of law officers.

"Do you . . . recognize this man?"

I turned and looked at SA Mathais Smikle, who stood close to me. I think. I was still working on my depth perception.

"Is this the, uh, is he the individual who—"

"Shanked me, Smikle? That what you're asking? This the guy who shanked me?"

Smikle stood looking at me same as if he was looking at the most boring television program on the face of the earth, and here he was without a remote.

I hated doing Smikle's work for him; making a positive ID on the body. But I was the only one who had ever seen what the Mexican looked like, truly his only surviving vic. That face. No matter he was nuts, I could see why Corina could not send him over. He looked kind and he was, I guess, good in his own evil way. He had protected Corina. He had used his wicked knife against deserving people.

Haxton told me the police had gotten an anonymous tip; where the rail killer was holed up.

Anonymous tip?

Poor Corina.

Did she leave him after she phoned it in? Could she, or would he have followed? Did she have to stay near, have to watch as Smikle led the Feds and the cops in? Guillermo's blade against their guns. One against twenty or thirty trained officers. Him against Smikle. He had no chance at all.

And now I had this final job: I say the word, and Smikle will have gotten his man. Haxton, for all his trying, will be left with jack but his mangled foot, his rail yard job. His wife who is not, oh, say, Elle Macpherson to go home to. A good many years of being nothing but a Bull to look forward to.

Smikle prompted: "Is he the one who stabbed you?"

"Yeah, that's the guy."

Smikle didn't say anything in the form of confirmation or salutation. He didn't say anything. He and the agents with him just left; Haxton and I not worthy of any comment at all. I wondered what it would take to get Haxton to slip his gun from his holster and hand Smikle a couple of bullets to the back. God, I hated him. I wanted to hurt him. I wanted to shred him. I wanted to let George do his trick and end his life. All I could do is watch him go and hope that someday I would pick up a newspaper, turn a page, read an article about the horrible death of Special Agent Mathais Smikle.

I said to Haxton: "Sorry."

"Got nothing to be sorry about."

"I know how badly you wanted to catch this guy."

"Not as bad as I just wanted him caught. He's done, and that's all that matters."

"Kind of a shame. Yeah, he was a murderer, but he's so young. Kid like that, maybe if things had been different for him—"

"That girl of yours gonna be all right?"

"I don't know," I said. "After all this, I don't know if she'll ever be good again. And she still has those drugs in her body. Sooner or later . . ."

Haxton nodded.

I looked to Guillermo again. Marveled again: "Looks so young."

"In his thirties."

Thirties? Didn't believe it. It showed on my face.

"Got his records from Mexico. He's slow, mentally. Got a history of petty crimes. Guess he got around to murder."

"Jesus, he looks like a . . . He looks so—"

"Looks don't mean nothing." Haxton brought the bloody sheet back over the Mexican. End of story.

And it felt like it was the end of me and Haxton. In the short history of us, all Haxton and I shared was a moment of getting high and the search for a killer. Getting high was a onetime thing. The killer was dead. Suddenly it was as if we were strangers at a cocktail party embarrassed by our lack of conversation.

"I'm heading to Spokane. Things I can do there," Haxton said, shattering the freshly formed ice. "If you want to come along . . ."

I said no to Haxton's offer, told him I wanted to stay in town. For a while anyway. With Kessler dead, his crew dead and/or scattered, maybe Corina had gone on, gotten away from this place. Probably she was still here and still needing help.

"I have to try," I said. "One more time, I have to."

"Well . . . I'll be in Spokane a couple of weeks or so. If you pass through, do me the favor of at least saying good-bye. Nothing else, I can get you on a train. Up in the Unit, even. Get you where you're going safe."

I looked around some. Not much to look at except bodies. Still looking around: "I just want you to know I'm sorry about things."

Haxton did not hesitate in accepting my apology. He did not lord it over me. "No issues, Brain Nigger. You acted how you thought right."

"I'm sorry anyway."

Haxton put out his hand. I shook it. I did not say it, but I hoped this would not be the last time I saw him.

And then he left.

I remained with the dead.

Progress through patience.

It was something . . . well, no. Can't say that. But it *sounded* like a slogan the Central Committee would have plastered all over Red Square back in the day to distract the proletariat from the latest famine: Progress through patience. It's pretty much what my life had been reduced to.

11:30 a.m. to 1:00 p.m.

I sat in a booth in the IHOP in Pullman over a single cup of tea that had cooled to room temp, having nursed it beyond its usefulness.

I waited.

I'd gotten me a couple of new spray cans, gone out through Pullman and marked territory; left signs for Corina:

IHOP LET'S GO HOME BNC

And again I passed that hour and a half between eleven-thirty and one staring at the tabletop, thinking about nothing.

I waited.

I waited with the couple whose lives had gone stale and the Home Guard who gave life to eating and the old woman who spent her life looking out the window and the happy waitress who'd saved my life. We all passed time in our own abutting universes. We all waited separately together for a week. A seven-day week, not a workweek. We all waited four more days. On the fifth day, the twelfth day in total, in the last half hour of my vigil, Corina came through the door of the restaurant. No hesitation this time. This time she came right to me, sat across from me, held her pack on her lap the way a little girl clutches a favorite doll she's selected to take on a long, long trip. She looked quite tired.

She said not one thing about how I looked. I looked, I expected, like a black man who'd spent too much time on the High Line—a lot of slow-healing damage. Fresh scars that would never fade.

I asked a useless question: "How are you, Corina?"

"I'd like to go home, please."

I started to get up. Corina stopped me and asked if she could have some pancakes. It would just about send me to Tap City, but I said yes.

I ordered pancakes from the happy waitress. When she brought them I told her thank you and she told me it was no problem, sugar. I didn't elaborate, but I had meant thank you for saving my life. I could do without a "moment." I let her think I was talking about the food.

Corina ate the pancakes.

Done, we left the others to their waiting.

Time was of the essence. Previously, when proactivity was beyond me, time was good for nothing except slogging through. Now there was none to waste. I had Corina, and I had to get Corina home so Walt could get her to a doctor.

But

There was the other thing I needed to do.

Needed

or

Felt compelled to do.

Haxton.

Haxton had wanted me to say good-bye.

I didn't have time for that.

But

I felt

I felt compelled to make time. Didn't like the feeling; the feeling of obligation. That was something which belonged to Charles Harmon and which Charles Harmon could not deal with and I had no room to carry.

But, like he'd said, Haxton could get me and Corina on a train, a hotshot maybe, and get us up in the Unit where we wouldn't have to worry about any train gangers finishing what Kessler had started. And he could probably do all that soon as possible. So how could I not make time to see Haxton? It wasn't fidelity that was siding me. My going to Spokane was merely expediency. I was Brain Nigger Charlie. Brain Nigger Charlie looked out solely for #1.

It was good to be me again.

Corina was okay with the idea; going to Spokane. Really, she didn't care what way we went home, and was mostly swayed by the words "fastest" and "safest."

I called Haxton's cell phone and he answered and I told him we'd be passing through Spokane after all. He was happy that I'd found Corina, that I'd be stopping over to make my good-byes. I couldn't tell him exactly when we'd be there. Catching out is not an exact science. He told me he'd be around most days, said he'd let people in the yard know a black man and a young girl would be looking for him.

Catching out of Pullman was work. It was for me with my broken body. Not for Corina. No matter we were catching a local rolling from the yard, she paced it with no effort, found an empty boxcar, floated in her pack, got a solid three-point grip, then eased herself up and in. She looked young, sometimes weak, but she was tramp to the soul. Getting me into the car was an ugly task completed only by Corina reaching down and hauling me in. I felt a little ashamed, but I reminded myself my condition was a result of journeying nearly to the end of the High Line and, now, back. That was impressive. It would make a good story to share one day with my

With no one, I guess. Still, it was a good story.

Once boarded, the ride to Spokane would not be long and it was mostly wordless between Corina and myself. She rode near the door staring out at the landscape and watching the sun fall until it set fire to the horizon.

In the near dark she looked to me, asked: "Brain Nigger, what's The Drift?"

I hesitated.

Corina started to repeat herself as if I hadn't heard her, or maybe didn't understand her meaning. "There were a couple of 'boes one time I caught out with talking about it."

"I don't . . . I can't explain The Drift any more than I can a good high. Except, it's better than a good high; an E trip, or dropping down the K-hole. When it takes you, it sails you for some whole other kind of place. If you've got good thoughts, it's about the most beautiful place there is. But if you've got shit that haunts you, it's hideous as Hiroshima when Little Boy came knocking."

Corina gave me a couple of seconds of blank face, then she turned, looked back out the door of the car, and watched the sun finish its work for the day.

We arrived Spokane at night. The yard near empty. Besides that it was off hours, yards are mostly automated now. Most everything run out of the CTC. Brakies aren't needed, neither are Switchers and Hostlers. About the only people rail companies need anymore are the accountants to tell them who's a good candidate for getting the ax. So never mind its size, the Spokane yard was mostly people free and overrun by rail cars in fifties sci-fi fashion: The Day the Trains Took Over. They lumbered through the yard, big dumb animals too stupid to know they were extinct. I walked Corina around in the dark—carefully around. Avoiding hot track—before hearing a Car Knocker and following the sound of his hammer whacking wheels. Strange. Haxton said he'd tell people we'd be looking for him. That meant Corina and I pretty much had an open pass to the yard. Still, to be a tramp on rail property and just saunter around as if you were free, white, and twenty-one . . . it was strange to me.

Anyway, I crossed to the Knocker, said plainly I was looking for Haxton Boole. The Car Knocker said the last he'd seen of him he was hanging around by track sixteen, counting south to north. I said thank you, and he told us, politely, to mind ourselves.

Strange. Pleasantly so.

Corina and I walked. Track six, seven, eight . . .

All around were the sounds of Units rustling, cars rolling in the dark. The ground rippled with the vibration, was matched in the air by the ever-present hum of the diesel-electric motors.

Thirteen, fourteen, fifteen . . .

Before I even got to track sixteen I could see Haxton sitting on an apple box, a space carved around him in the night by a lantern. An honest-to-God railroad lantern.

"Haxton!" I ran to him, never mind my aches, all smiles and excitement.

He stood, cool in his manner and distant in his mien. It ran counter to my enthusiasm, made me feel big and broad. And silly. I calmed myself. "Hey."

"This Corina?"

She stepped close.

"Yeah. Corina, this is the Bull I was telling you about, Haxton."

Corina nodded.

Haxton put his hand on his gun. To me: "Why don't you toss away your goonie stick."

"What?" I was smiling. I didn't know if what Haxton said was funny, or just so queer I had to laugh.

There was not even a slight bit of levity to him. "Trying to do this easy as possible. If things have to go the other way, I'm all right with that, too."

Corina: "Brain Nigger . . . ?" She said my name in a way that asked thirty-two questions, all of them owning the same preamble: What the fuck . . . ? What the fuck is going on? What the fuck is he talking about? What the fuck is he doing gripping his gun?

"Stay right where you are, miss."

By then I'd lost my smile and I wanted to know: "What the fuck do you think—"

Haxton unsnapped the safety strap on his holster, slid out his piece. He held it parallel to his leg. He didn't point it at either me or Corina. Just the ground. No matter. The threat was the same.

And then, like the situation wasn't bad enough, nutty enough, George Plimpton had to open his yap about things, told me to let him at Haxton; let him do his trick. He could take the Bull. He could take him real good.

Let you at him for what? I don't even know what's going on.

Guy's got a gun. What else you need to know? Let me at him.

"Brain Nigger . . . ?"

"The goonie stick; toss it."

Let me—

"Brain Nigger!?"

Just let me—

"Now! Throw it away!"

I flipped George Plimpton away from me.

George Plimpton questioned my manhood, cursed my name.

I swore at Haxton: "Goddamn it! Tell me what is going on! Whatever you think I did—"

"Don't think you did anything." And he looked toward Corina.

Corina: ". . . No . . ."

I echoed her: "No. She didn't do anything."

"Murder four times. That's something."

"The Mexican—"

"He was retarded, Brain Nigger. You could see it in his face. There's no way he could have—Stay where you are!"

Corina had begun to creep, had taken a step. Haxton shut her down.

"Brain Nigger, tell him I didn't hurt nobody!"

"Skinhead neo-Nazis trying to kill her . . ." I advocated on Corina's behalf. "I know. They tried to kill me. And they would've kept coming after her—"

"Unless they were scared off. A girl alone's not going to put much fear in them. A rail killer might. So she talks a slow Mexican into becoming one, or she did the work herself and kept him around to take the blame."

"That's not . . . he stabbed me."

"You got cut from behind. You know for sure who it was that stuck you?"

I saw Guillermo. I saw him.

But

I didn't see a knife.

But

Corina was screaming at him for stabbing me. She was screaming. Was she screaming? Was she screaming at him? Was she screaming at me for messing things up? Getting in the way?

Corina could read my thoughts on my face. "No, Brain Nigger. Guillermo was my angel. He saved me."

"He saved you," Haxton talking, "you con Brain Nigger into taking Kessler out, then you send the Mexican over and you walk. That how you had things worked?"

That couldn't . . . whatever doubt I might have had, that a plot so torqued with its own deviance could come from someone who was "Just a little girl. You think for a second she—"

"I don't care what she looks like. You know same as me she's full grown, pure woman."

"How can you not—"

"It's easy not to trust when a woman's involved. Takes no effort at all." Haxton would not convince. He would not be denied.

I would not stop trying. "What does it matter who killed them? They were Nazi drug dealers. They deserved to die."

"And Insurance Kid, he deserved to get stabbed and have his penis removed?"

"He tried to rape me!"

"Then it's self-defense. The law will go real easy on you."

Corina whipped her head around, sicced her voice on me. "God-damn you! You brought me here!"

I had. I'd brought her to the Spokane yard, but not for this. Only to say good-bye to Haxton.

. . . Jesus. Haxton. A Bull. Bulls have no authority off company property; no power to make an arrest. Anywhere else, all his theories would have been just that and no good against Corina. Anywhere else. I'd handed her right to him.

I let Haxton have my rage. "You used me!"

"Then we're even up."

"Haxton, if . . . *if* things are like you say, they're done now. What does it matter?"

"Same as you, I have an obligation."

"To what, your big fat corporation?"

"To doing what's right."

Oh, now I was laughing again. "What's right? They made her swallow drugs that are going to kill her. She's going to die and you want to put her in jail? Don't you talk to me about . . ."

I let it go. Even in the poor light I could see Haxton's curious stare as if the whole of me, even at my most fundamental level, was beyond his understanding.

He said: "What's got you so blind? You really think she's got drugs caught up in her?"

"You want to see what's in my pockets!?" Her fury was redlining. "You want to see what's in my fucking pockets!?" Corina jammed her hands into the pockets of her jeans, pulled them inside out.

I would say, I think, maybe a dozen little plastic bulbs came popping up into the air.

Haxton watched with conviction the bulbs do their dance. There they were like he'd always known; the drugs, supposedly stuck in Corina's body, that she'd just out-and-out stolen.

Haxton followed the bulbs as gravity caught them and they arced in the night. His mistake. The bulbs were nothing but a magician's misdirect. He did not see the real trick—Corina making a speed knife appear in her hand, flicking it open. Her hand whipped out. The blade snagged Haxton's neck. Opened his flesh. And the blood came running. It flowed, didn't pump. His jugular wasn't severed. He grunted, didn't gurgle. His trachea was still intact. He was cut bad, but not deadly bad.

Haxton didn't know that.

All he knew was that his throat has been slashed and reacted accordingly. He dropped his gun, clutched his wound, and started to melt groundward.

I moved for him.

Corina's knife met me halfway. I felt it slip into my body. Below my ribs. On my right side. I felt it, but it didn't hurt. What hurt was when she pulled the blade free. I was looking down, I saw the steel exit my flesh, saw blood spurt like water punching its way from a busted dike. Out of all the nastiness I'd encountered recently, scaled from a kick to the head all the way up to my eyelid getting removed, this was the first bit of violence against me that I had actually witnessed, was able to see for myself. My mind composed an appropriate hurt to go with the image. I took to my ass, sat, shocked. I was opposite Haxton, who flopped wildly on his back with fear of dying. We were both useless.

Corina owned the moment.

What she chose to do with it was get down on her hands and knees, scurry around—frantic—scooping up all her meth bulbs, and

"Don't listen to him!"

"You believe something like that could really happen?"

"All he wants . . . there's reward money out there. He's trying to get a piece of it."

He had said that: Haxton had previously told me he was only in this for what he could get out of it.

"Please, Brain Nigger. I'm dying, and he just wants to make money off me."

"Then how about we look in your pack?"

"Yeah. Okay." Corina was happy to comply. "I'll show you." She started to open the pack.

Haxton's gun came swinging up. "No ma'am!"

Corina to me, desperate: "He won't let me show him!"

"Haxton, Christ—"

"There's nothing in here!"

"You let me open it up."

She hesitated a little. When she did I felt sick. "God, Corina . . ."

"There's . . . there's nothing . . ."

"Then let him see it!"

Haxton beckoned with his unoccupied hand; the one without a gun.

No defiance. No anger. With more of a petulant "let's just do this" attitude, Corina held out her pack.

Carefully, real carefully, his gun keeping its eye on Corina all the way, Haxton took the pack, fumbled it against his body, sent his free hand digging through it. Some clothes fell out, canned chili, toothbrush, a messed-up copy of *In Style* magazine . . . Not much of anything in particular. Specifically, no drugs.

Corina let Haxton have it. "You son of a fucking bitch!" She seethed with a high poison. "You goddamn bastard. Both of you! All of you!"

God, I hurt. I should've just taken her straight home. I should have . . . Fucking Haxton!

"You all treat me like shit for nothing! You treat me—"

"Now let's see your pockets."

"Damn it, Haxton!"

get them back into her pockets. Her knife stayed in her right hand. Dirt caked the blood that covered her wrist, formed a muddy red gauntlet.

With no other bright ideas, I moaned, weakly: "Help me, help us . . ." My voice didn't carry over the slow-rolling Units and cars.

People couldn't hear me.

Trains didn't care.

What was happening: Corina paused, getting ready to let her psychosis run free. No ranting, no wild talk. Her insanity was silent. Her blade would do the speaking. Then she went to work, went for Haxton, crept up over his legs. Her empty hand pulled at his belt, undid his pants.

Christ . . .

I tried to tip to one side. I just fell over. I started to squirm along the ground.

Corina, quiet, just going about her business. Going about her sick business.

Haxton knew what was coming, tried to yell. All he did was give a bloody sputter. He swung at Corina.

Her left hand made a fist, pounded him in the head, face, went back to his pants. Opened his fly. Tore at his underwear.

Wasn't she supposed to be dripping from the mouth? She was demented, wasn't she? Wasn't she supposed to be screaming? Fuck you! Fuck you all! Fuck you for what you've done to me! You'll never fuck again!

I squirmed on, kept pulling myself. My hand wormed the earth, frisked it. Panicked. Desperate.

Haxton, screaming. An awful blood-soaked wail. In my grave I'll hear it. In my grave I'll hear that noise.

But people couldn't hear.

Trains didn't care.

My hand touched wood.

I said it.

I said a prayer good and loud.

I said a prayer of salvation.

I said: "Save us, George Plimpton."

And George did his trick. A twist. There was the sound of metal scraping metal as I separated George's innards from his body. I pulled . . . and I threw. Sharpened steel bit air, shrieked with the hideous glee of a beast long held in captivity now set free. George flew without fault and was true. A sound. A sound like a shovel breaking ground. Like it, except; steel shearing flesh. Corina, manic, quiet no more. Hide rented, the demons she kept let loose. They left her in a wail that went on and on and on and on. She rolled, twisted, howled and howled. God, the sound. Body writhing, reaching for George, reaching to pull him free. He would have none of that. George wouldn't let go. Bit harder. If anything, he bit harder. Corina went banshee-pure insane. The wild wail hit fever pitch.

Trains didn't care.

And Corina spun and twirled.

Trains didn't care.

Corina gyrated.

Trains didn't care.

Corina flipped and wrenched and stumbled.

Track fifteen.

The trains did not care. They just rolled on.

I would say in all my time it was just about the most horrific thing I had ever personally witnessed.

Haxton was screaming again. Not again. He had been. Steadily. I'd lost his noise under Corina's. Now I could hear him. Screaming. I wanted to help him, to do something. I could do nothing but lie on the ground and bleed and hope that someone would find us.

Before we died, I meant.

I was three days in the Garfield County hospital. Back in, I should say. Back with the doctors and nurses who gave me all the love and attention to be handed out for free at a public medical facility. The staff was amazed at how well I seemed to continually recover from being beaten and stabbed and tortured. They were amazed, or they just told me I was doing great so I wouldn't give them any lip when they released me after only three days.

Haxton would be in the hospital a couple days longer than me. He'd bled out more than I had. He also had insurance. I didn't. On day three, the day I was mobile enough to go home, I went round to Haxton's room. His wife was there. She'd come to Spokane right after the yard had called, told her her husband's throat had been slashed and his balls had been almost but not quite removed. As Haxton had promised she was no, oh, say, Elle Macpherson. Not even close. But she sat by her husband's hospital bed for one hundred twenty hours back to back, didn't freak out that her husband's wang would look Frankensteinish for the rest of forever. Was just happy he was alive and would one day be well enough to go back to working the yards for crappy but honest pay. Didn't know for sure, but figured that was more than you could say for most supermodels.

The good thing that happened: it got out—got to the papers—about what went down in the yard; the truth about Corina and how, one way or the other, she was the brains of this whole rail murder mess. It got out that no matter all the police presence and all the Feds doing work on the taxpayer's dime, Haxton, a private Bull, had figured things, lured the nutso girl to the yard, put his life on the line to bring her down. Reporters started coming around reporting all that, making a big deal out of all that. It was good copy. Good copy sold papers.

SA Smikle came around trying to glom some of all that. He had the nerve to show up at Haxton's hospital room spouting phraseology about the successful cooperation of government and the private sector and a job well done, and could you possibly get a picture of me shaking hands with Haxton so it'd look like I had something to do with anything?

With me just sitting in the room, watching? Listening? I don't think so. I started piping up to the journos about an incident in a sheriff's substation right there in Spokane; nastiness done with a stun gun and how a tiny little excuse for an FBI agent had tried to—

A hand on my wrist; Haxton pulling me back down into my chair, saying without saying: Let it go. And if Haxton, who I'd lied to, who'd had his throat carved and his nuts trimmed, if he was benevolent enough to let Smikle do some credit-grabbing and self-aggrandizing . . . well, hell, I'd only been electrocuted by the guy. So I sat and watched Smikle put on his little show and get his photo taken, watched him hang around for what felt, to him, the appropriate amount of time, then leave. And still he did not acknowledge me. I felt rage and I felt hate. I could only think, again, of a newspaper article printed sometime in the hopefully near future that reported Special Agent Smikle's untimely and quite horrible death. And I felt calm.

I stayed with Haxton, with Mrs. Haxton—Whitney was her name—for a while. I stayed until I figured they were sick of me sitting around, although they were two who would never say so. I got up to go. Me and Haxton both worked hard to avoid playing out some treacly good-bye scene, acted like we'd see each other again one day, though we both knew our dialogue to be wholly untrue. Haxton asked if there was somewhere he could write me. As there was reward money coming in, he thought I should get—that I had earned—a piece of it. I still had forty-some dollars in food stamps. More than I was likely to spend in a good while. I told Haxton thanks, but don't bother. A guy like me was hard to be found.

I left Haxton and Mrs. Haxton—Whitney—to each other and limped off to catch out.

I had not yet closed out things on Corina. Didn't know how to close things. The last of her would be the hardest. I wasn't sure if Corina was damaged before she ever caught out, or if she'd had her damage starved and beaten and raped into her by the rails. Maybe she was just a greedy little girl who wanted to steal a handful of meth and didn't care if she had to stab a few guys and give them deep circumcisions along the way. I knew she could be sweet at times. Seemed so. I also knew she had a deviousness to her and a wickedness in her that was ninety-nine-point-repeat-nine percent pure. And I knew the only world where she belonged was the one which ultimately drove her insane and swept her to her death. What I did not know, standing outside a trailer inside a trailer park in a bad section of St. Louis, MO, was how to break any of that down for Chocolate Walt.

He came to the rusty-metal door of his mobile home wearing his Folgers-can crown. He looked kind of stupid. Not kind of. Stupid. Queen Elizabeth didn't get as much mileage out of her headgear. But then, she's got the gig for life. Walt could only milk it for a year. Probably the only good year he'd had in fifty or more shitty ones. And I had returned at the top of it to tell him that the only person alive he cared anything about was alive no more. I could think of no easy, no soft way to do the job. I didn't try to find one. I just said it. Just told Walt Corina was dead.

"You sure?"

I'd killed her. I'd staked her with the trick goonie stick Walt himself had given to me. I watched her do a dance of death into the path of a train.

"Yes."

Walt took a beat, then he shrugged with his voice: "Well, that that. Got some pizza rolls cookin'. C'mon in if you want some."

My jaw fell just a little. Pizza rolls? Was shock blocking him from getting what I was saying? "Walt, did you hear me?"

"Standin' right here. How'm I not gonna hear you?"

"Corina's dead." I said it again, trying to will the proper response from him. Walt had sent me to find his niece and I had ended her life. No, he did not know that; he did not know his charge to me was a signature on her death warrant. But I knew, and my guilt and frustration demanded something more from him than an invitation to snack.

"Yeah. She dead. Figured. Girl alone on the High Line? She was dead before she first caught out."

". . . Don't you care?"

"Course I care. Need closure on a situation. Had to know one way or other. Had to. That why I sent you, Brain Nigger. Had to know. But she gone, and ain't no way to make her any less dead. No way I know. Do any good to dwell on it, you show me how." Then: "Shit! Pizza rolls's burnin'!"

Walt ran back into the trailer. The crown fell from his head, took the floor with a clank. I heard some noise. I heard him swear as he burned himself saving the pizza rolls from a toaster oven. I could smell their blackened crust. I could hear the sizzle of the grease as it bubbled and popped and ran from the food. At that moment life was very vivid to me.

Walt yelled: "Got some Tang if you want it."

From St. Louis I caught out. I did not bother with my rail book; did not try to figure where the trains were headed. I picked the first freight I saw, hopped a car, and let it take me wherever it cared to go, my actions confessing my lack of direction. In my years of travels I had told myself I rode the rails for their freedom alone. I rode looking for nothing and taking whatever came. I had told Stupid Dumbass, when Stupid Dumbass was my friend, in the time before I most likely ended his life as I would later Corina's, that there was no point in looking for answers on the rails. Answers were not to be found. But each word I spoke was a piece of a deception well built that gave life to the lie that fooled even myself. The truth: from the moment I first caught out from Cali answers were all I'd been questing for. How do I make good the defects I carried? How do I atone for the sins that I owned? In our time together my wife had given me the harshest gift of all; her love. I carried her devotion like a burden, repaid her affection by breaking my every vow. I abandoned her, I abandoned a child I had never known. The scars of separation would be mine forever. And no matter my denials, from that moment on the search for redemption was my sole occupation. I thought I had found it in the task of returning a lost girl to her home, but my mission of mercy was nothing more than a mercy kill; a living parable staged to prove all my plans were no more than castles made of snow, and July just around the corner. What I sought could not be earned on any schedule. What I needed would find me in its time; when it was ready for me, not when I was ready for it.

There is no control. Proactivity is a lie.

Progress through patience.

So I rode. Alone. George Plimpton crushed under the wheels of a slow freight, having given his life in saving mine.

Night came.

Above me was miles and miles of dark salted with stars. Beneath me I felt the roll of the wheels over the joins in the rails, the gentle rock of the car on its couplings. Way up front the whistle of the Unit rippled off to nowhere. The air clean, naked of smell other than the suggestion of rain. And then I was in The Drift. I did not fight it. I did not try to hold it off with the false love of my ladies. I let The Drift take me. And when it had, when it gave me sleep, it showed me the vision. My child. My child with three eyes. But this time, different from every other time, the vision was altered. This time, different from every other time, my child's third eye was not crystal blue. It was brown. All my baby's eyes were brown as a black child's eyes should be. And with that alteration, for the first time the vision—the vision which had driven me from my life and from my mind—gave me a sense that maybe one day, even if my world would not be perfect—it would never be perfect—it might just get a little better. Though lonely and lost, living outdoors and eating from garbage, I might just find reason to live. The vision gave me the one thing I so desperately needed in all my life.

It gave me

Hope.

## A NOTE ABOUT THE AUTHOR

John Ridley is the author of four highly regarded novels and a former producer on NBC's *Third Watch.* He wrote and produced the film *Undercover Brother*, wrote the story for *Three Kings*, and wrote and directed *Cold Around the Heart.* His novel *Stray Dogs* was made into the movie *U-Turn*, directed by Oliver Stone. He is also a regular commentator for National Public Radio.